# THE FLAME AN

C000172879

JOHN BLACKBURN was born in 1923 in
the second son of a clergyman. Black
College near London in 1937, but his ........... ... ...............
onset of World War II; the shadow of the war, and that of Nazi Germany,
would later play a role in many of his works. He served as a radio officer
during the war in the Mercantile Marine from 1942 to 1945, and resumed
his education afterwards at Durham University, earning his bachelor's
degree in 1949. Blackburn taught for several years after that, first in London and then in Berlin, and married Joan Mary Clift in 1950. Returning to
London in 1952, he took over the management of Red Lion Books.

It was there that Blackburn began writing, and the immediate success in 1958 of his first novel, *A Scent of New-Mown Hay*, led him to take
up a career as a writer full-time. He and his wife also maintained an
antiquarian bookstore, a secondary career that would inform some of
Blackburn's later work. A prolific author, Blackburn would write nearly
30 novels between 1958 and 1985; most of these were horror and thrillers,
but his output also included one historical novel set in Roman times, *The
Flame and the Wind* (1967). He died in 1993.

GREG GBUR is an associate professor of physics and optical science at the
University of North Carolina at Charlotte. He writes the long-running
blog 'Skulls in the Stars', which discusses classic horror fiction, physics
and the history of science, as well as the curious intersections between
the three topics. His science writing has recently been featured in 'The
Best Science Writing Online 2012,' published by Scientific American. He
has previous introduced four other John Blackburn titles for Valancourt
Books.

*Cover*: The cover is a reproduction of the first edition's jacket art by Bill
Botten. Botten started out in advertising at age 16 and spent the next 17
years in advertising and publishing, including working as art director for
Sphere Books. He later became a freelance designer and designed dozens
of dust jackets in the 1960s, '70s, and '80s for books by many well-known
authors, including Kingsley and Martin Amis, J. G. Ballard, and Margaret
Drabble, and for the Booker Prize winners *Troubles* (1970) by J. G. Farrell
and *Midnight's Children* (1980) by Salman Rushdie.

# By John Blackburn

*A Scent of New-Mown Hay* (1958)*

*A Sour Apple Tree* (1958)

*Broken Boy* (1959)*

*Dead Man Running* (1960)

*The Gaunt Woman* (1962)

*Blue Octavo* (1963)*

*Colonel Bogus* (1964)

*The Winds of Midnight* (1964)

*A Ring of Roses* (1965)

*Children of the Night* (1966)

*The Flame and the Wind* (1967)*

*Nothing but the Night* (1968)*

*The Young Man from Lima* (1968)

*Bury Him Darkly* (1969)*

*Blow the House Down* (1970)

*The Household Traitors* (1971)*

*Devil Daddy* (1972)

*For Fear of Little Men* (1972)

*Deep Among the Dead Men* (1973)

*Our Lady of Pain* (1974)*

*Mister Brown's Bodies* (1975)

*The Face of the Lion* (1976)*

*The Cyclops Goblet* (1977)*

*Dead Man's Handle* (1978)

*The Sins of the Father* (1979)

*A Beastly Business* (1982)*

*The Book of the Dead* (1984)

*The Bad Penny* (1985)*

* Available or forthcoming from Valancourt Books

JOHN BLACKBURN

# The Flame and the Wind

'A gentle breeze gives life to the flames,
a stronger destroys them.' Ovid

With a new introduction by

GREG GBUR

VALANCOURT BOOKS
Richmond, Virginia
2013

*The Flame and the Wind* by John Blackburn
First published London: Jonathan Cape, 1967
First Valancourt Books edition 2013

Copyright © 1967 by John Blackburn
Introduction © 2013 by Greg Gbur

The Publisher is grateful to Mr Bill Botten for permission to
reproduce his illustration for the cover of this edition.

Published by Valancourt Books, Richmond, Virginia
*Publisher & Editor*: James D. Jenkins
*20th Century Series Editor*: Simon Stern, University of Toronto
http://www.valancourtbooks.com

ISBN 978-1-939140-70-8
Also available as an electronic book

All Valancourt Books publications are printed on acid free paper
that meets all ANSI standards for archival quality paper.

Set in Dante MT 11/13.5

# INTRODUCTION

THE 1967 novel *The Flame and the Wind* represents something of an anomaly in the writing of John Blackburn (1923-1993). It is the only example of historical fiction amongst Blackburn's works, which otherwise consist of a collection of mysteries, thrillers, and horror novels set in contemporary times. *The Flame and the Wind* is set in the ancient Roman Empire and Near East during the turbulent years following the death and supposed resurrection of Jesus of Nazareth, and explores the immediate consequences of that event. The novel is, however, still a mystery and thriller, though such a simple classification does an injustice to the unusual nature of the work. Despite its dramatic departure from Blackburn's traditional themes, a closer inspection shows that it is paradoxically in fact also an almost perfect representation of them, as we will see.

An investigation of Blackburn's personal history suggests that *The Flame and the Wind* is a particularly unusual novel for the author. He was the son of a clergyman, Charles Eliel, who had immigrated to the United Kingdom from the Seychelles in the Indian Ocean. By all accounts, Eliel raised John Blackburn and his brother Thomas in a very strict and cruel environment. John did not write about his own childhood in any detail, but hints of the brothers' treatment is found in his niece Julia Blackburn's memoir[1] about her father Thomas. Julia notes,

> Eliel was the son of a missionary who had declared that his task in life was to 'stamp out copulation' among the natives of Praslin and as a result of his efforts the family had to leave the island in a hurry because a sorcerer tried to kill them all with a voodoo spell.

Eliel seems to have renounced his own family when he left the islands, but he brought with him a sense of self-loathing coupled with his father's abnormal views of sexuality. Julia further writes,

---

1 Julia Blackburn, *The Three of Us* (New York: Pantheon Books, 2008).

*Worst of all was the terrible metal contraption designed to control wet dreams, which had been especially ordered from a supplier in Mauritius. It was strapped across the boy's naked groin at night, and if he had an erection it would clamp down on his penis, thus waking him out of his state of sin.*

Thomas Blackburn suffered lifelong psychological trauma from his childhood. Brother John fared much better, working a collection of jobs before marrying and taking a job as the manager of Red Lion Books in London. His first novel, the horror thriller *A Scent of New-Mown Hay* (also reprinted by Valancourt Books), appeared in 1958 and was an instant success. Blackburn became a full-time writer, though he and his wife Joan Mary Clift also ran an antiquarian bookstore on the side. *The Flame and the Wind* appeared in 1967, just before Blackburn wrote some of his most powerful novels of horror such as *Nothing but the Night*, *Bury Him Darkly* and *Devil Daddy*. It is surprising that John wrote a novel about religious history, considering his abusive childhood at the hands of a clergyman, but it is reasonable to view it as Blackburn's attempt to come to terms with his religious heritage.

The novel is set six years after the death of Jesus. It follows the investigations of Sextus Marcellus Ennius, Roman officer in the Empire's Department of Vigilance, an organization of spies dedicated to uncovering and destroying internal threats to the Empire. As the story begins, Sextus travels to the estate of his wealthy uncle, where he is tasked with an unusual mission: discover the true nature of the supposed King of the Jews, Jesus of Nazareth – was he a god, or a charlatan? The quest is of importance to the entire Roman Empire: the cult of Christ is spreading rapidly through the provinces, and its followers preach a seductive gospel without fear. Together with his colleague Eros Dion, a freed Greek slave, Sextus will travel throughout the lands of the Middle East, both cities and wilds, and eventually to Rome, in search of the truth. Along the way he will encounter a number of figures from history and find the most unlikely of allies. Eventually the investigators settle on a diabolical and desperate plan to completely discredit the Messiah, and it will bring them to the feet of the Emperor himself.

Blackburn focuses the Romans' investigations on the so-called

'Unknown Years of Jesus', a period of his life from the age of twelve until the start of his ministry at roughly age thirty that the Bible does not document. The only mention of this period comes in the New Testament at Luke 2:52: *And Jesus advanced in wisdom and stature, and in favor with God and men.*

Biblical scholars have generally assumed that Jesus worked as a carpenter during this quiescent period, but others have come up with more fanciful ideas. In medieval times, a story appeared that said that Jesus had visited Britain as a boy, and this tale became entwined with the Arthurian legend. More recently, French author and enthusiast of Indian mysticism Louis Jacolliot noted similarities between Christian and Hindu stories in his 1869 book *La Bible dans l'Inde, Vie de Iezeus Christna*. Though Jacolliot did not argue that Jesus traveled to India, the idea of a connection to distant lands was made. In 1887 a Russian war correspondent named Nicholas Notovich claimed he had found evidence that Jesus spent the missing years studying in Tibet. Notovich later admitted to fabricating his evidence, but it seems that he had planted a seed in the imagination of would-be scholars and mystics. Blackburn, who clearly knew much about the Bible himself, took the 'mystery' and turned it into the focus of his novel.

Though *The Flame and the Wind* is under 250 pages long, it is Blackburn's longest book and it is truly epic in scope. Christianity is well depicted as a massive intangible power spreading rapidly through the Roman Empire at the same time that the Empire is collapsing under the weight of its corrupt leaders. Much of the novel focuses on the ascension of the Emperor Caligula in 37 A.D. and his rapid descent into madness when in power. Though the true extent of Caligula's depravity has been debated by historians in recent years, it is well known that he undertook a policy of executing anyone whom he perceived as a possible threat. He also spent the Roman treasury on lavish gladiatorial spectacles as well as extravagant and often wasteful construction projects, including a pair of massive personal pleasure barges;[1] his spending precipitated a financial crisis only two years into his reign. Not long after,

---

1 These barges were actually rediscovered at the bottom of Lake Nemi in Italy in the 1930s, though they were destroyed during the Second World War.

Caligula started representing himself as a deity and – in an event that has serious implications in *The Flame and the Wind* – reputedly had a statue of himself erected in the Temple of Jerusalem, much to the ire of the Jewish population. His violence and excesses would catch up with him quickly – Caligula would be assassinated in A.D. 41.

One other deity makes an appearance in *The Flame in the Wind*: the ancient god known as Moloch, worshipped by a variety of peoples in Northern Africa and the Middle East. The worshippers of Moloch were reported to sacrifice their own children to an effigy of the god, which is often depicted as a massive bronze statue with outstretched arms and the head of a bull. In one description, a child would be bound to the arms of the idol, which would then be heated until the sacrifice was burned to death. In Blackburn's novel, the people of the Roman Empire live in fear of Moloch, as many of their captured soldiers were reportedly sacrificed to it.

The story of *The Flame and the Wind* marks it, despite its unique setting, as very much in line with Blackburn's other thrillers and tales of horror. It is really so much more than that, however, as even literary critics of the time appreciated. Writing in the March 17, 1967 edition of *The Guardian*, crime fiction reviewer Francis Iles notes,

> It seems a pity, too, to denigrate John Blackburn's The Flame and the Wind (Cape, 21s) to the level of a mere thriller, as his publisher does. This is an historical novel in the grand manner: the period, Rome under Caligula; the theme, the denigration of Jesus and the extirpation of the Christians; the picture broadly painted and fully peopled with historical figures like Caligula . . . A lot of research must have gone into the work, and the result is wholly satisfactory.

There is one other way in which *The Flame and the Wind* fits remarkably into the oeuvre of Blackburn. Many of Blackburn's plots involve the spread of a deadly plague, and the hero's efforts to contain it. The spread of the contagion is highlighted, and tension built, with small vignettes showing the impact on innocents. Consider the following passage from Blackburn's 1976 *The Face of the Lion,* in which a young girl visits her grandmother's house and gets an unexpected welcome:

> *'Oh, Gran. Where are you, Gran?' she whimpered, and then broke off abruptly, realizing she was not alone. The kitchen door was closed and from behind it came a sound. A grunting, guzzling, slobbering sound which reminded her of pigs jostling around a swill tub. A sound that made her forget about Gran and think of her own safety, though she couldn't run away. Tears were blinding her, her feet seemed to be nailed to the floorboards, the pills dropped from her hand.*
>
> *Outside in the garden the dog whined twice and then bolted off down the hill. Inside the cottage the sound increased. The kitchen door opened.*

This passage can be compared with a vignette from *The Flame and the Wind* about the spread of Christianity:

> *At about the same time that Eros was dictating his letter, a man was speaking in a square at Alexandria. He was a young man, but his voice was strong and self-confident and the words carried easily to all his audience.*
>
> *He spoke to them of a god who had revealed himself in Palestine and was the only true ruler of mankind. He appeared to be a strange fellow, this god, because he demanded very little from his followers; no sacrifices, no priests, and no offerings except complete belief in himself and his teachings, which were stranger still, for they stated that it was the poor and downtrodden who would rule the earth.*
>
> *The collection of Egyptians, Greeks and Africans listened politely enough, the well-to-do cynically and the poor with a mixture of hope and disbelief. Only a little group of Jews seemed to take him seriously, and after a time one of their members asked the young man a question. The answer meant nothing to the majority of his listeners, but it appeared to goad the Jews into a fury and stones were lifted from the ground and thrown at him. As all sane people knew, Hebrew quarrels are best left alone, and the preacher was obviously a Jew himself. It was not an affair for outsiders and the others hurried away. Only one thing appeared strange to them. As the stones ripped open his face and knocked him bleeding to the ground, the young man smiled.*

It is not difficult in reading the novel to see Christianity as a 'plague' spreading through the Roman Empire, and Sextus and Eros the heroes seeking to stop it before it consumes all. But is every contagion an evil that must be stopped? Blackburn seems to have been pondering this question; readers of *The Flame and the Wind* will have to judge the answer for themselves.

GREG GBUR

*August 3, 2013*

# THE FLAME AND THE WIND

*For Joan with love*

# One

'There, my lords; the house of the Governor.' The guide reined his horse at the top of the slope and pointed across a wide, rocky valley. 'This is as far as I was paid to take you, so go with the gods.' He lifted his arm in a slightly mocking salute and turned back towards the town.

'Then that is your inheritance, my friend?' Eros Dion raised his eyebrows. Even in the distance there appeared to be something mean and squalid about the place, though the building itself was large enough. An 'L'-shaped block of limestone, so low and rugged that it looked like part of the natural landscape, with outhouses and huts dotted around it, and the whole enclosed by a tall wooden fence. The general effect was more of a military camp than a nobleman's mansion.

'Let us hope only part of the inheritance. My uncle is supposed to have other properties.' Sextus Marcellus Ennius grinned at his companion, thinking how inaptly Eros had been named. The wrinkled, keen-eyed face bore no resemblance to that of the sightless god of love, and his squat body was knotted with muscle. He had counted Eros a friend for a long time, but he never felt that he really knew him, because there was something in the man's make-up which repelled intimacy; a mocking cynicism that hid all emotion except a burning loyalty to the state and an efficiency which had won him his freedom and the favour of two emperors.

'I think it is an inheritance I shall have to earn, however.' Sextus urged his tired horse forward. When he had shown Eros the letter in Rome, he had expected him to be politely interested, but for once the Greek's face flushed with excitement. 'Yes, I must go with you,' Eros had said, and Sextus had never seen him look so eager. 'Please let me go with you. I will help you to earn your money, and you may help to answer a question which has troubled me for years.'

The house was getting closer now and they could see the enormous blocks that formed the walls, the low sagging roof with a wisp of smoke from a chimney and the mean huts surrounding it. Dogs and cattle lay in the compound and a few human figures lounged in doorways. This was the home of a man who had once governed an imperial province. For the hundredth time Sextus' fingers ran across the pocket of his tunic, feeling the thick parchment crinkle under the cloth, the letter that had made him ride eight hundred miles through the stifling weather, all the way through Italy and across the passes that Hannibal's elephants had taken four hundred years ago into the squalor of central Gaul.

'To Sextus Marcellus Ennius, my sister's child, greetings.' The writing was feeble and spidery and now and then sloped wildly across the parchment. His uncle was reputed to be one of the richest men outside Italy, but was apparently too mean to employ a scribe.

'I am old, Sextus, and have been warned that I am soon to die. Since my wife was taken from me, I have no heir . . .' She had died raving, Sextus had heard: cursing the gods, prophesying disasters and continually washing imaginary bloodstains from her hands. 'For the memory of your mother, come to me, boy. Come to Gaul and help me.'

'We will earn it, Sextus. If there is an inheritance, you shall have it.' Eros Dion's body looked as though it were a part of his cantering horse, and there was a prim smile on his face. As he watched him, Sextus longed to look through the leathery skin and see what went on in his brain. How long had he known him now? Three years? No, nearer four; when he'd first been transferred to the Department of Vigilance, and he'd hated him at the beginning. He, the officer of a legion, being forced to take orders from a Greek freedman, and serve an organization of spies and informers. It was months later before the work started to fascinate him and he realized its importance. Since Julius Caesar, Roman strategy did not envisage the defensive. Rome's aim was to forestall hostilities by offensive or preventive measures, and this could only be done by having an efficient intelligence service.

Yes, he and Eros had travelled far in those short years. In Anglesey on the western edge of Britain they had risked their lives together: crawling through bracken and watching men garlanded with oak leaves staring at the sky till a glimmer of dawn fell on a slab, and the stone axe came down on the throat of their god.

In Germany too; crouched in the depths of the Teutoburger forest while tribesmen crooned around their camp fires and, high above, legionaries screamed as they roasted to death in the wicker cages. The air had been thick with smoke and he'd had to fight back a cough till Eros Dion's dagger touched his throat and he heard him whisper, 'You can't cough, Sextus. You can't make a sound. Before you open your mouth, I will have killed you.' Eros had saved his life many times, and how he wished that he really knew him.

They were almost there at last. The gates of the stockade were open, and beyond them dogs had started to bark and a group of ragged figures were staring suspiciously. Everywhere there was an air of disorder and neglect. The estate of a man who had once ruled a province!

A man who obviously liked his privacy, though. Some of his retainers carried clubs and rusty swords and looked as though they would enjoy using them. Tall, fair-haired Celts mainly, but a few small, dark men from the south. Women and children too, scowling from the doorways as though their greatest pleasure would be to see the strangers torn to pieces.

But at least there was one friendly face. The door of the main building had burst open, and an enormously fat man was hurrying towards them with a strangely smooth gait that made it appear as though there were wheels instead of feet under his rumpled toga. His mouth was set in a wide beam of welcome and tiny, pig-like eyes gleamed above the bulging cheeks.

'Greetings, lords. Welcome to the kinsman of my master.' He paused before Sextus, straightened his shoulders, and brought up a podgy hand in a military salute.

'No, there is no doubt at all. The resemblance is quite uncanny, Sextus Ennius. I could see the family features from the doorway.

'And what are you thinking of, fools? These are our guests. Our honoured, long-awaited guests.' As he was speaking, the retainers had lowered their weapons and the scowls had left their faces. Now, grimy hands almost dragged Sextus and Eros from their saddles and others hurried to unload the pack horse.

'Please forgive our reception, my lords.' The fat man wasn't actually drunk, but his speech was slurred and there was a thick tang of wine on his breath. 'We were not expecting you for at least another two days, and this is an isolated community. Since his last illness my master has set great value on his privacy and these people have been told to discourage strangers.' He belched loudly and Sextus drew back before the reek of stale wine.

'Allow me to present myself, however. My name is Gaius Vinius, once centurion of the second regiment of the Tenth Legion. A man of some authority then, but that was a long time ago.' Again the huge shoulders straightened as he pronounced the rank and then he grinned. 'Yes, a very long time ago. Now, I am as you see me. An old, broken fool, serving another fool who is equally broken.

'Oh, do not be alarmed, my lord Ennius.' The grin grew to a chuckle. 'I said your uncle had been ill, but there is no immediate need for concern. He is in excellent physical condition and can ride twenty miles a day, or walk ten. His sickness is here – in the head. A certain worm which he says the gods have placed against his brain to trouble him.' The man's fat cheeks joggled up and down in his merriment.

'But I am forgetting my duties, my lords.' There was a slight accentuation in his voice as he studied Eros, obviously wondering, slave or freedman? 'You must be very tired after your long journey. Please let me take you to your quarters.' He turned and led them towards the doorway.

If the compound had been squalid, the interior of the house was unspeakable. Its long, gloomy corridors were unwashed and littered with rubbish, and half-naked children played on tiled floors so dirty that their patterns were invisible. At the end of the last corridor a drunken man lay sprawled before a door and, without altering his smooth, wheel-like gait, Gaius kicked him to one side and pulled it open. The room within had two stools and two couches, and a copper basin was heating over a charcoal stove. Two sluttish girls were bent over one of the couches. They looked up, giggling, as the men entered.

'So, these are our quarters.' Eros glanced briefly at the nearest couch, and then crossed to the stove, filling the shovel with charcoal and blowing on it.

'What are you doing, fellow?' The fat man reached out as Eros pulled back the bed-clothes, but the Greek pushed him to one side.

'Something that should have been done a long time ago.' The coals glowed as he scattered them on the mattress and Sextus saw the little grey bodies of lice hurrying away to safety.

'But I know you, don't I?' Eros threw down the shovel and took a knife from his belt. 'Gaius Vinius, sometime centurion of the Tenth Legion, who got into trouble. You became drunk once too often, Gaius, and struck a superior officer. First they flogged you and then dismissed you without a pension.' Not taking his eyes from the smouldering mattress, he raised his knife till it pressed against the man's throat.

'Now you work for an old, sick master whom you cheat and despise. You also call me *fellow*, not knowing whether I am a slave or a freedman, so I will tell you what I am.

'Put it out now, woman.' He nodded to one of the girls and she hurried to the bowl and poured water on the couch, steam hissing and drifting across the room like fog.

'My mother was a Greek prostitute, belonging to a man who hired her out to anyone. When she was too old and ravaged for her trade, he kept her to clean the rooms in the brothel and she did it well. Just as you will see that this room is cleaned, Gaius, as clean as though you expected the Emperor himself to sleep in it.' The point of his knife was digging into flesh now and the fat man was quivering.

'At seventeen my master realized I had certain small talents and he sold me to the imperial civil service. At twenty-five I was freed by the Empress Livia, and at thirty I was granted citizenship. I am now a senior member of the Department of Vigilance, answerable only to the Emperor and Naevius Macro, Prefect of the Praetorian Guards. Do you know what that means, Gaius?' He withdrew the knife and smiled pleasantly. 'I could kill you now and nobody would dare to lift a finger against me. Do you understand that?'

'Yes, yes, lord.' Like a huge fish the man bent down and kissed Eros' hand. There were tears in his eyes and blood trickled from the puncture in his throat.

'Please forgive me, lord. I did not understand, and you were not expected so soon. It is so difficult now. These are a dirty, rough people, and they are out of hand. Since my master's illness, we can do nothing with them.

'But in one thing you are wrong. I do not cheat my master, Eros Dion. I love him and I humour him in every way. That is all I can do. When you have seen what he has become you may just realize . . .' He broke off as a gong sounded somewhere in the far distance.

'And that is the master now. He must have heard of your arrival, so please follow me. I had hoped he would rest for a little, but . . .' Gaius turned and almost ran out of the room.

The next wing of the house was as squalid as the first. More children playing on littered floors, unkempt women giggling at them, more drunken figures huddled in doorways, but finally they came to a big, brass-studded door with a bell-pull beside it. Gaius rang three times and then dragged back the door as the gong sounded in answer. It opened slowly, creaking on unoiled hinges, and behind there was no daylight, but the flicker of torches and a blazing fire. In front of the fire, an old man was sitting on a couch massaging his hands before the flames.

'Master, they are here. Your guests have come, as you said they would.' Sextus was struck by Gaius' tone. He sounded oddly paternal; more like a tutor with a stupid but well-loved pupil than a servant before his master. 'This is your nephew, Sextus Ennius, and his friend Eros Dion. They have come to help us and there is nothing to worry about any more.

'Allow me to present my master, lords.' He ushered them forward to the still figure by the fire, drew himself up to his full height and bowed.

'His Excellency, Pontius Pilate, formerly Governor and Procurator of Judaea.'

The room was vast, probably occupying a quarter of the entire wing, but the low ceiling gave it a strangely tomb-like appearance, as did the marble busts lining the walls, the big brass gong, and the almost motionless figure of its owner before the roaring fire. Toy soldiers were spread out on a table beside his couch.

'Pull back the curtains, Gaius, so that I can see our guests.' Pilate's voice was full of quiet command, but it lacked something, and his face was just the same. A big hooked nose, a heavy jaw, a domed forehead, and all carved by years of service and authority. But, as the sunlight streamed in through the windows, Sextus felt he was looking at a wax dummy, or a man from whom all character had been removed by some horrible process of surgery or torture. His skin was almost dead white apart from a vein that lay like a blue worm across the centre of the forehead.

'You may leave us now, Gaius.' Pilate eased himself round in the couch and stared up at them. Perhaps because of the sudden daylight, his eyes did not appear to focus quite correctly and he waited for the door to close before he spoke again.

'Sextus Ennius, my sister's child, and Eros Dion, a freedman of Livia, of whom I have heard a great deal. Both of you are very welcome here.' As he spoke his eyes kept flicking over the soldiers on the table.

'The last time I saw you, Sextus, was fifteen years ago when you were only a boy. Do you remember me at all?'

'I think so, uncle, but I can't really be sure. As you say, it is a long time ago.' Sextus had a vague picture of that lined face smiling down at him from above a magnificent scarlet cloak, but he didn't know if it came from memory or from what his parents had told him. The Ennius family were of the patrician class, but poor and without influence, and Pilate's position had been a considerable feather in their cap. He could still hear his mother boasting to friends. 'My brother, the Governor, told me . . .' 'As I wrote to the Procurator of Judaea last month . . .'

Not that Pilate's career had been at all distinguished. The Jews were probably Rome's most troublesome subject people and the country was administered by Procurators; Treasury officials who were largely concerned with taxation and lacked the authority of full provincial governors. Most of these men had been weak or self-seeking and Sextus' uncle was one of their worst examples. He had vacillated with the Jewish elders one moment and been unduly harsh the next, till the province was on the verge of rebellion. The Emperor had recalled him in disgrace, not actually exiling him to Gaul, but making it clear that he would be wise to stay there.

'And before that I saw you at Pompeii; a baby with a wet nurse.' The old, characterless voice ground on through the sunlight. 'Your

mother always was a fool, Sextus, and that was typical of her;
letting her only son be reared on the milk of a slave-woman.

'Come here and let me see if you are a fool too.' He motioned
them to the table beside his couch. With the hot sun outside and
the blazing fire, both Sextus and Ennius could feel sweat pouring
down their faces.

'You did your military training with a famous legion and are
now employed by the inner section of Vigiles; the Intelligence
Branch of the civil police. How would you dispose your forces in
this case?' The toy soldiers were laid out across the table, horsemen in two 'V' formations and Roman infantry scattered at
random.

'In the only possible way.' Sextus started to form the foot soldiers
into position. Front ranks locked, shields raised against arrows in
the centre, short swords forward; the classic formation of muscle
and metal and leather that had cowed every nation which dared
to face it.

'Yes, that is correct, of course.' Pilate nodded. 'The disciplined
wall that breaks everything it meets.' He got up and smiled down
at the glittering square.

'But if discipline failed, Sextus. If the officer here did not give
the correct orders. If this man ran. If this fellow had developed a
conscience against killing. What then?' He lifted the figures from
the table as he spoke. 'Will your wall still hold?'

'It will collapse, of course, but what you suggest is impossible.
The Roman soldier does not break.' Sextus frowned at him. Pilate
really was sick, he thought. In disgrace and exile the brain had run
down and he had come eight hundred miles to talk to a madman.

'He does not break now, Sextus, but I think your uncle is trying
to look into the future.' Eros gave his little prim smile. 'Am I
correct, Governor?'

'Perfectly correct.' Pilate nodded again. 'At least my nephew has
the sense to choose wise friends, Eros Dion, and I am delighted
you accompanied him.

'But please help yourselves to wine. There is some local brew
on the shelf behind you. I am not allowed any myself these days,
but I remember it was pleasant enough.'

'Thank you.' Sextus forced back a frown as he poured it out.

The goblets were grey with dust and, though the wine ran like thick treacle, its taste was thin and sour.

'And now, nephew, I will show you the bait that brought you here.' There was a drawer under his table and Pilate pulled out a long roll of parchment and handed it to him. At first glance Sextus saw that it was some kind of legal document, covered with seals and the signatures of witnesses, and after reading a few lines he felt his heart start to beat a little faster.

For, though his uncle chose to live in squalor, the stories of his wealth were true enough. Three villas in Italy, a grain farm in Egypt, two marble quarries in Sicily and half a million gold pieces locked away in a Roman vault. All legally certified, and all had come into his hands during a period of ten years. The loot of a province accumulated through his long term of office, by bribery and extortion and the sale of positions, and Sextus realized why he had constantly vacillated and given in to the Jewish hierarchy at the end. Half of them must have had the evidence to break him.

'All yours, boy – every silver piece will be yours soon. Whatever my doctor says, I haven't long now.' Pilate bent over the fire, rubbing his hands together as though washing them in the glow of the flames. 'My body is cold all the time, and this thing in my head is torturing me.

'That's right, read what it says at the bottom. "To Sextus Marcellus Ennius, only son of my sister, the Lady Octavia Lepida, I leave my entire estate."'

'But you haven't signed yet, Governor.' Eros glanced at the document. 'Without that it is valueless. What must Sextus do to earn your signature?'

'Truth.' The word was like a gasp and, as Pilate turned from the fire, they could see the vein twist in his forehead. 'He must find out the truth for me. That is your job, isn't it, Sextus? That is why your department exists. Just tell me the truth and you will have it all. Everything that I own.

'Now come over here.' He walked heavily across the room, with his feet dragging on the floor as though they belonged to a man much older than one of his sixty-three years. On the far wall, between busts of Julius Caesar and the god Augustus, hung a huge

coloured map of the Empire, with parchment shields pinned to
the borders to show the forces that held them. The Rhine legions,
those along the Danube, and the mass of auxiliaries in Syria.
Beyond the shields the canvas was completely blank.

'Yes, that is what we have made. The Roman peace, all the civilized world.' Pilate's hand ran east across the Danube. 'The only
really stable force of law and order and discipline that mankind
has ever known.

'Tell me, Sextus. Can it ever be broken?'

'Not from outside alone.' The reply was automatic; the stock
answer of the Department, and Sextus knew it was true enough.
Since the reign of Augustus, the boundaries were sealed. Pyrrhus
had broken them in the past, Hannibal and the Gauls, but that was
long ago. Now the frontiers were impregnable.

But from inside; that was a different story. If there was a weakness behind the bastions – if the Germans had attacked while
Caesar and Pompey fought each other at Phasalia, or the Gauls
marched in during the slaves' revolt under Spartacus – then there
could be no guarantee of security. That was one of the reasons
why the Vigiles existed. Why Eros Dion, the son of a Greek prostitute, could make senators cringe before him. Why he, Sextus,
was proud to take orders from Naevius Macro, a man he despised
socially.

'No, not from the outside alone.' Pilate nodded convulsively as
if his head had been jerked by a cord. 'But if something were to
come in. A thing which seems harmless now, but is working against
us all the time. A rot in timber – hidden springs washing out the
foundations so that the house becomes weaker and weaker.'

'And you know what this thing is, Governor.' Eros wasn't
smiling any more, and his face was keen and eager and reminded
Sextus of a dog's before a rat hole. There was a dusty expanse of
wall beside the map and he started to trace something on it with
his finger. 'You are also sure that it is here already, aren't you? May
I ask how you know that?'

'Because . . . because . . .' Pilate's words came gasping out, and
there really did seem to be a worm in his head: the blue vein wrig-
gling behind the pale flesh.

'I know that thing is here, because, may the gods forgive me,

I let it in.' He staggered back to his couch as Eros stepped aside to show what he had drawn. A long scaley fish with its jaws wide open as though snatching at a bait.

'I suppose one could say he is mad, but what is madness? A joke of the gods, a punishment from heaven, or a physical sickness? A real worm in the brain that gnaws out reason. Don't ask me. I am not a physician or a priest.' Eros paced backwards and forwards across the floor of their room. His words to Gaius Vinius had borne fruit and it was spotless now, the tiles polished and fresh bedding provided. Even the maids who had waited on them had procured new dresses from somewhere.

'Whatever the cause, he claims that it all started merely because a man was sentenced to death six years ago.' The memory of Pilate's voice repeating the story kept droning on in Sextus' head. The terrible dreams that racked him. The feeling that blood was sticking to his hands. How his wife had died raving. And all the time that vein had twisted and throbbed in his forehead and tears dribbled down the cheeks till at last he had lain back exhausted and begged them to leave him.

'Why should it worry him? He must have sentenced hundreds of people to death in his time.'

'Hundreds, or more probably, thousands.' Eros nodded. 'Have you ever seen a crucifixion, my friend?'

'Once, but it was a long time ago.' Sextus tried to remember the details. The criminal had been a runaway slave who richly deserved to die, for he had killed his master, an old, kindly man who treated him well, and violated his young daughter. The cross looked as though it had been used many times before, and he had been surprised how small it was. The man's feet were barely off the ground when they tightened the cords with water. Because his crimes were so bad, a sedile had been fixed in position: a wooden peg between the thighs on which he could support himself, but the object was not mercy, but the extension of agony. It took a very brave man to hold himself forward from it and let rigour shorten pain, and that slave had not been brave. For two days and nights he had hung there moaning.

'But this Jew your uncle sentenced demanded such death,

Sextus. That is the point, I think. He asked to be crucified. Is that correct, Gaius?'

'In a manner of speaking, my lord.' The pleasant effects of drink had obviously worn off, and the fat man was paying for them now. His face was mottled and his whole body trembled.

'My master never wanted to execute him; why should he? The fellow had broken no law of ours that we could see. He was just a wandering preacher – you find dozens of them in the east – who had come up to Jerusalem with his followers for what they call the Feast of the Passover. His people claimed that he could work miracles; heal the sick, turn stones into bread, that kind of thing; and the temple authorities arrested him for blasphemy. It was none of our business.'

'And did you believe in these miracles, Gaius?'

'I, my lord! I was a Roman, a soldier, a follower of Mithras.' There was something pathetic in the way the huge bloated creature pronounced his calling and his faith. 'I know nothing of Jewish superstitions, though later my master had certain inquiries made. The man was a Nazarene, the son of a carpenter named Joseph, and he had left home at an early age. It seems that he had probably joined one of their monastic orders, perhaps the Essenes, and then started this cult of his own. Most likely he got his delusions of power from self-starvation or hashish.

'Oh, there was a lot of talk about miracles; blind men healed, water turned into wine, even that he'd risen from the dead, but never a scrap of real evidence. Just stories, my lord. Folk tales for very simple people.'

'And he claimed to be a god too, I think. Wasn't that the blasphemy that the Jewish elders really objected to?'

'Well, a sort of god, I suppose. The Messiah they call him, but it's difficult to know what they mean. A headache to us he's been in the past, though. The story goes that he will come down one day from heaven and lead his people to freedom. Almost every petty revolt in Judaea used the story as a rallying cry. This Jesus-bar-Joseph claimed to be he, and that's what annoyed the priests. What the Messiah actually is, I can't tell you, I'm afraid. The son of their Jehovah perhaps, or some deity who takes human form, as Jupiter and Mercury are said to do.'

'No, not like Jupiter, Gaius. Not at all like Jupiter.' Eros turned and stared out of the open window. The sun was going down now and long shadows were creeping across the valley like the ranks of an advancing army. Soon the world would be in darkness, and as he watched the dying of the light, he tried to marshal his own fears.

The frontiers of the Empire were firm and secure, as Augustus had made them, but would it always be like that? Could there be a rot inside, as Pilate said, that was already weakening them? Could this cult of the Nazarene be the tiny seed which would one day destroy the civilized world?

The Slaves' Revolt less than a hundred years ago had almost done so. Spartacus had destroyed two consular armies before Crassus crushed him at Apulia, and Spartacus' followers had been a rabble, with no cause except the longing for freedom and the pleasures of rape and loot and destruction. If they had had a religious belief or a faith to support them, the campaign might have had a very different ending. Chaos would have come and his world would have gone dark, just as the valley outside was darkening now.

And it was his world. Though he was the son of a slave, it was he and the new race of freedmen who were taking over now. Every government department was full of them, and though Rome might be corrupt and savage, it would improve under their rule. Mad or sane, the emperors relied completely on his kind, and their extravagances in the city itself were quite unimportant. The city wasn't Rome. Rome was an idea, a faith, a belief in authority and order. The only civilizing force in the world, stretching from the northern seas to Africa. Rome was the one hope that mankind could develop and prosper, and always the barbarians outside were waiting for a crack in its walls. The shutters rattled and he pictured a spark falling on dry leaves and glowing harmlessly till a breeze sprang up and fanned it into flames which burned down the forest. Let this doctrine of equality, this hideous notion that humanity owed no allegiance except to God take root and chaos would come. A second image of unmanned forts and ragged horsemen pouring unchecked between them flicked across his mind, and then Eros looked at Gaius again.

'Go on, please. The Nazarene was arrested by the Temple guards and brought before the Governor?'

'That's right, lord, but a deputation of priests came first. Caiaphas their leader was called; an old, grizzled fellow with his shoulders bent by poring over texts for most of his life. He told my master that this Jesus had claimed to be the Messiah and the people would revolt unless he was executed before the Passover.

'The Governor laughed at first. He said that he'd always tried to please the elders but this was ludicrous. Only the Roman authorities had power to pronounce a death sentence and what had the man done? Blasphemed against their Jehovah!

'"That is true, Excellency," Caiaphas answered, giving a bow and a little smile. I was standing behind the throne and heard everything that passed between them.

'"All the same, the revolt will come unless you do what we ask, and I do not think Caesar will be pleased to hear of it." He had one of the most persuasive voices I have known. "Surely it is better for one man to perish than the whole race be destroyed."

'I could see that my master was disturbed by that, and he listened to what the priests had to say, and then had the man brought in. Very tall he was, but stooping because he'd been beaten about quite a bit, and I remember there was blood on his face. A strange face it was, like . . . like . . .' Gaius broke off as if unable to find the right comparison.

'Anyway, my master repeated the evidence against him and then asked the question which the priests had prepared. "Are you a king?" Three times he said that, and the fellow refused to deny it. There was nothing we could do to help him after that. It was an insult to Caesar, a clear statement of treason, and . . .'

'So the Nazarene won, Gaius. He forced Pilate to do exactly what he wanted and you crucified him.' Eros sat down on a couch and he suddenly looked tired and drained of strength.

'His gospel demanded he die that way and you Romans did everything to support it. You crowned Jesus-bar-Joseph in mockery, and took him up to a hill outside the city, and crucified him between two brigands. Probably because he had been bribed, the officer in charge of the detail used nails instead of ropes to support his body, and all the prophecies about the Messiah were fulfilled. He died quickly, and was placed in the tomb of a certain merchant named Joseph of Arimathaea from which the body vanished some time later. What do you think happened to that body, Gaius? Did it really come to life again as his followers claimed?'

'Of course not, my lord. I don't know what my master told you just now, but he is sick. He imagines the execution of the Nazarene brought a curse on him. At the time it seemed clear that the body must have been removed by the merchant you spoke of, Joseph of Arimathaea. The Jewish priests wanted us to put him to the torture, but he was a rich and influential man and we refused. The whole business appeared quite unimportant.'

'Yes, I suppose it did at the time. All the same I wish I had been in Jerusalem then. However influential he was I think I could have found a way to make that Joseph talk.' Eros lay back on the couch with his hands folded as though in prayer. Through the window before him the dark streaks of night had become a huge purple carpet slowly spreading across the valley and obscuring everything.

'Now, six years after he was executed, the memory of a Jewish criminal has driven your master mad, and brought me all the way here.

'I imagine that is all you can tell us, Gaius, so pour us out some wine and then you go and sleep off what you have had yourself.' He grinned as the shaking hands filled their glasses and the man stumbled gratefully away, and then looked at Sextus.

'Yes, my friend, I think you will get your inheritance, but I wonder how long you will be allowed to enjoy it.' Eros sipped the wine and stretched himself still further on the couch. In the thin moonlight his face was like tarnished silver.

'Listen very carefully, Sextus, and I will try and explain why I wanted to come here with you. I want you to realize the danger that threatens us. The evil which has been born, the flame rising against the Empire, merely because your fool of an uncle sentenced a maniac to die on a cross.'

The wind had blown up in the night, bringing clouds and scattered rain from the north, but at the moment there was a glimmer of moonlight through the shutters. Sextus lay on his couch staring at it and trying to review the events of the day. He was very tired and they all seemed unreal; half-remembered incidents from a dream, or things that had happened to other people.

But wealth was there. That sealed parchment had lain in his hands with its promise of gold in Rome and properties in three provinces, if he could only tell his uncle about some quite unimportant truth.

For it did seem unimportant, whatever Eros Dion might think. He trusted Eros' judgment, but in this case he couldn't see any cause for real alarm. Internal squabbles amongst the Jews brought about by a group of people whose symbol was a fish and who recognized each other by joining two 'L' shapes together to form the sign of a cross. There had always been crazy sects in the east and these Christians were no different. 'The Followers of the Anointed One' would be a fair translation of the word, he supposed, and they claimed that a dead criminal had come alive again and was a god who would reward his adherents with eternal bliss. By Eros' own admission they were largely drawn from slaves and the lower orders, and entirely confined to the Jews. 'What is there to worry about?' he had kept asking while Eros discussed them. 'Let the poor dolts keep their absurd superstition if it gives them any comfort.'

Now, as he lay there, staring at the moonlight through the shutters, he was beginning to wonder if he had been wrong. Eros was no fool, and for three years he and Naevius Macro had been studying the cult. From what their agents told them it had been almost wiped out in Palestine but was spreading rapidly to the north and into Asia Minor. Again and again the elders of Jewish communities had asked the local Roman officials to take action against it, but the Christians were well-behaved as far as civil law was concerned, and nothing had been done.

'Why should they act against them?' Sextus had broken in. 'The internal squabbles of the Jews are no concern of ours, and Rome does not fear foreign gods, because she accepts them. That is one of the reasons why we have been able to colonize the world. We do not antagonize our subject peoples by insulting their deities, but absorb them with our own. The god of the Nile is shown as another form of Father Tiber. A German sea nymph is regarded as Venus. In time that is bound to happen to this Messiah.'

'My friend, I wish you were right, but I'm afraid it will not happen.' Though he usually drank very little, Eros had got up and poured himself another cup of wine.

'Our gods, Jupiter, Minerva, and the rest, are merely symbols; divine figures in human form to explain the cosmos to simple people. We love and respect and fear them, but we never completely sacrifice ourselves in their service. You, for example, Sextus. Would you make a public protest if Tiberius were to place his own head on Jupiter's statue?'

'I certainly would not.' The very thought of offending the aged Emperor made Sextus wince. 'I would be insane if I did.'

'Of course you would be, because Jupiter might not protect you, and you would die very painfully and for nothing.

'This Messiah – the Nazarene your uncle executed – is different, though. He demands complete obedience from mankind, but he rewards it with the promise of eternal life and happiness. That is the first terrible thing about him.' Sextus had never seen his friend look so tired since their days in the German forest.

'The second thing I fear is this. During his very short ministry, Jesus preached to poor and humble people, and he told them that all mankind is equal in his sight, and loyalty to God is far more important than loyalty to a human master.

'Don't you see what that means, Sextus? The greater part of humanity live wretched lives which they accept because they fear authority, pain, and the mystery and finality of death. But take away that last fear and the others become meaningless. Give them the promise that death is not something to be dreaded, but an eternity of happiness, and human life and authority won't count for much.

'I know what you are going to say.' He had gripped Sextus' arm as he tried to break in. 'This cult is confined to the Jews now, but I don't think it will remain so for very much longer. And if once it starts to spread across the Empire, we might have a movement that could undermine the whole structure of governments, and bring down law and order like a house of straw.

'Remember what happened to Spartacus. He was outnumbered by Crassus, because many of his followers were a frightened rabble who deserted him. But, if they hadn't been frightened; if they had had a faith that removed the fear of death and promised them heaven by their dying for it. Then I think there would have been a different result at Apulia.'

Well, Eros might be right, Sextus supposed. It was a horrible possibility, but he was too tired to think about it any more. He lay back, considering pleasanter things: gold in Rome, a farm in Egypt, and properties in Italy and Sicily and Gaul. Outside, little flurries of rain pattered on the shutters and the wind sighed over the house, lulling him to sleep.

'Wake up and listen.' He opened his eyes and saw that Eros was out of bed and standing beside him. The Greek had a sword in his hand and was staring at the door. There was a light showing beneath it, and from somewhere in the distance they could hear a noise. A long, muttering, rumbling chant, as though a hundred voices were repeating some formula and beating their feet in time to it. They spoke in a rough provincial dialect, and the words were incomprehensible at first. Then Eros pulled open the door and they could hear clearly. 'Crucify,' the chant went. 'Crucify . . . Crucify him . . .'

'Take your sword, Sextus, but I don't think we will have to use them.' Eros stepped out into the corridor which was lit by oil lamps set in niches along the walls. Thick tarry smoke was drifting down it from the courtyard beyond, and as they walked forward the whole building rang with more cries of 'Crucify him.'

'So that's it.' Eros nodded as the corridor turned to the right. 'The madman acts out the story again.' The yard in front of them was packed tight with humanity, and the smell of unwashed bodies merged with the stench of torches. Every retainer, slave and hanger-on in the estate appeared to be assembled there and they clearly were taking part in some well-drilled ritual. They were silent as Eros and Sextus pushed through the archway, and then an old man at the front raised his arms and all of them, men, women and children, threw back their heads and shouted, 'Crucify him', again.

'No, no, do not ask me to do this. I can find no fault in the man. Please do not ask it of me.' Pilate stood on a stone platform at the end of the courtyard with his hands stretched out in supplication. He was dressed in the full robes of a provincial governor, but the gold laurel crown and staff of office were dull and tarnished, and his robe was crumpled. The whole effect was immensely pathetic; a poor actor trying to please a rabble. Behind him stood Gaius Vinius: the mockery of a centurion, with sagging flesh bulging out over his breast-plate.

But it wasn't the human figures that horrified Sextus. Between the crowd and his uncle, two dummies had been placed. They were made of cloth, stuffed with straw or sawdust and, though roughly sewn together, they had obviously been conceived by an artist and suffering was clear in their every feature. The backs had been striped with paint to simulate the marks of a whip, the thongs seemed to be cutting into the wrists, and the heads were bent forward as though staring hopelessly at the ground. The one to the right of the platform was squat and broad, but the other was very tall and, though its face was invisible, the wreath of briars around the forehead gave it an oddly stag-like appearance.

'Well, whom shall I release unto you?' Again Pilate stretched out his hands. 'It is your right to ask for the life of one criminal on your festival, so who shall it be? The robber, Barabbas, who has killed and pillaged and brought shame on all your race, or this man with whom I can find no fault? I beg you to let me release him to you.' His words were drowned by a roar of 'Barabbas', and flaxen-haired Gauls screamed and shook their fists in mock fury. Pilate watched them for a moment and then slowly lowered his hands. As he did so, two men stepped forward to the right-hand figure, untying its wrists and hoisting it on to their shoulders, while the crowd shouted in triumph. It was clear that they were no mob, but a well-drilled company of actors, paying for a life of idleness by indulging their patron's crazy whim.

'And what of that man? Your king? The King of the Jews?' There was a final roar of 'Crucify him,' but much more subdued, because the climax of the entertainment had obviously been the release of Barabbas. Already women were gathering up their children and starting to file away. The actors had paid for their keep till the next performance, and could go to bed.

'Then I am innocent of the blood of this just man.' The yard was half empty when Gaius lifted a bowl of water and held it out to his master.

'Leave that alone.' Eros walked forward with the torch-light glowing on his set face. 'You are not innocent, Procurator, and your hands will never be cleaned by water. But the blood on them comes from Rome, not from this.' His left hand grasped the remaining dummy, and the sword in his right slashed and hacked at it. Sawdust gushed out from the cloth and the thing started to shrink.

'The man is dead, Procurator. He died on a cross in Judaea and his followers stole the body to create a legend. He never rose from the dead, and you have nothing to fear from him.' Eros stepped up on to the platform with the almost empty sack in his hand.

'But there is still a curse on you, my lord. Though the Nazarene was a poor deluded fool, you didn't realize how dangerous his teachings could be. Now, because you gave him the death he asked for, they have started to spread; a disease that could eat into the whole body of the Empire unless we destroy it.' He threw the sack away from him and motioned Sextus up the steps.

'Well, Procurator, you sent for your nephew and here he is. How must he earn his inheritance? What is the truth you want him to find for you?'

'I want to know who the man really was.' Pilate didn't look at Sextus, but stared down at the heap of crumpled cloth on the ground.

'After his death, when the body disappeared, I thought like you, of course: that his followers had stolen it from the tomb to create a legend. I started to have inquiries made, though, and later I wasn't so sure.' Pilate's voice was without any expression and it might have been a dead man talking to them.

'The Emperor recalled me from Jerusalem before I could discover anything, but it did seem to me that the man might be what he claimed. Even in his boyhood he was supposed to have had strange powers. And later, during his ministry, there were a dozen stories of healing and miracle working. Only one thing appeared to show that he was a charlatan, and I never had time to check on it.'

'Go on, man. What was this thing? Tell me how we can discredit him.' Pilate had broken off, as though too tired to continue, and Eros grasped his shoulder. 'What was it that you couldn't check on?'

'It was the years – the years between.' The old man swayed on his platform and only Eros' grip held him up.

'We knew about the Nazarene's childhood. We know when he appeared out of the wilderness to begin his ministry. But in between . . .' Pilate's voice was so faint that Eros had to lean forward to make out the words.

'For eighteen years. From the age of twelve to thirty, nothing is known about him, nothing at all.'

To Naevius Macro, Prefect of the Praetorian Guard and the Department of Vigilance, from his friend and servant, Eros Dion, greetings.

Eros had procured a scribe in the village where they were staying and he nodded approvingly as the man's hand ran quickly across the parchment. He hated slow dictation. He hated everything that was slow and inefficient.

Sextus Ennius and I left his uncle's house yesterday. There is nothing more to be learned from Pilate, and we hope to find a ship at Marseilles which will take us directly to the east. In my opinion, there is not even time to call at Rome and report to you personally. Once this cult, which preaches human equality and an obedience to a god who rewards by eternal happiness, leaves the Jews and starts to spread we will have to act quickly.

My last letters from Rome tell me that Tiberius is very sick and before long Gaius Caligula must take his place. When that happens, you, my old friend, will be the most powerful man in the Empire. I pray that you will use your powers wisely where these so-called Christians are concerned.

We both recognize their dangers, but I do not agree that civil suppression is the solution to the problem. People who hope for martyrdom, who believe that they will gain bliss by dying for their insane faith, will go cheerfully to the cross or the stake and provide a most unfortunate example to others. As I see it, the only way to destroy the movement is by discredit or ridicule.

Fortunately the possibilities of this are favourable. It appears that after the death of Jesus-bar-Joseph, Pilate started an investigation into his life. This showed that his later years were as we already know, and he was just a wandering preacher who deluded himself into thinking he was a god, and died on the cross.

His early life is clear too. He was the precocious son of poor but respectable parents, living at Nazareth till the age of twelve.

However, it is the middle years of the man's life that should concern us. As we both know, people only conceal their pasts if they contain something discreditable, and this 'Messiah' must have had something to hide. From the age of twelve to thirty when he appeared to the man called John the Baptist, nothing is known about him. He did not even tell his closest followers where he had been or what he had done, and unless my knowledge of humanity is very poor, he must have had a good reason for this.

That is why I am going to Judaea. It is my intention to open up the hidden period of this man's past, and discover what he had to conceal. I have no doubt that I will soon supply you with enough evidence to bring down the whole hateful superstition in a flood of ridicule, laughter, and contempt.

Now, may we consider the other discrepancies of the story? Concerning the nails . . .

At about the same time that Eros was dictating his letter, a man was speaking in a square at Alexandria. He was a young man, but his voice was strong and self-confident and the words carried easily to all his audience.

He spoke to them of a god who had revealed himself in Palestine and was the only true ruler of mankind. He appeared to be a strange fellow, this god, because he demanded very little from his followers; no sacrifices, no priests, and no offerings except complete belief in himself and his teachings, which were stranger still, for they stated that it was the poor and downtrodden who would rule the earth.

The collection of Egyptians, Greeks and Africans listened

politely enough, the well-to-do cynically and the poor with a mixture of hope and disbelief. Only a little group of Jews seemed to take him seriously, and after a time one of their members asked the young man a question. The answer meant nothing to the majority of his listeners, but it appeared to goad the Jews into a fury and stones were lifted from the ground and thrown at him.

As all sane people knew, Hebrew quarrels are best left alone, and the preacher was obviously a Jew himself. It was not an affair for outsiders and the others hurried away. Only one thing appeared strange to them. As the stones ripped open his face and knocked him bleeding to the ground, the young man smiled.

# Two

'A month, my lords. Yes, it must be over a full month since you arrived here, and you have learned precisely nothing.' Marcus Cato, the Tribune commanding the single regular cohort in Judaea, had no connection with his famous namesake and owed his high rank to strict regard for detail and the fact that he had survived some of the bloodiest battles in modern history.

'And, if I know anything about this country, you won't learn much either. It's the only province I've served in where I've felt that the population actively hated us.' Cato was technically on duty and dressed in full uniform though the weather was stifling, and his armour clanked loudly as he walked across the room of the inn.

'The Jews are a hard, stiff-necked people. Merchants and simple craftsmen on the surface, but underneath, every one of them is a religious fanatic and a revolutionary: Zealots who pray to their god to drive us out, and even the common brigands rob under a guise of religion. Sicarii – the Knifemen – they call themselves. We kill a few of them, we drive the survivors out into the desert, but they always come back reinforced.'

'Your garrison is under-strength, I have heard.' Eros smiled sympathetically, but the Tribune snorted with disgust.

'Under-strength. That's putting it mildly. Before Augustus re-organized the army, there was a full legion in the province. Now what have we? My lads and a company of Balearic slingers here in Jerusalem, two half-strength auxiliary cohorts of Syrian Greeks up in Galilee, a few frontier police and one good cavalry regiment at Jericho. Three thousand men and half of them raw recruits or veterans, too old to march, let alone fight. Augustus cut us down, and Tiberius beggared us.'

'But in our latest letters from Rome it appears that Tiberius is a sick man. You may find his successor more generous to the army, Tribune.'

'And let's hope your letters are correct, Sextus Ennius.' Cato nodded in hearty agreement. 'Yes, when the old goat dies, Gaius Caligula is bound to take his place and then we will have a real emperor. Little Boots, the son of my first general, Germanicus. He won't forget his soldiers. Did I ever tell you how he used to parade with us on the Rhine when he was a child, dressed up in a little uniform and a pair of miniature legionary's boots that got him his nickname?'

'Yes, you have done, Tribune.' Eros refilled his own and Sextus' glass. Though a heavy toper in his free moments, Cato never drank while on duty, which was one of the reasons he held his rank. 'And you still haven't found one Christian for me?'

'I haven't, Eros Dion, and I don't think I ever will. My belief is that they've all been driven out of Judaea by now. Can't see any harm in the poor blighters myself, whatever you may say. This country's full of crazy sects and always will be. The Christians are no worse than any of the others, though their leader appears to have made a thorough nuisance of himself. He came riding into Jerusalem, more like a conqueror than a holy man, with his followers cheering themselves hoarse and throwing leaves under his donkey's feet. I wasn't here myself, of course; I was up in Syria; real soldiering that was. But, from what my predecessor, Quintus Flavius, told me, it was a good job the priests took the law into their own hands and forced the Governor to stretch him up.' Cato raised his arms above his shoulders, hung his head down and groaned, as though in extreme agony.

'Yes, a weak man your uncle must have been, if I may say so, Sextus Ennius. Now, if Marcus Crassus had had his job and the blighters had tried to tell him what to do, there'd have been some fun: crosses from here to Samaria I shouldn't wonder. My old leader, Germanicus, had a way with rebels too, my lord. I remember what happened to . . .'

Jerusalem was a dull city, Eros thought. Cato had launched into a long military reminiscence, and he turned and stared out of the window. The Mount of Olives might be pleasant enough, but most of the buildings were small and drab, and the temple they boasted about would pass unnoticed in Italy. Its roof had been repaired some time back and had an oddly piebald appearance. Even the hills surrounding the place looked dispirited, and a wind was blowing from the south, bringing the stench of the garbage pits in the Valley of Hinnon.

Still it was here that the story had ended, and here that they had to start to piece it together, though the first month had been fruitless. There had been visits to monasteries and to the Jewish elders who denounced the man passionately as an apostate, but always denied knowing him; confessions obtained under torture which were later proved false, long hours poring through old files, and the false trails of informers after gain. 'Do not repeat it to anybody, lord, or I will be killed. Yes, I did know that bad man and for just two gold pieces, I will tell you all about him.'

So far they had discovered nothing of value; not a single fact to help them. They knew all about the Nazarene's boyhood in Galilee, but from the age of twelve, when he was said to have left home, there was nothing. Not one single clue as to where he had been or what he had done. It appeared that he had not even mentioned his middle life to his closest followers, and it was like an enormous void; almost as though he had vanished from the earth for eighteen years before appearing to the hermit named John the Baptist at the age of thirty.

All the same, they would discover the truth in time. The man had to have been somewhere, and it was just a matter of patience and research. Macro had promised to send him a dozen trained agents from Rome, and with their help he would find a crack in the wall and the void would start to fill. Eros was still completely confident of that, and he was also sure that the Nazarene must have had a very good reason for concealing his past. Somewhere during those eighteen years there had been an incident of discredit or shame: the evidence to set the world laughing and destroy his religion with ridicule.

'The sun is behind the temple, Tribune, which means that you are off duty.' He interrupted Cato's long-winded account of an uprising which Germanicus had crushed with great brutality. 'Won't you drink a glass of wine with us now?'

'Thank you, but I'll have Posca instead of your Falernian.' He watched Eros pour out the strong, sour liquid which formed part of a legionary's rations, and took the glass from him.

'Ah, that's soldier's tipple, and it never harmed anyone, whatever they say.' Before raising it to his lips, Cato clanked over to the window to make sure he was off duty.

'As I said before, I don't think you'll find any of your Christians in Jerusalem these days. The poor devils either keep their beliefs to themselves or have hooked it. I can't say I blame them either.' He pointed across the square.

'There was a man stoned to death at that very corner only a few months ago. A revolting affair, and my lads had to stand by and pretend it wasn't their business. We just haven't got the strength to risk provoking a full-scale riot.

'When I first came out here, I had a slave who became a Christian . . .' He broke off, grinning at the sudden eagerness on Sextus' face.

'Oh, no, I said *had*, didn't I? There's nothing to help you there. When people heard about it, I couldn't even send him to market without knowing that he'd come back with a black eye or a mass of bruises; that's what your pious Jew does to Christians.

'The fellow was an unsatisfactory servant too. Quick and willing enough, but somehow I never felt that he really regarded me as his master. I finished off by selling him to a Greek merchant who was on his way home to Corinth.

'And, though it's not my place to complain, I hope you'll be a bit tactful with your inquiries. The General was saying the same thing only this morning. Oh, we don't mind lending you a few clerks and handing over the files, but we can't afford any trouble with the Jewish authorities. Everybody in Jerusalem knows what you're here for, but they can't take in the real reason. Because it's not Rome's policy to interfere with the internal affairs of her subject nations, some of the elders accuse us of favouring the Christians, and this country could be ripe for trouble.'

'I understand, Cato.' Eros nodded, but he was smiling to himself. Until the right time came, that was exactly what he wanted people to think. They must appear completely open-minded towards the Christians: earnest seekers after truth who were interested in the story of the Nazarene because he had founded a novel and benevolent religion. Only when the necessary evidence had been collected and checked would they come out into the open and destroy him.

'We'll be very discreet, I promise you,' he said. It would never do to turn Cato or his superiors against them. The Governor had been easy to deal with; a mild, easy-going man, who delegated authority whenever he could. But the General, Rufus Aquila, was a very different matter. A black-bearded, irascible professional soldier, preoccupied with policing his province with a token force, and full of contempt for their mission.

'I'm glad to hear that, my lord.' Was it imagination, or had Cato's manner changed suddenly? A moment before he had been scowling, but now there was a slightly furtive look in his face.

'This is really good Posca, and could never do anybody any harm. Do you mind if I refill my glass?' Sextus had taken in his expression now and moved to one side of the doorway with Cato following. Almost miraculously the Tribune's armour had ceased to make a sound.

'No, good wine never hurts you. I remember a standard-bearer of the Eleventh Legion, who could knock back a couple of jugs at a sitting and be as fresh as paint for the next parade.' Sextus pulled back the door and Cato's hand shot out.

'Please – please, master. Great lord, do not hurt me.' The boy wriggled in his grasp like an eel. He looked about twelve, but his expression could have belonged to a bitter old man. His matted hair was spoiled with ringworm in places and two of his front teeth were missing. He was dirty, not so much from mud and dust as from being habitually unwashed.

'Am I hurting you, lad? Do you call this really hurting?' Cato's grip tightened on his ear and the boy screamed in agony. 'I am just playing with you, but soon I may really start to hurt.

'Now, why were you listening outside the door? Who told you to, and what were you hoping to hear?'

'I wasn't listening, master.' Tears were trickling down the soiled cheeks. 'I came with a message, and the girl told me where the room was. I was frightened for a moment and didn't like to knock.'

'I see. We will have a word with the girl, but first you can tell us what your message is.'

'It is for them, master; for the noblemen from Rome.' He suddenly twisted out of Cato's grasp and flung himself down in front of Sextus.

'My Lord, you want to hear about the great rabbi; the Anointed One?'

'Perhaps I do.' Sextus drew back slightly. The thin body stank of sweat and was obviously crawling with lice. 'What do you know about him?'

'I know nothing, lord. I am too young and stupid to understand such mysteries. But I have been told to lead one of you to a person who does. Just a silver piece it will cost, and then you will hear everything you want to know.' A grimy hand stretched out, palm uppermost.

'Give it to me, lord. One silver piece and I will take you to the Mother of God.'

It was dark now, with the sun far behind the hills, and the wind had dropped, leaving a thick blanket of cloud to cover the city and seal in its heat and stench, so that the atmosphere was barely supportable.

The Mother of God! Sextus considered the title as he followed his guide through the streets. He had smiled when the boy had pronounced it, but Eros had leaned forward eagerly and said: 'I never heard of God having a mother.' The reply had been completely assured. 'Their God has.'

Well, soon he would know if this was just another false lead, or the first piece of luck to come their way. They were going north; the temple was on their right, and Herod's palace and the citadel behind them. The heat seemed to increase with every step as they walked down narrow alleys into the Valley of the Tyropoeon which divided the city into two almost equal sections.

Probably the first assumption was correct, Sextus thought, and this was a mere ruse of some petty crooks hoping to profit by Roman credulity, because the boy's story was sketchy, to say the least. His name was Balek, an orphan who lived in the ruins of the lower city and existed by begging and taking on any odd assignments which came his way. That afternoon two men had approached him in the street and given him his present task.

They had told him of a woman who came from the north and now lived with them. She was old and very wise, and could heal the sick, for she was the mother of the Messiah. Balek said he had been frightened then, for everybody knew who the false god was; the Apostate from Nazareth who had broken the law and was an abomination for ever. He had also seen what happened to people who acknowledged him.

The men had been kind though and very persuasive. They had bought him sweets and promised him money, and in time he had agreed to do what they wanted. He was to go to the inn and ask for the Romans who were lodging there. He would then take one of them with him, following a prepared route to the north of the city, and the silver piece he received in payment would be his own.

'Only one of us!' Marcus Cato had broken in with a scowl. 'Oh, no, my lad. We're not going blundering into your slums without an escort. You will take us to this woman, but there will be a detail of soldiers too.'

'But that is impossible, master.' Balek had obviously been prepared for the question. 'I do not know where the woman is. I have to follow a route and the men will meet us somewhere on the way. If I have more than one person with me, they said they will not show themselves.

'You are the one who must come, my lord.' He had looked up at Sextus. 'They said it must be you. The tall, young man with a face that resembles the old Governor's.'

There had been no choice. In spite of Eros' anxiety and Cato's formal protest, Sextus had handed over the coin and followed his guide. He felt no anxiety himself, for however dangerous their teachings might be, the Christians were not thought to be violent. Besides, one Roman nobleman with a sword was a match for any rabble.

It was a rabble, too. Stalls with flaring tapers lined the alleys, and the sweepings of a dozen races thronged them. Tall, long-bearded Jews, who stared at him with open resentment, Nubians bearing tribal scars on their cheeks, Syrian Greeks holding each other's hands and chattering together like girls, and men from the East with fierce hawk-like faces that could give a child some bad nightmares.

'One moment, my lord.' A company of soldiers had turned out of a side lane, and their officer halted and saluted him. 'Don't think

I'm impertinent, but this is a bad area. There's nothing of interest to see either, unless . . .' He had grinned and made a gesture with his hands. 'If that's what you're after, my lord, why not come back with us. I can show you a much better place near the citadel. It's clean and . . .

'Very well, my lord. But don't say I didn't warn you.' He shrugged his shoulders as Sextus thanked him and hurried after the boy.

But there was no doubt what he had meant. They were in a brothel area now, and cheap scent joined the stink of corruption. Women of every race and colour and type leaned leering out of windows, and pimps crowded round him till he drew his sword half-way out of the scabbard and they fell back.

'Come on, master. This way, great lord.' The boy hurried up the far side of the valley. 'It cannot be far now. Soon the men will meet us. Soon you will see the Mother of God.' There was a square at the top of the slope with more stalls, and the air full of bargaining voices and the smoke of flares. Beyond it lay a patch of waste land heaped with bales of cloth and dried fruit; a caravan due out in the morning. Tethered camels beside them groaned in complaint, and the Nubian guards wore swords that were so curved that they looked more like ornaments than weapons.

But if the men existed, and the whole business wasn't just a trick of Balek's, they would show themselves soon, for this was one of the outskirts of the town. A dying area, with half of the hovels unoccupied and decayed, as though not worth the trouble of repair. Sextus had the feeling of enormous antiquity as he walked between them. Jerusalem might be a mean unlovely place, but it had been a city before Rome was thought of.

And what was he going to see, if Balek was telling the truth? More impostors trying to deceive them for a little gain? A crone performing conjuring tricks, or the one person who might help them to fill in the blanks? A woman whose son had preached a gospel that could threaten the Empire? The sweat on his forehead was suddenly cold, and his feet stumbled on the uneven ground. There were no stalls here and, apart from a dull glimmer of moonlight through the cloud, the area was in darkness. Its ruined houses looked like overgrown bushes in the gloom.

'We are here, my lord.' The boy had scrambled on to a crumbling wall and was looking down at him. 'I lied, master. There are no men, but I can take you to her, and the house is very near. Give me another coin first though. Just one more silver piece to see the Mother of Our God.'

'Very well.' Sextus pulled it out. So, he was right. Balek had tricked him. There was obviously no woman and he had brought him on a fool's journey. All the same he intended to recover what he paid. 'You can have the money, Balek, but you must come down and take it from me.'

'Oh, no, lord. Throw the coin here.' Balek grinned like a monkey from the top of the wall. 'Only one more silver piece and I will take you to her.'

'As you wish.' Sextus judged the distance in the gloom and tossed the coin towards him but just out of his reach, and as the boy tried to catch it, rushed forward to grasp him.

'Pig – Roman pig.' Sextus missed his hand by inches and Balek dropped over the wall to safety. 'Roman pig who crucified our God.' Sextus started to climb after him when the stones came.

So, that was it. He reeled back with blood pouring down his forehead. Marcus Cato had been right. He had blundered into an ambush and his attackers were all around him. The stones flew from every side, beating the sword out of his hand, knocking his legs from under him, and they still fell as he twisted on the ground. The blood from his forehead obscured what little light there was, but he suddenly remembered the local legend of David and Goliath. A typical Hebrew trick, that. A man challenges you to fight with swords, and you meet him with a sling.

'Brothers, do not kill him.' Just before he lost consciousness, he heard the voice. It seemed to come from a long way off, but was so cold and full of bitterness that he would remember it till his dying day.

'Even the killing of a wicked man is against the master's law. Hurt him though. We will hurt him very badly indeed.'

'Try and remember, Sextus Ennius. I know that you are still very weak, but it is vital that you tell me exactly what happened.' Cato's face was bent over him, as though suspended from the ceiling, and

Sextus closed his eyes again, trying to force memories together: to make one story out of a jumble of shadowy events.

At the beginning there had only been pain. The stones beating him to the ground, a pair of hands dragging him to his feet, and that bitter, authoritative voice giving more orders as the world faded into oblivion.

But that had only been the beginning of pain. After he came to, he had been bitterly cold, though from somewhere nearby there was a glint of flame and the smell of hot metal. When pain returned it wasn't brutal as before, but administered gently as though by an artist. Long, thin fingers had opened his hand, somebody had laughed, and the smell of heated metal had come closer and closer. Then his own scream had drowned the hiss of burning flesh and it had been dark again.

'We have to find these people, my friend, and you are the only one who can help us. You are a Roman citizen and they have dared to attack and torture you. Though I warned you against going with that boy, they must be rounded up and punished.' There was a strong tang of Posca on Cato's breath.

'Don't you understand that? If they are allowed to escape, the whole population will laugh at us. Surely you can describe some of them.'

'No, all I can remember is a voice. Their leader spoke in Greek. I would know him if I heard it again.' Sextus opened his eyes and looked around the room. He was obviously in a sick bay of the barracks, and a middle-aged man in a blue gown was standing behind Cato.

'It was dark, you see. All the time it was dark. But afterwards . . .'

Afterwards, there had only been pain for a long time, and intense cold and the strange way his body kept shaking. He was lying naked in a ruined building, and quite alone, though he seemed to think he had seen a child glance at him through the doorway and scurry off.

Then people had come and helped him. About five of them perhaps, but he couldn't be sure. They had put him on a litter and taken him to a house where an old bearded man and a girl had looked after him. He could remember them all right. The man seemed to be a doctor and he had rubbed ointment into his wounds and bandaged them. The girl had reminded him of a statue of the corn goddess; tall and full-breasted and warm. The very sight of her made his coldness worse. Though they placed hot bricks under the couch he might have been lying on a block of ice, and his teeth had chattered like sparrows.

The doctor gave him some bitter stuff to drink, and soon he felt sleep coming, but fought against it, knowing that he would never wake, and trying to hear what the doctor was telling the girl.

'It is the only way – remember David.' Several times he mentioned the king who had fought the giant, while the girl kept shaking her head as though in horror. 'Mercy comes before everything, my dear, and without your help the man will die.'

The doctor had gone then, and he was alone with the girl. She wore a long purple dress, and her hair was like red gold, which was unusual in a Jewess. She had come slowly towards him, slipping off the robe as she did so, and her naked body shone like that of the goddess. He had watched her pull back the blankets and climb in beside him, and as their flesh touched, warmth and sleep came together.

'Who were the others, Tribune?' He took Cato's arm and pulled himself up to a sitting position. 'The people who helped me?'

'We've no idea, but it's quite certain that they saved your life. When you didn't return that evening, we naturally combed the city, but there wasn't a trace of you. Then early this morning, a letter was delivered at the barracks. We followed its instructions and found you in a ruined temple near the Horse Gate, wrapped in blankets and heavily drugged. Your benefactors obviously want to remain anonymous, but I think I'm right in saying that you would have died without their help.

'Do you agree, Doctor?' Cato nodded to the other man. 'This is Marcellus Cinna, our regimental surgeon.'

'You are perfectly correct, Tribune.' Cinna had short grizzled hair and a face like a cat's. 'Sextus Ennius is a very strong fellow and a lucky one too. The man who patched you up was obviously a doctor and knew his business. I would very much like to meet him.'

'So would I. Also . . . .' Once again Sextus saw that white glowing body moving towards his bed.

'It's the others I want to meet.' Cato was fingering the hilt of his sword. 'These Christian devils who have dared to assault a Roman citizen. And to think that I defended them to Eros Dion just the other day.

'But I was forgetting. Dion asked me to give you his good wishes and apologies for not being here. He waited till Cinna was sure you were out of danger, and then went off to Tyre. It appears that one of your agents there has come up with a lead that might help him.

'Yes, a Roman citizen stripped, tortured and left to die of exposure. And I thought they were harmless.' Cato's face flushed with anger and his speech was slurred.

'We may be short-handed, but they won't get away with it. The general has recalled the cohorts from Galilee, and when they get here we'll turn every rat hole of this town inside out. That's one job that the priests will help us with too.'

'Are you sure they were Christians?' The boy, Balek, had mentioned the crucified god, and he had heard that bitter voice speak about 'the master's law', but that was the only evidence.

'Oh, we're sure enough. At first I thought it might have been a band of Zealots or Sicarii, but there's no doubt at all. Remember what they did to you. Surely that's ample proof.' Cato broke off frowning.

'My dear boy, you don't know, do you? You haven't seen what was done. I'm afraid this is going to upset you a good deal, but I think you had better look for yourself. Do you agree, Cinna?'

'Since you have mentioned it, I agree, though I would have preferred to wait until he was stronger.' The doctor shrugged his shoulders and stepped forward.

'This is not pretty, but the disfigurement is the only thing to worry about.' He lifted Sextus' left hand and started to unwind the bandages. 'Your hand will be out of action for a time, but the muscles are not damaged and the wound is healing well. As I said, the man who looked after you knew his business.' The last dressing came away, and he motioned Cato to hold him back.

'No, no.' Sextus gasped out in horror and fought against Cato's arms. He remembered the smell of hot iron and the pain, but he had been half-conscious and hadn't taken in what it meant.

'Not to me!' He'd seen slaves branded a hundred times, watched the process with amused interest when he was a child, but he'd never imagined it might happen to him.

It had happened, though. The open palm was a mass of scar tissue and in its centre, deeply burned into the livid flesh, was the mark of a cross.

'Tyre stands out in the sea as the palm of the hand does from the wrist', a poet had written, and Eros considered the description apt. Though the city had never fully recovered from its sack by the Macedonians more than three centuries ago, it was still one of the great ports of the world and breathtakingly beautiful. Egyptian grain ships lay at anchor in the harbour formed by the island and the causeway that Alexander had built, and the tall houses of the island city rose in tiers to walls which could obviously stand a considerable siege. More ships were unloading on the quay before his window and a war galley had started to round the island, her white oars rising and falling like the wings of a bird in the blue-green sea.

It was very pleasant to be here after Jerusalem, Eros thought, watching bearded Phoenician merchants strolling arm in arm and little ladies chattering together in their gaily draped litters. The tart, strangely exciting smell of rotting shell-fish, from which the famous dye was made, hung over everything. Tyre looked as though its prosperity would last for ever.

That was just a dream of course. Since the new naval base had been established at Caesarea, half of the town's importance had vanished, and trade was falling away fast. Cheap Egyptian products were bringing down the price of dyes and purple glass, exports were declining, and it was merely a matter of years before 'Tyre the Magnificent', as they had once called her, ground into obscurity. Those ladies in their litters were laughing in ignorance of the city's fate, and their husbands, so grave and self-assured, were probably negotiating loans or talking wistfully of the days when Phoenicia ruled the seas and their great daughter, Carthage, was the mistress of the world.

Still, it was restful to forget the dust and heat of Judaea for a while, and pleasant to feel one was not loathed and despised as a servant of the occupiers. Eros leaned back on his couch and smiled to himself, though he was very worried about Sextus. The doctor had promised that the wound would heal cleanly, but the scar might remain in his mind as well as on the palm. All the same, there was no denying that the attack gave them a useful lever. Before it, Cato and his general had sneered at their fears of the Nazarene cult, but now they would change their tune and take whatever action he considered necessary. Also, the Jewish authorities could be invited to co-operate with them. Eros had no intention of acting openly against the Christians at this juncture, but that cross burned into his friend's flesh gave him the power to arrest whoever he wanted.

What would he learn in Tyre, he wondered. The summons had sounded important enough to make him hurry there, and he just hoped the informant would prove reliable and not another romancer out for petty gain. Was a chink beginning to appear in the Nazarene's hidden years at last? Something cruel, or criminal? Better still, something merely comic or pathetic.

The House of the Sea really was a pleasant inn, or perhaps guest house would be a better name for it: one of those new establishments which had sprung up everywhere since the reign of Augustus, and catered for Roman tourists and well-to-do merchants. It was a little dowdy, perhaps, rather ultra-respectable; parties of young naval officers were not encouraged, and the vomitorium was well in the background and rarely used. But the food and service were excellent, and he had never slept on a more comfortable couch.

'Your merchant appears to be late.' Eros glanced at the hourglass set in an alcove. 'I think you said he would be here by noon.'

'Do not worry, master.' Pallas Pelleus, the Department's representative on the Phoenician Coast, was a short, stout eunuch just approaching middle age. Although technically a slave, very few people knew this, and he was answerable only to Rome. After a few moments' conversation Eros had judged that he was both efficient and devoted to his work.

'Hanno is a man of enormous self-importance, as you will soon discover. He will keep his appointment but it will give him pleasure to make us wait.

'An objectionable fellow, I'm afraid. He lives by any villainy which comes his way: usury, blackmail, and the introduction of young men to certain addictive vices are a few of his trades. He is very rich, but works a full twelve hours a day because he enjoys his vocation; the kind of man who loses money to ruin a business rival for the mere pleasure of it. I could name twenty people in this city alone who pray daily for his death, and only heavy bribes to the magistrates keep him at liberty. Judge for yourself, master.' Pallas pointed down to the quay. An enclosed litter was approaching with an escort of armed Nubians marching at either side. It was a huge thing decorated with brass and silver, which should have had twelve bearers to support it, but was carried by only eight who gasped and staggered beneath their enormous burden. The carriage of a man who was frightened and ostentatious, and either mean or deliberately cruel.

'I understand,' Eros nodded as the litter swayed into the courtyard of the inn and passed out of sight. 'Not the most reliable of witnesses, I would have thought.'

'I am not sure about that, master. Hanno is too rich to have invented a story for money, and too cautious to risk our displeasure with a clumsy lie. He said that he had two motives for approaching us. One was the simple wish to gain favour with Rome and the other to satisfy a deep personal hatred of the Christian cult. I am prepared to believe that he has some information about the Nazarene to give, but I think he will exaggerate the details you wish to hear.' Pallas stood up as the door opened and two people entered the room. 'May I present Dela Hanno, merchant of this city. My superior, Eros Dion, freedman of the Empress Livia, and the most trusted servant of our lord Tiberius himself.'

'I am delighted, Hanno.' Eros studied his guest. The man was grey-haired, of middle height, and wore the typical curled beard of his nation. The face above it was a mask which gave no hint of his thoughts, though the eyes and mouth looked mean and vicious. The woman behind him also appeared middle-aged at first glance, but a second showed Eros that she was still young, and the illusion came from the bitterness of her expression.

'Your servant, my lord.' Hanno bowed and lowered himself on to a couch, spreading out his purple gown so as not to disturb its folds. His right hand was deformed and rather horrible. The fingers had only one joint and their nails grew where the knuckles should have been.

'You will take wine, Hanno?' Pallas had already filled a cup and offered it to him, but the Phoenician pointed to the girl. 'Give it to her first.'

'You use a female to taste against poison?' Eros watched the woman lift the cup. Her hand shook slightly and her expression had changed to one of deep anxiety.

'I do, Eros Dion. Areté shares my couch, so why not my food? Drink more deeply, girl. Let me see you swallow.' Hanno grinned at the dread in her face and then took the cup himself.

'Forgive the precaution, my lords. I do not suspect your intentions of course, but I am a man of many enemies and some of them may be employed at this inn.'

'Please do not apologize.' Eros had rarely disliked anybody so much at first acquaintance, and he tried to look through the mask of Hanno's face and see if he could be trusted. The fellow's nose was obviously at a hundred rat holes and he might well have discovered something. All the same, his information would have to be treated with suspicion.

'And now to business, Hanno,' he said. 'You claim to know something about the Hebrew apostate, Jesus-bar-Joseph, who was executed while Pontius Pilate was Procurator of Judaea. Why did you not give the information to Pallas and save me the journey?'

'I do not confide in slaves, lord, and I am probably the only man in Tyre who knows our friend's status.' His eyes mocked the eunuch's anger.

'No, Eros Dion, the story is a good one and I wish to tell it to a person in authority. When I heard that Pallas was seeking information about the man, I said I would only repeat it to his superior.' Hanno lifted the cup and sipped the strong, sweet-smelling liquid, rolling it around his mouth before swallowing.

'You also told him that you required no favour in return. Why is that, Hanno? I have heard that you are a man of business.'

'There are many forms of business.' Hanno pointed to the floor and the girl knelt down at his feet. 'I will be glad to tell you my motives when I have heard yours. Why are you interested in this Jesus, Eros Dion? Do you want to encourage his cult and use it as means to humiliate the Jewish nationalists, perhaps? Or are you merely a student, interested in novel religions?'

'Neither of those.' As he mentioned the Nazarene by name, Hanno's mask had left him and open hatred was clear on his face. He was obviously a potential ally, and Eros told the truth. 'I think his teaching is the most dangerous thing the world has ever known, and he must be discredited.'

'Good. I am your ally, my friend.' Hanno smiled, showing brown teeth worn almost down to the gums. 'I too fear his gospel and realize the dangers involved. But it is the man himself I hate. The boy I almost regarded as a son, till he betrayed me.'

'You hate a man who died, Hanno? Surely you do not believe in the story of his resurrection.'

'No, it was the memory I meant.' The girl shuddered because the little deformed hand was resting on her shoulders and its nails dug and kneaded into the flesh. The practice was clearly a common one for her skin was marred by a criss-cross of other cuts and bruises.

'I knew your Jesus, and his very name offends me. I want to make it a term of insult and abuse till the end of time, and with your help, I have the means to do so.

'Oh, such a pupil he was when I befriended him. Just a runaway apprentice, but as sly as myself and twice as ruthless. Given the chance that boy would have torn out a man's eyes to reclaim a debt and taken the sockets in place of interest.

'Fetch me more wine, woman. My anger makes me thirsty.' He handed his cup to the slave and she stood up to refill it, clearly welcoming a moment of mercy from those kneading fingers.

'Like a son, that Hebrew boy was. Quick and clever and cunning and I thought I had a partner for life. But he betrayed me, of course. Even I, his benefactor, he sold for gain because he was incapable of honesty or love, and my heart broke when he left me.' The woman returned with the cup and, after she had drunk some, Hanno drained the remainder of its contents with a single quick motion.

'But we found him again, didn't we Areté?' He twisted her face towards Eros and she nodded. 'Yes, years later I found that boy. He'd grown into a man and age had changed his ambitions as well as his body. Power and wealth he'd wanted before, but now his claims had become much more exalted. Standing on a hill in Galilee he was, and proclaiming that something called the Kingdom of Heaven was at hand.'

Hanno told his story well at the beginning, and Eros treasured every word, for it was exactly the kind of thing he had hoped to hear. A runaway apprentice joining forces with a man who dabbled in any villainy which would yield a profit. For three years Jesus had worked for Hanno, showing such aptitude for fraud and vice and the enticement of fools that the Phoenician almost acknowledged him as his master. Then one day he simply vanished, taking all their joint savings and notes of credit as well.

Yes, that fitted, Eros thought, as Hanno paused for the girl to refill his cup, again watching her sip from it before drinking himself. He was still not sure if there was any truth in Hanno's tale, but the Nazarene had mentioned a similar incident himself. A discharged steward who sold back pledges to his master's creditors. Just the kind of incident he had hoped to hear, and Eros smiled out at the big war galley coming in towards the causeway. She looked very lovely, brightly painted and gilded, with the blue eye of Apollo at the bow.

From then on, Hanno's account became more vague and almost rambling at times. He wasn't sure of the dates or even the reason for his visit to Galilee, though he thought it was about ten years ago and he had been on his way to the City of Tiberius to offer a loan to certain merchants. Eros wondered why he did not consult the woman who had accompanied him, but he obviously regarded her as a mindless animal, only worthy to satisfy his body and protect it with her own.

The atmosphere sounded correct though. The dusty road along the Sea of Galilee, the smell of goats and dung fires, and tarred fishing nets drying in the sun. Just after Magdala, the road was blocked by a crowd filing up towards a hillside on the left, and he heard talk of a great rabbi who was going to address them. Hanno wished to have his money safe in Tiberius before dusk, but he was also an inquisitive man. He sent his escort on ahead and he and the girl, Areté, followed the crowd.

'Are you unwell?' Hanno had broken off, and shook his head when the girl reached for the cup. The mask-like face looked flushed and he was sweating heavily.

'I am all right, Eros Dion, but your wine is very strong and it is a hot day. Besides, that is unpleasant.' He broke wind and pointed towards the harbour. The galley was tying up against the mole now. Half her beauty had vanished with the loss of motion and she had obviously been a long time at sea. The breeze brought a foul stench from the unflushed slave decks.

'And it was that man.' Hanno continued the story. 'Standing up on the crest of the hillside, he was, with the crowd spread out around him. More than ten years had passed since Jesus-bar-Joseph left me, but I recognized him all right. He kept spreading out his arms to the people while he taught them blasphemy in the name of the Jewish God. If only my escort had been with me, we would have carved a way through to him and his memory would not trouble you, Eros Dion.'

'More wine, Areté. My thirst is terrible.' Another bubble of wind burst from his mouth and the forehead was running with sweat. If he hadn't seen the girl sample every cupful, Eros would have suspected poison.

'Yes, such evil my former partner gave those people, and knowing his nature I sensed he was laughing at them from behind the skin. The humble and poor should become the masters, he said. No woman could be divorced save for adultery. A man should not seek revenge against an enemy. He who had robbed and almost ruined me dared to say that.' Hanno's face really was a mask now, the flesh rigid as metal, and the neck and jaws might have been moving on hinges.

'A kingdom, he promised those simple fools. A place of eternal ease and joy in return for faith in himself and a denial of the rulers of this earth. Such a gospel he taught! Even if the man had remained my friend, I would have hated him for it.'

'What is it, fellow? You must be ill.' Hanno's body suddenly arched back like a bow and as Eros leaned forward, a sweet sickly smell joined the stench of the galley. 'Tell me what is the matter with you. Should we send for a doctor?'

'A doctor would be no comfort to him, lord.' For the first time the slave girl spoke. The sad, bitter expression had left her face and she was smiling up at the straining, retching figure on the couch. 'My master is dying and I must finish the story for you.'

'You poisoned him, girl.' Eros dragged her to her feet. 'But how? I saw you drink from his cup each time you filled it.'

'That is true, my lord, but I ate unleavened bread before coming here. I shall share his death, but the poison will take a little longer to affect me.' She held out her arm and he saw a sachet sewn into the sleeve and the sprinkle of brown powder. 'I am a Dacian, lord, and in our country there grows a certain tree which produces red berries. Grind those berries very finely, mix them with a man's drink, and you get that.' She laughed as Hanno's chest arched still higher, and Eros imagined the years of pain and disgust and humiliation which had caused such hatred.

'Why, woman?' For a brief moment the spasm passed and her master's horrible little hand clutched out at her. 'I know you hated me, Areté, but I have owned you since you were a child. Why now?'

'Because I wish to finish the story, Hanno.' Eros saw that Areté was beginning to feel the poison herself now, but she still smiled.

'There was no partner who betrayed him, lords; no Jewish boy who stole his money. Only the end of the story is true, and I was there to witness it. A man who talked of love, and human dignity, and promised that there was a kingdom of peace and rest for those who suffered; a place where there would be no more shame or degradation. That rabbi was the only man who gave me hope in all my life, and this pig hated him.' Her fingers shot out and three red lines appeared on Hanno's face.

'He was frightened, lords. The rabbi's message terrified him. Night after night, I have heard him scream while he slept and felt the couch grow damp with his sweat. Then, when he learned you sought information about the cult, he made up this story of a partner who defrauded him.' As if an upright rack was stretching her spine, she turned rigidly towards Hanno.

'Listen, pig,' she said. 'Listen, great master, who takes such pleasure in pain.' Hanno lay quite motionless and Eros imagined he was already dead.

'The rabbi made another promise, didn't he? Gehenna, he called it; the place of retribution for the evil-doers; the fire to burn those who torture children.' Taller and taller her body grew and blood crept out of her mouth like a scarlet snake.

'I was a child when you bought me, Hanno, so burn.' She tilted forward into the dead man's arms and her voice sounded like tearing parchment. 'Burn in my rabbi's fire for ever.'

'Of course we are prepared to support you, masters. We always have been.' The three representatives of the High Priest bowed in unison.

'It is merely the means of suppression that we are not agreed upon.' Their leader, Esdral, was a very old man with a white beard and red-rimmed eyes ruined by a lifetime of study. He kept fingering the Star of David around his neck as if the feel of the metal gave him confidence.

'You, who represent Rome and the state, consider that at some future date these so-called Christians may become a political threat to your empire. I agree entirely, but the threat to us is not in the future. It is already here, ravaging, desecrating, destroying our law, our faith, everything we love and worship. For years we have begged you to give us a free hand against these people and it has taken an assault upon one Roman nobleman to make you consent.' He smiled bitterly at his hosts. Sextus lay on a couch by the window, his hand still bandaged, and Eros and Marcus Cato faced him from behind a table.

'I do not like the expression "free hand", Esdral.' Cato's fingers drummed quietly on the table top. 'We wish your masters to have the authority to arrest suspects for questioning, but that is all. We will not tolerate any incidents similar to the one which happened out there.' He nodded towards the window. It was just down the street that the ritual had taken place, and when he had heard the details, surprise had been Cato's first reaction. Stoning suggested quick movement. A man fleeing before a mob, or twisting inside a circle as he tried to avoid the missiles hurled at him. This had been long and slow and formal: the body stretched out on the ground, surrounded by naked figures holding rocks, and the crowd awed and silent. Then priests had intoned a malediction and the first figure had stepped forward, raised his rock and brought it crashing down on the victim's feet.

Yes, very slow that death had been. The next rock fell on the thighs, then one on the genitals, another on the chest, till finally mercy came and the skull was shattered. The strangest thing was that at no point did the victim cry out. He had smiled to the very end, as if incapable of feeling pain.

'This is a Roman province, my lords, and no freedman may suffer death unless he has broken our laws; certainly not for blasphemy against your god.'

'With your permission, Esdral.' The youngest of the three men stepped forward. 'There is no need to remind us of that, Tribune, and I too am a Roman citizen. My name is Saul – Saul of Tarsus.' Though very young and of less than average height, he gave an impression of age and power, and Sextus had the sudden feeling that he had seen him before.

'You sneer at the blasphemy against our god, but your own gods are involved too. The followers of the Apostate have not only stolen parts of our religion, but mixed them with alien beliefs to make the superstition attractive to all mankind.

'Think of the story of Jesus for a moment, my lords. He was born of a virgin and a god, as was Minos of Crete, and shepherds visited his cradle as they did for Mithras. He suffered death as our Messiah must do, and he finally rose from the dead as does Osiris of the Nile.' Saul ticked off the points on his fingers.

'And the symbols of the cult are a lamb and a fish; the Golden Fleece of the Persian Sun God and a beast sacred to your own Apollo.

'Don't you understand, my lords? Can't you see the spark that has fallen and is already glowing in the wind?' Saul suffered from some nervous complaint and his face trembled as he spoke. 'A monstrous plot to spread the superstition to every nation on earth.

'Oh, I know it is confined to our people now, but how long will that continue? Soon, very soon, I think, a man will come forward and offer the gospel of the Nazarene to the Gentiles, and then . . .' Saul had spoken quietly at first, but his voice rose to a scream.

'When that man appears, the fire from Galilee will swallow the world.'

'I entirely agree with you, Saul of Tarsus.' Eros smiled at him. 'But the problem is to decide what action to take against these people. You have listened very patiently to the account of what happened in Tyre, and though Hanno was merely a liar, my journey was of some importance, I think.

'That slave-girl killed her master, not only out of hatred, but because she hoped to profit by her act. Hanno had invented a story which we could use against the followers of the Nazarene, and the Nazarene had promised her eternal life and happiness in return for serving him. Had Areté survived the poison herself, she knew she would have died by torture. But she didn't care, did she? She was willing to risk two agonizing deaths in return for the assurance of happiness in an after-existence.

'That is the strength of the movement, Saul. The man promised everlasting bliss in return for a simple devotion to himself, and I don't think any amount of physical persecution can compete against such an offer. By the very nature of things, life must be hard and wretched for the vast majority of people, and if a man believes that he will gain an eternity of ease and happiness by dying for a cause, he will go very gladly to his death. The fellow who was killed out there proves my point, I think, and such deaths are bound to attract followers.

'There is only one way to stop this movement. We must discredit it and expose its founder as a deluded fool or a cunning imposter. We must laugh him out of existence, in fact.' Eros broke off as the street outside rang with the tramp of marching feet: the cohorts from the north which the General had recalled to Jerusalem.

'I have heard all this before, Eros Dion.' Saul's voice was low and relaxed again, and once more Sextus had the odd feeling that he should recognize him.

'You want to discover what the Nazarene did between the age of twelve and when he appeared to John the Baptist in the Wilderness of Judaea many years later.

'Well, don't you think that we also want to know that? Don't you imagine that we have combed the whole countryside and questioned every Essene community? There is nothing to be found, I tell you. It even seems that the man never mentioned that period of his life to his closest followers.' The tramp of feet grew louder and louder and Saul frowned, hating the thought of more foreign troops entering Jerusalem, though he was obviously proud of his Roman citizenship. 'The only sane course is to move against the sect here and now.' He glanced again at the parchment before Cato, still unaware of its contents; the right to arrest any person suspected of Christianity, to hold trials in their own courts, and obtain confessions by torture. The Governor had been infuriated by the attack on Sextus and refused to alter the orders, though Eros had personally pleaded with him.

No, Eros knew that that was not the way because it had been tried before. 'Better one perish than the whole race,' the priests had said, and they were wrong. The Nazarene had accepted death as proof of his promise and the race was already infected by the example. The single thing the movement needed was a crop of martyrs, and it was going to get them. He could almost hear groups of slaves and poor people discussing a man's end. 'For hours they tortured him, brothers, but he still smiled, certain of his reward. The prophet said that we belong only to God, so why obey our masters any longer? What is earthly pain compared to an eternity of rest and contentment?' The rot in the timbers, the sickness of delusion which could bring down the whole structure of government. Their only defence was to expose this self-styled deity as a maniac or a mischievous charlatan.

'How can we discover anything unless you give us complete authority, my lords?' The old man, Esdral, broke in. 'After the Apostate's body was stolen from the tomb, we asked the Procurator for emergency powers, but he said that he would conduct his own inquiry and hardly anything was done.

'If we had been able to interrogate the persons concerned; the fisherman called Simon, the rich merchant, Joseph of Arimathaea, the centurion in charge of the execution party . . .'

'What was that?' Cato scowled at him. 'You are questioning the conduct of a Roman officer, Hebrew?'

'No, Tribune. I intend no disrespect, though the circumstances of that crucifixion were unusual, to say the least. All I mean is that the details of the man's death and supposed resurrection are surely more important than what he did during his middle life, and we are wasting our time over it.' Esdral edged towards him as if he were longing to snatch the scroll from the table.

'Give us the authority to take action, lords, and you will never regret it. Let us round up the followers of the Apostate now. Nothing is known about the man himself except the reason why he left home and what he did after being baptized by John.'

'You know why he left home?' Eros leaned forward. 'Please tell us about it, Esdral.'

'Of course, lord. You speak for me, my son. I am an old man and the day is very warm.' He looked pleadingly at Marcus Cato, but the Tribune made no move to offer him a seat. He had to work with these people, he had to hand over authority to them, but that didn't mean he would provide for their comfort.

'It happened when he was twelve years old.' For the third time Sextus felt he should remember Saul's face. 'The Apostate's parents brought him up to Jerusalem for the Passover, the greatest feast of our year. They were pious people in those days and well-to-do. The poor, humble carpenter story is a lie to attract the masses.

'Even then he was a precocious boy, and he talked to some elders in the temple who were astonished by his knowledge of the law. One of them was named Silas of Hazor; a very good old man, though a falling wall had injured him as a child and he was badly crippled.

'The boy, Jesus, had the arrogance to contradict him on some matter, but Silas forgave the rudeness because he had taken a fancy to him. He even approached the parents and offered to take him on as an apprentice – he was a silversmith – and instruct him in the law.

'As you can imagine, it was a wonderful opening and the parents naturally jumped at it. But not Jesus. No, that would have been too much to expect.' Again Saul's voice became harsh and strident and his face trembled.

'He refused completely and, when his father said the terms of apprenticeship had already been agreed, he ran away. Climbed out of the window of the inn and vanished completely. Yes, even at that age, he betrayed his parents and his would-be benefactor, just as later he was to betray his god, his nation, and the law.'

'That is all you know?' Eros tucked the information neatly away in his brain for future reference.

'Yes, that is all, my lord. And now, Tribune, will you give us the

Governor's orders? We have been with you for over two hours, I think.

'Thank you.' Saul reached out as Cato reluctantly slid the scroll across the table. His face was quite blank as he started to read and then broke into a wide beam of triumph, and he turned to his companions.

'This is exactly what we hoped for, brethren; we have been given all the powers we need.' He bowed stiffly to Cato.

'Please thank the Governor on our behalf, Tribune, and tell him that he will never have cause to regret what he has done. I will send a detailed report from Damascus.'

'You are leaving Jerusalem then?' Sextus was not particularly curious, but he wanted to look Saul full in the face in the hope of remembering where he had seen him.

'I am leaving, my lord. There is little for me to do here. Do not worry about the people who put their mark on you. They will be caught, but they are merely dupes obeying orders. My belief is that the ringleaders fled to the north months ago.

'No, I have no proof of that yet, but something tells me it is the truth. The voice of God himself ordering me to Damascus where I will find the people who really matter.' He was flushed with excitement and didn't look completely sane.

'And once I have found them, once I have found the ringleaders, we, Jew and Roman, will destroy this cult of the Nazarene together.'

It was after midnight, but very few people slept in Jerusalem. Lines of torches were moving down the street, and from the balcony Eros could hear screams and the crash of splintering timber as a party of Temple guards forced their way into a house. Since early evening, the arrests had been mounting up and already the prisons were packed to over normal capacity.

'Do you think he will help us?' Eros glanced back into the room. The inn was under the protection of Mithras and Sextus was kneeling before the little altar of the god.

'I wasn't praying to Mithras.' Sextus stood up and walked towards him. 'I was trying to talk to my lost youth.'

'But you are still a boy!' The Greek frowned and then looked at his bandaged hand and nodded. 'Yes, I understand. Since they did that to you, you feel old.

'You came here for two reasons, didn't you, my friend. Because the department ordered you to, and because you hope to earn that inheritance from your uncle. Now, it is quite different, I think. The matter has become a war.

'And with me it is the same too. At first I merely looked upon this movement as a danger to security which had to be removed. Now the Nazarene is like a personal enemy who has to be destroyed if I am to sleep again. Sometimes I almost feel that he is still alive.'

'Yes, I know. As though one could hear his footsteps behind us, or his breath on one's cheek.' Sextus leaned out over the balcony. Somewhere in the south a building was on fire, and the glow lit up the bruises on his face.

'But what did you think of that man Saul? Does he really know that the ringleaders are in Damascus?'

'Possibly. The fellow is a religious fanatic, but he didn't strike me as a fool.' Eros wiped the sweat from his forehead.

'And what a crazy religion it is! One small, petty nation who have done nothing important in history imagining themselves to be the chosen of an all powerful god! To think that they objected to our bringing the standards into their miserable city!

'What a people! Priests and Zealots and common brigands, and every one is a maniac where their religion is concerned. I'm not a gambler but I'd risk a small bet that one day this country will be stripped of timber to provide crosses for the lot of them.

'Look over there.' He pointed across the street where a party of guards were driving an old man forward with their spear points. 'This isn't merely a round-up of suspected Christians. The priests are paying off every old score they can remember. People who have worked on their sabbath, people who have eaten meat they consider unclean, people who have neglected their temple dues.'

'But in a way, we're responsible.' Sextus glanced at his hand. The wound had healed cleanly, but it still throbbed a little under the bandage. 'My blundering off alone and getting this forced the Governor to take action, and you asked for co-operation with the Jews.'

'That is quite true. I wanted them to bring in suspects for questioning, but I never intended anything like this.' Eros looked towards the fire again. It appeared to be spreading fast, and more buildings would catch if somebody didn't act soon. 'I never thought that old fool of a governor would give them a completely free hand.'

'I'm sorry. I shouldn't have said that. But what more do we know about Saul? Is it true that he is a Roman citizen?'

'I believe so. Cato said he received it from his mother's side. But what's your interest in the fellow; you've been bringing him up all evening? He's of no importance; just a tent-maker who has managed to curry favour with the priests.'

'I'm not sure, but I feel that I should remember him.' Sextus paused as a troop of cavalry clattered past, and he tried to push back time. A face in a crowd? A certain expression? A manner of smiling?

'All the time those men were with us, I had the feeling that I'd known Saul before. That I'd seen him somewhere and it was important that I should remember where.'

'You probably have seen him; in the street perhaps. This is a small town and all these people with their long beards that have never known a razor look pretty much alike.'

'Ah, and about time too.' Eros nodded as two water-carts drawn by mules lumbered slowly towards the fire.

'No, not like that. Not in a street or a crowd. I seem to feel that I knew him well, and it's very important that I remember him.'

'Just a moment, though.' The throbbing in his palm quickened suddenly and he stared at Eros. 'Did either you or Cato tell them exactly what was done to me?'

'Of course not. You asked us not to. We merely said that you had been attacked and badly injured.'

'But he knew, didn't he? Saul knew about my hand. He said "they put their mark on you". And there is only one way that he could have known.' He felt himself stagger and Eros reached out and gripped his arm.

'I remember now. It was he, Eros. All the time it was Saul, and it wasn't his face I thought I recognized, but his voice.' The room seemed to darken, and he was back among the ruins with the stones beating him to the ground till that bitter authoritative voice came out of the shadows.

'No, brothers, do not kill him. Even the killing of a wicked man is against the master's law. Hurt him though. We will hurt him very badly indeed.'

They started at first light, as soon as Cato had provided them with an escort, and travelled across to Jericho and then up the Jordan valley through little dusty villages with outlandish names. At each village they heard the same thing. Saul and his companions were in front of them. Four men mounted on mules who had passed by eight hours before.

It wasn't a bad journey at first. A sea wind kept them cool, but after they reached the borders of Samaria it dropped, and the heat became like a furnace, baking the sweat on their foreheads, so that every mile was a misery. Sextus and Eros were well mounted, but the three troopers were heavy men riding young horses unused to the climate, and they could barely keep up a slow trot. Also Sextus was still very weak and, though he made no complaint, Eros insisted that he stopped and rested frequently.

And who was Saul? Which side was he on? Again and again Eros asked himself the questions as another innkeeper pointed up the road and said, 'Eight hours ahead, my master. Four men on mules.'

Why had he organized the attack on Sextus and put that mark on his hand? Was he a traitor? A Christian spy hiding in the ranks of their enemies, or was there another reason for what he had done? A cunning plot of the Jews to force the Roman authorities to give them the powers they craved?

But whoever he was, whatever his motives, they would know the truth before long. Eros grinned slightly as he considered the infinities of pain that humanity had devised. In his own way, this Saul appeared to be an artist, and an artist would supervise his death and make sure that he talked.

They had to catch him first, of course. Damascus was a huge city and the man and his companions could easily disappear if they reached it before them. They were still eight hours ahead too, and the horses of the escort were almost spent, while Sextus' face was grey under his tan. Four men against five. The odds would be fairly equal when they met.

Beyond the new city of Tiberius, the country became hostile.

Brown mountains reared up in the north-west and to the east lay desert. The road had been busy till then, but now there were only a few herdsmen who scowled at them with open resentment and every outcrop of rock could be sheltering brigands, or the dreaded 'Knifemen' that Cato had mentioned. A country that had always been invaded, always occupied; by Assyrians, Persians, Greeks and Romans, but never submitted to any of them. Eros felt a deep and personal hatred for it and its peoples.

At a place called Meron, on a lake where the river divided, they told the escort to follow as best they could and went on alone. Saul was still the same distance ahead, and with the slow horses holding them back, he was bound to escape. Eros would have liked to put one of the troopers on Sextus' mount but he couldn't suggest that. His friend had been branded like a slave and the man who did it was somewhere ahead of them. It was his right and his duty to follow him.

A few miles from Meron a stone pillar marked the border of Syria, and they turned into the desert. From then on there was no shade and no water, and the road was a causeway: a narrow rope of stone stretching endlessly over the sand which threatened their horses' hooves. They had to go on at a walk. The heat was something neither of them had imagined possible, and they slumped listlessly in their saddles. Sextus' hand had opened again, and little blue flies rose up from the stunted bushes and swarmed over the blood-stained bandage. He still did not complain, though, and Eros realized the power that kept him going. He himself had been branded, the mark was still there on his arm to shame him, but he had been a slave who expected such treatment. To a Roman nobleman the humiliation would be unspeakable.

But, however great his will for revenge, Sextus couldn't go on much longer without shade and rest. He was almost clinging to his horse's neck when at last they came to a tributary of the Jordan forming a little green valley in the centre of the desert.

There was a ford across the river, and a settlement on the opposite bank; low huts surrounding a stone farmhouse with vines growing on the slope behind, and the pleasant music of pigs from a paddock. The place looked friendly and innocent enough, but they approached it cautiously. On either side the road stretched away, bare and deserted, and the nearest Roman outpost was twenty miles distant. For all they knew a band of Sicarii might be waiting to rush them from the farmyard.

They need not have worried. There were no men in the yard; only a grotesquely fat woman who lay stretched on a couch against the wall, with a little Nubian girl crouching at her side. She took in the situation at a glance and clapped her hands loudly. When two labourers appeared she pointed to Sextus and then to a doorway, and they lifted him off his horse and led him into the house.

'No, lord. You will remain here.' The woman had made a kind of low clucking sound with her lips, and the girl stepped in front of Eros. 'Your friend will be looked after and it is better that you wait for him.' She went back to her mistress and helped her to rise from the couch and waddle painfully after Sextus.

So, this was probably the end of the journey. Though these people seemed friendly, he couldn't leave Sextus alone with them, and in any case what could one man do against four? The only hope would be to outride them and inform the first Roman officer he found. There was little chance of that either, Eros thought, as he led the horses across to a drinking trough. They were both completely worn out and could hardly carry him another five miles, let alone catch Saul before Damascus.

'Your friend is sleeping, my lord.' The fat woman had returned at last, and the slave helped her back on to the couch. 'For just a little while he will sleep, and when he wakes, he will be strong again. We have put new dressings on his hand, and given him something to restore his strength.' It was the girl who spoke, though the woman smiled up at him. Her face was so bloated that it gave no hint of her age, but her hair was still dark and glossy. She was obviously dumb, and communicated through her servant by signs and that odd clucking noise.

'My mistress says that you need not worry about him, lord. She is a very great healer. All over Syria people speak of the powers of Adah, the Sorceress.'

'I have heard of you, lady.' Eros gave a little bow. It was a lie, but he was a firm believer in politeness. 'We are most fortunate to have found you, and are grateful for your help.' One of the labourers hurried over with a stool and he sat down facing her. 'How long will it be before my friend is able to travel? We have urgent business in Damascus.'

'Soon, very soon. And my mistress knows all about your business. Your friend talked before we made him sleep. She wishes to know what you will do to these men when you catch them?'

'You are obviously a woman of imagination, lady.' Eros smiled and spread out his hands. 'You know what happened to my friend, so think of the worst death you can, and it will be theirs.'

'Good. Adah says that is very good.' The girl crouched beside the couch staring up at the woman, who was smiling widely and her fingers trembled in the air as though playing some stringed instrument.

'These are evil men, lord. They halted here for a time, but refused our food as unclean and derided the powers of my mistress. Also ...' She broke off, concentrating on what Adah was telling her. Awe was the only word to describe her expression. Not the fear of a slave for an owner, but religious dread like a person before the Oracle.

'Years ago, before my mistress had learned her powers, men like these, Hebrew fanatics, accused her of blasphemy. She suffered from them as your friend Sextus Ennius has done. Look for yourself, lord.'

'I am sorry; bitterly sorry.' Eros repressed a shudder as the mouth opened to show what was left of its tongue.

'If it is in my power, the men we follow will pay for what their fellows did to you.'

'Good, again that is very good.' A soft white hand reached out and took his and he could almost feel her fingers talking to him. 'But how do you intend to catch them? It is almost three hours since they left here and your horses are spent.'

'Only three hours!' At least they had gained a little time. Eros looked up gratefully as another girl appeared with a jug of wine and two silver goblets. 'Can you sell us fresh horses perhaps?'

'We have horses, but not fast enough to help you. And you are not the one to punish these men, Eros Dion. My mistress can read your destiny through the skin, and your hatred is centred on someone else; a man who died. It is Sextus Ennius who must pay his own debt.'

'But he is weak; so very weak. A man who died! You know about that? About the Nazarene?' The wine was heady and potent, and taking effect on his empty stomach, while the sound of rooting pigs mingled with the flow of the river. Eros had the strange feeling that everything was part of a pleasant dream.

'But naturally, lord. She is Adah, the Sorceress, and can read all your thoughts.' The girl looked slightly put out at the question, as if offended by a blasphemy. 'As she told you, your friend will soon be strong, and there is a way for him to catch the men who branded him. A ship that can cross the desert faster than any horse. Its name is Beelzebub.'

Beelzebub – the Lord of the Flies – the Prince of the Hebrew devils. As she had said the name, there was a sudden, rasping, grunting noise from beyond the pigs, and Eros' feeling of unreality increased. He sensed that the wine had been drugged, but it didn't bother him. Nothing was important except the girl's voice, and that pale bloated face smiling into his eyes.

'Yes, he is a devil, my lord, as your friend may find out, if he isn't careful. Look for yourself, though.' She pointed to the right and Eros almost dropped his goblet in astonishment. Waddling down a path from behind the house came an enormous yellow beast, with arrogant red eyes, and half-chewed cud hanging from its sneering mouth.

'So, there is a way to catch them.' Eros stared at the animal with admiration. Its shoulders were a good six feet tall and muscles like a ship's cables rippled under the glossy coat. It bore as much relationship to the crawling drudges of the caravans as a war galley does to a merchant ship. This was the real racing dromedary of the desert which in time will outrun anything that runs.

'Do you think you can ride him, my lord?' The woman was looking at Sextus, who had appeared at the doorway and was walking towards them. Like Eros he appeared slightly drugged, but there was colour in his face now and his steps were firm.

'I can ride him, Adah.' He stared up at the camel, as a groom hurried forward with a saddle. 'You may have to tie me on, but he will take me to Saul.'

'Don't be a fool.' Eros stood up and gripped his arm. 'You are still weak; far too weak to ride. It is only some drug that makes you feel stronger and soon it will wear off. Let me go, and there might be a chance of passing them before they reach Damascus.'

'No, Eros Dion, it is his destiny to go.' The woman shook her head and smiled again. 'You are right in saying our wine is drugged, but it is a good drug which will carry him safely across the desert.' The brute had sunk groaning to its knees and the groom was fixing the harness to its towering hump.

'There is more wine under the flap of the saddle, and you will take one mouthful whenever you feel you are about to fall. Be careful with Beelzebub, though. He has been kindly treated and is unused to pain. Hold his head to the road, but do not beat him unless you wish for death.'

'I will remember that.' Sextus pulled his arm away from Eros and climbed into the saddle. The animal swung its head and glared viciously at him, and even in the kneeling position he seemed a long way from the ground.

'Thank you for all your kindness, Adah. And don't worry about me, Eros, old friend. Follow with the troopers and we will meet in Damascus.' He reached out, but before their hands touched, the groom let go the bridle, the camel rose to its feet with a grunting roar, and he was off.

At the beginning it was agony. The animal's gait was quite unlike that of a horse; a swinging mixture of trot and canter with the legs of either side moving in unison. His body was hurled madly from left to right and, even with the high pommels, it took all his strength to remain in the saddle. After a single mile he felt he had been flogged.

But it would be worth the discomfort. Before he slept, Adah had promised him that he would find the men, and she hadn't lied in saying that her drugs would give him back his strength, and her animal could outrun any horse. The road was dead straight and Beelzebub had settled into a stride that no other creature could keep up for more than a few miles. Its huge padded feet pounded silently on the hard surface with no risk of a broken hoof, and its body seemed incapable of fatigue. The farm and the valley were well out of sight when Sextus reached under the flap of the saddle and took a sip of wine from the flask. At once pain vanished and the camel's gait appeared almost pleasant. He hummed to himself as he watched the milestones appear in the distance, grow large, and then flash past.

'You will find that man again,' the little slave-girl had repeated, while Adah's face bent over the couch and the sleeping draught started to take effect. 'You will meet with Saul and have the means to revenge yourself, and there is nothing to fear from him.' His eyelids had closed as she spoke and the voice seemed to come from an enormous distance. 'It is written that the only person you need to fear is a close friend.'

That was nonsense, of course. He had only had two real friends in his life. One had died of fever, and the other was a cinder in a German forest. Eros Dion might be called a friend, he supposed, but not a close one. He respected Eros deeply, was fond of him, but he had never felt the real intimacy that comes from deep friendship. Adah was a wise woman, but the only true prophet was the Oracle at Delphi. She had either been trying to impress him with her powers, or he had misheard her. He pushed the memory away and concentrated on counting the milestones.

The desert was a terrible place. There was no shade, no cultivation, no sign of man except the road stretching endlessly to the north-east over the baked earth, and now and then little climbing wave-like hills. The road along which the invaders had come; Assyrian, Persian, Babylonian, hurrying down to the sea and leaving their dead behind them. Even today, death was common in that wilderness, and now and then he passed the whitened bones of animals, half submerged in the sand like the timbers of wrecked ships. Monotony was almost as bad as the heat and it took all the power of Adah's wine to keep him awake in the saddle.

Then at last, and Sextus had no idea how long he had been travelling, for he had ceased to count the milestones, and the sun appeared to be hung stationary over his head, he saw that the country was changing. On the far horizon to the north a triangle of blue hills was rising up, and he knew they were the heights of Anti-Lebanon which guard Damascus on three sides. The dromedary was still keeping up its effortless pace, but he had to restrain himself from increasing its labours with the flat of his sword. Less than twenty miles away was the great plain of Barada, and Saul and his companions could vanish for ever in its teeming towns and villages.

But there! Yes, there was something at last! Towards the top of a slope which was rather higher than the others, four tiny dots were moving. Sextus took one final mouthful of wine and grinned in triumph. Even at that distance he could see that they were travelling very slowly, though one was a long way in front of the others; obviously better mounted and hurrying on to Damascus alone. Something told him that that man was Saul.

But, however well mounted he might be, he still had a long way to safety, and no mule could escape the relentless, effortless swing of the camel. Sextus threw the empty flask away and prepared to enjoy the sight of Saul's face as he swung round in the saddle and saw him ride past. There was bound to be a Roman post near by and they would take care of him.

But what was happening? Had that final mouthful of wine been too much for him, or was the sun really becoming hotter and far brighter? And Beelzebub was slowing too. The canter had fallen to a trot and then to a walk, and the brute suddenly gave a deep groan and stopped dead, almost throwing him over the pommel.

'Come on, boy. Come on you great hairy devil.' He shook the nostril-ropes encouragingly, but it was no use. The animal stood stock still, groaning again, and he could feel its body trembling beneath him. In the far distance the dots still moved forward under the blinding sun.

'Come on, you brute. Only a little way to go.' In spite of Adah's warning, he drew his sword and belaboured the animal with the flat. He might have been beating a stone for all the effect it had.

'All right, you asked for this.' He turned the blade and drove the point into its rump.

That worked. Beelzebub screamed in pain and rage and shot forward like a bolt of a catapult. For a moment Sextus thought that all was well again, when it suddenly stopped dead and lurched forward on to its knees. He flew over the saddle, the sword dropping from his hand, and the road came up, knocking the breath out of his body. He had just time to turn his face away when the neck swung down, long yellow teeth gripped his shoulder and the world went dark.

He couldn't have been out for long. The dromedary was still in sight, pounding back along the road for home with the same effortless stride as before. Sextus stood up and felt his shoulder, thanking the gods for the toughness of his jerkin. The skin was unbroken and, as everybody knows, a camel's bite contains deadly poison.

Just why had it behaved like that? A few moments before the animal had seemed completely willing and tractable, almost as though it were enjoying the chase. He could understand the cunning way it had taken its revenge for his sword-thrust, but what had made the brute stop in the first place? He turned and looked towards Damascus, shielding his eyes against the glare of the sun. Three of the men had halted and were standing beside their mules, but the fourth was riding on. Soon he would have topped the rise and be out of sight.

What was that? Somewhere from the north-west he could hear a strange humming sound, rising and falling on the wind, though the air around him was quite still.

There it was again. Soft and irregular, as if an unskilled musician was trying to play on a flute but was uncertain of the tune. And something was moving across the sand. A grey, snakelike shape, twisting over the ground in spirals, and at first he didn't know if it was small and close to him or very large and far away. Then it rose higher and higher, and he knew what it was. A dust storm raised by some freak local wind, climbing into the sky.

That was why the camel had refused to go on. It had heard the swirling sand long before he did, and realized the danger ahead. The noise was a high-pitched scream now, and the three men had remounted and were trotting away out of its path.

Not the man in front though. He must be blind, or deaf, or insane, because he was still riding slowly on, straight into the eye of the storm.

And if that man was Saul, Sextus was going to have a horrible revenge. The cloud was a towering pillar, and in the blazing sunlight, its greyness turned to a shimmering mass of colour. A bolt from heaven rushing to destroy that tiny human figure riding towards it. As he watched, Sextus saw the shape of the thing start to change, the cone splitting into five separate columns and bend forward. It was merely the trick of air and atmosphere, but a sudden terrifying sense of dread took hold of Sextus and he dropped down on his knees. The rider still moved blindly on, and the pillars of dust swirled nearer and nearer. Just as it reached him, the cloud had almost the shape of a clutching hand.

'The men escaped you? Somehow they managed to pass through that dust storm and reach Damascus, where they disappeared.' The Governor's hand beat up and down on his desk.

'Perhaps you would like to know what has been happening here in your absence. Oh, yes, we did what you asked. We gave full powers to the Temple authorities and every rat-hole in this miserable town has been turned inside out. And where has it got us?' Normally Appius Vinicius was an easy-going man, noted for his pastoral verses and a fine collection of Etruscan pottery, but now he was flushed, and he scowled angrily at Sextus and Eros.

'I will tell you, Eros Dion. We have had murder, arson, attacks upon completely innocent people, and courts set up in the Temple claiming the right to pronounce the death sentence.' Again his hand tapped sharply on the table, and beside him Rufus Aquila, the area commander, glowered like an old ill-tempered bear which has been suddenly aroused from its hibernation.

'And not one person they arrested has been proved to be a member of this cult of the Nazarene! Not a single one! All your request has achieved is to bring the country into a state of anarchy.'

'With the greatest respect, Your Excellency.' Eros leaned forward with a little bow. 'I must point out that it was you who insisted on giving the Jews a free hand. I merely asked that they should be encouraged to co-operate with our forces.'

'And do you think they would have?' The General broke in with a growl of contempt. 'Without the authorization to try prisoners in their own courts, these people would have done nothing to help us.

'I have only a token force to police the entire province, but until you arrived, it did the job moderately well. Then, because a Roman nobleman was foolish enough to go blundering into the ruins and get himself attacked, I had to turn the town inside out to find the culprits. Do you think I could have done so with the troops at my disposal?

'I will tell you what I think, my lords. The sooner you both return to Rome and leave the running of this country to people who understand it, the better it will be for everybody.'

'Please, Rufus. There is no need for personal criticism.' The Governor shook his head, remembering Eros' credentials. Whatever happened he didn't want to quarrel with the Department of Vigilance. The Emperor was old and sick, and the life he led at Capri made his early death a certainty. Soon Gaius Caligula would take his place, and it was well known that Macro and the Vigiles had his personal protection. If he hoped for a long and pleasant retirement, he must not offend them.

'Personal recrimination will get us nowhere, my friends. What we have to do is to restore normal order as soon as possible. Whoever this Saul of Tarsus is – a Zealot who organized the attack on Sextus Ennius to force us to give the priests powers against the Christians, or a Christian spy who had managed to deceive the Jewish authorities, as they themselves claim – it seems clear that he spoke the truth in one thing. The leaders of the Christians do appear to have left Jerusalem and it is the responsibility of our authorities in Syria to round them up. I am sending letters to the Governor of Syria to that effect, and I intend to withdraw the emergency powers of the priests forthwith. You agree?'

'I agree about the emergency powers, my lord.' Eros shrugged his shoulders. For six days the city had been in turmoil. Buildings burned down, shops looted, old scores paid off by hired killers, and courts presided over by fanatics who would pass a death sentence for some minor infringement of the law. That had to be stopped, but there was something else which was more important.

'Regarding your letters, my lord. I would be grateful if you would ask the Governor of Syria to take no further action against the Christians for the time being. It is important that this movement is not encouraged by examples of martyrdom, and the agents we expected from Rome have now arrived. The Department will be able to do all that is necessary without outside help.'

'Just like that!' Rufus got up and stared at the smoke drifting across the city from some smouldering building.

'You force us to bring the province into turmoil because of these so-called Christians and now say that no further action should be taken against them. It is not good enough, my lords. Since I called in the provincial garrisons both Galilee and Samaria have been rife with brigandage.' He turned from the window and bowed formally to Vinicius.

'May I have permission to return those troops to their normal stations, Your Excellency?'

'You have it from this moment, General.' The Governor nodded and then frowned as a secretary hurried into the room. 'What is it, Crito? I told you that we were not to be disturbed.'

'I know that, Excellency, but there is a messenger from the high priests waiting outside. I have heard what he has to say and I think it may be important.' Though a slave, the man was obviously an old and trusted servant who had little fear of his master.

'Very well.' Vinicius adjusted his robe and sat up straighter as an officer of the Temple guard appeared in the doorway. He was a very young man, probably under twenty, but his flowing uniform and unshaven beard gave him the air of a priest rather than a soldier. He spread out his hands in obeisance and bowed.

'Greeting, Lord. My name is . . .'

'Never mind your name, Captain.' There was no expression at all on the Governor's face. 'Merely state your masters' message. It had better be important if they wish to regain my favour.'

'At once, lord. The message is in two parts and the first concerns your visitors from Rome.' He turned to Sextus and Eros, his dark eyes glistening like over-ripe grapes in the youthful skin.

'We understand that you are hoping for news of the man, Saul.'

'You know we are.' His hand was almost healed now, but as Sextus heard the name, the scar tissue seemed to throb slightly. 'He has been found?'

'No, lord. He escaped from our people in Damascus, but we know what he was now and have proof of it; a Christian spy who betrayed us all.' None of them had seen so young a man look as bitter.

'Oh, yes. Saul of Tarsus has come into the open. He has not only proclaimed himself as a follower of the Apostate, but done more, much more. He has declared in public that our God, the God of Moses and Jacob and David, is not ours alone any more, but belongs equally to every race and nation in the world.'

'And there is proof of this? You are sure?' Eros gripped the arm of his chair. So, the thing he dreaded was coming true. The doctrine of man's equality, the promise of eternal life in return for a simple belief, the denial of human authority were no longer Jewish heresies, but open to all races of mankind. The fire that could spread across the world and destroy everything he believed in.

'We are quite certain, lord. The man preached it openly before fleeing from Damascus.'

'I see.' Eros nodded, and he remembered what the woman, Adah, had told him while he waited for the escort to catch up with him, her fingers running over his hands and face while the slave translated for her. 'This thing you fear will soon start to grow, Eros Dion, and I can see that it is your destiny to fight it till the end. One thing I cannot see however. Is it the Nazarene or yourself who will finally conquer?'

'And now state your message to me, fellow.' Vinicius interrupted his thoughts. 'In my opinion, enough time has been wasted over this man already.'

'If you say so, Excellency.' There was open mockery in the guard's face as he turned to him. 'The elders wish to know if it is true that you intend to rescind the powers which you gave them?'

'It is perfectly true. Your masters have abused those powers shamefully. They were asked to co-operate with our forces and promised to do so. Instead they have acted as if they were the independent rulers of the city.' He got up and paced across the floor.

'How many houses have been burned during the last six days? How many shops looted? How many innocent people killed? Over fifty according to my last report, Captain.'

'Fifty-two, to be exact, Lord.' The boy smiled as Vinicius used his title. 'They were not innocent, though. Every one of them had broken the law.'

'Your law, fellow; not ours.' The Governor suddenly looked very tired, and Sextus realized that he must have conducted scores of similar interviews in the past.

'What do we care for your law or your tribal customs? Women stoned to death for adultery! Houses burned because their owners ate certain foods! Men tortured for working on the Sabbath! I am sick of hearing about your law, and you will give this message to the priests.

'From sunset this evening all Temple guards will be confined to the areas where they belong.' He paused in front of Rufus Aquila and nodded. 'You, General, will see that an adequate Roman force is on hand to ensure my orders are carried out.

'Is that clear, Captain?'

'It is very clear, Excellency.' The ripe, glistening eyes turned to Eros again.

'But regarding the followers of the Nazarene in this city. There we have some little news for you.'

'Another false confession under torture? Another excuse to try and hold on to your powers?' Eros' voice was both savage and bored, but it was only to himself that he felt the bitterness. You fool, he thought. You are responsible for the blood bath and the failure. You should have waited till Macro's agents arrived and tracked these people down with cunning; informers hanging about the inns; scraps of stories pieced together from women's gossip; every tiny lead examined and checked till a truth started to appear. Because of the attack on Sextus, because he had been impatient, the Christians in Jerusalem were warned and had slipped through the net. Time was running out too. The man, Saul, had offered the doctrine to the Gentiles, and they had to discredit the Nazarene before it spread.

'No, my lord. There has been no torture and the person has not confessed to anything.' Like his eyes, the captain's lips were soft and glistening; red fruit in the darkness of his beard. 'We rather thought that you might like to witness the interrogation for yourselves.

'As you may remember, the Apostate, Jesus, had many misguided followers, but most of them did not matter because they were merely ignorant and gullible people. Twelve of them did matter, however. Twelve evil men to whom he was supposed to have given magical powers.' Though far the youngest person in the room, he had the manner of a schoolmaster before his class.

'After the Nazarene died, a Galilean named Simon, who calls himself "The Fisherman", became leader of the group . . .'

'I know all this, Captain.' Eros raised his hand as if to stifle a yawn. 'There were twelve disciples who each represented one of your tribes. What about it? It is too much to expect that you have located one of them.'

'In a manner of speaking, lord. Seven are thought to have gone north, with that Fisherman amongst them, and four to Egypt and Africa. Only one remains in this city.'

'You mean you have found him?' Eros wasn't yawning now and his face was keen and eager. 'You have located this twelfth man?'

'Only in a manner of speaking, as I said, my lord. The fellow died before his master, you see.' The boy stroked his beard and smiled at them. 'All the same, he may still be able to help us, because we have found his daughter.

'Yes, masters, though she changed her name after his death, Judas Iscariot had a daughter.'

The prison was in the east wall of the Moriah, the outer temple area: a squat, unlovely building of crumbling stone, dwarfed by the aqueduct which curved gracefully away to the right, and obviously far too small for its present number of occupants. As they approached, Sextus and Eros caught the smell of unwashed and tightly packed bodies.

'This way, lords.' The Jewish captain dismounted gracefully before the gateway which was flanked by Temple guards, while from across the street a Roman detail glowered at them. They were like two packs of dogs waiting for an order to fly at each other's throats.

'One moment, please.' Eros walked over to the Romans. He and Sextus had come alone and he wanted an escort to show their authority. After a moment's conversation the sergeant and three men formed up behind them: tough, hard-bitten regulars with faces as brown as their leather tunics.

'That is not necessary, lord. You are our guests, and this is temple property. We wish to welcome you as friends.' The captain was still smiling, but his eyes were cold.

'You wish to question this woman, and you may do so. You will have all the information she can give, but she is our prisoner, and we are helping you as allies, as friends. It is not lawful that your common soldiers enter our property without permission from the priests.' The sentries fingered their weapons as they listened.

'Your property! Temple property!' Eros sneered at him. 'Let me tell you something, boy. We allow you to use this prison, we allow you to worship in your temple, but you own no property. You own nothing at all, because this is an imperial province, and everything is leased to you by us. Remember that if you wish to remain a captain for long.' He nodded to the sergeant who gave an order, and the main Roman detail spread out; the rear rank composed of small dark men holding leather pouches taking position between each soldier; Balearic slingers who could clear the street in minutes.

'Now, you may take us to the prisoner.'

'As you wish.' The boy spread out his hands in resignation. 'Come with me please, but my masters will protest to the Governor about this.' He turned and led them through the gate.

The smell had been bad enough in the street, but inside the building it was unspeakable; stale and foul and cloying, like a leper's blanket wrapped over their faces. The prison was designed to hold fifty people, but four times that number must have been crammed into it. Through the iron grilles they could see that each cell was packed tight with bodies, and filth dribbled out into the corridor. Apart from a low collective moan which was almost masked by their marching feet, most of the prisoners were silent, though somewhere in the distance a man was cursing at the top of his voice. Sextus had little Aramaic, but he could hear the word 'Gehenna', the name of the refuse pit in which the evil dead would be buried, being repeated over and over again.

'This way, please.' The captain passed through an arch and led them into a courtyard. The aqueduct towered above it, and the building opposite appeared to be the garrison's living quarters. A tall man stood by its entrance and hurried forward as he saw them.

'Greetings, masters.' His hands fluttered in the long black sleeves. 'We welcome you as the Governor's representatives. My name is Malchus and I am the servant of the high priests. We had hoped you would come as friends, however.' He glanced at the four soldiers and frowned slightly. His face was elderly, but surprisingly handsome, though it had one blemish. He was lacking a left ear, but appeared to regard it as an honourable scar, because his hair was brushed back to show the naked hole and ragged tissue.

'We are Romans and we come as we please.' There was all the

arrogance of a self-made man in Eros' voice. 'Now, take us to this woman.'

'Of course, masters.' Malchus bowed and ushered them into a room at the side of the building. It was low and narrow and very dark, with only a single window, though a fire was burning in the far corner. A man was crouching before the fire holding a metal bar in the coals, and Sextus winced as he smelled hot iron again.

'There she is, lords. Rachel, the adopted daughter of a Greek physician named Lucius Timeus, sometime resident in this city. Her real father's name, however, was Judas Iscariot, one of the intimates of the Apostate.'

'Thank you.' Eros stepped forward. The woman stood against a wall with her arms raised and her head bent forward and hidden in shadow.

'I thought you said that she had not been tortured.' As his eyes grew accustomed to the dim light, he saw that her feet were off the ground and the straps that held her to a hook in the wall were cutting into her wrists like knives.

'Torture, my lord.' Malchus grinned slightly. 'I do not call that torture, but only the preparation. The torture is to start now.' Still grinning, he turned to the man by the fire and then suddenly screamed as Sextus swung round and sent a fist crashing into his face.

'It is she: the one I told you about, Eros. The girl with the doctor who saved my life.' Sextus hurried to release her body from the wall, and his sword sliced through the thongs. He helped her to a chair, tearing his tunic to bandage the bleeding wrists, and then looked at Malchus.

'You will pay for everything you have done, fellow, but first fetch her wine. Fetch it quickly unless you wish to lose your other ear.' He raised his sword and the man scurried over to a niche in the wall and produced a flask.

'And now leave us – both of you.' Sextus watched the torturer shamble out after his master and held the flask to the girl's lips. Her eyes flickered for a moment, and then she stared at him in complete bewilderment.

'You – it is you – the poor branded Roman.' Her voice was just a whisper. 'But you are one of them? All the time you were one of them and . . .'

'No, we are friends. We are here to help you. You saved my life when you came to that couch, and whatever happens I will protect you.' There was an embarrassed flush on her face and Sextus realized she must have thought him unconscious when she crept in at his side. 'Rest for a moment, and then we will take you out of here.'

'I am all right.' At each word there was a little more strength in her voice. 'But you, my lord? Did your wound heal?'

'His wound healed, but his brains appear to have deserted him.' Eros was looking out through the doorway. The four soldiers had locked shields in front of it, and Jewish guards were pouring out of the archway and shouting abuse at them.

'You know what you have done, don't you?' He scowled at Sextus who was kneeling beside the chair bandaging her wrists. 'That man was not merely a servant of the priests, but a priest himself, and you struck him.

'Oh, I'm not blaming you. The girl saved your life, but surely you could have kept your temper and demanded that they hand her over to us.' There were more than fifty guards at the far side of the courtyard now, and the man Malchus was standing beside the captain waving his arms in fury and shame.

'We may have conquered the world, but we haven't destroyed this people's spirit yet, and violence to one of their priests has to be paid in blood, even if they hang on crosses for it.

'You, break rank and come in here.' One of the soldiers was young and slim, and Eros pointed to the window. 'See if you can climb through there and tell the lads outside to get round quickly.' He watched him remove his helmet and start to wriggle into the tiny space, and then he smiled at the girl.

'Well, Rachel. You saved my friend's life, but it appears that we may all have to pay for it. Do you think you are strong enough to walk?'

'I can walk, Eros Dion.' She stood up and came towards him. As the light fell on her face he saw that Sextus had been right in describing her as a corn goddess.

'Good. But how do you know my name?'

'Sextus talked about you while he was delirious.' She smiled back at him. 'He said you were like a little grey wolf.'

'Did he? And if we get out of this alive, he may find that I am a very vicious wolf.' He grinned bitterly at Sextus who was trying to help the soldier at the window. The man was twisting like an eel, but he didn't seem able to get his shoulders through the frame. From across the yard the guards' voices were a steady chant of abuse. At any moment they were bound to rush the door.

'But tell me, Rachel. Is it true that you are a Christian?'

'I, a Christian!' Her smile was far more bitter than his. 'No, perhaps I wish to be but if you knew my story, you wouldn't even bother to ask. I am the Accursed.' She made the statement as though it were completely natural; as if she were giving her age, her nationality, the town where she was born.

'I see. That is a pity. I would have liked to have talked to one Christian before I died.'

'Good lad.' Sextus gave a sudden heave and the soldier wriggled out through the window. They had a chance now, but a very small one.

'Come on then.' Eros picked up the man's shield and walked to the doorway. The chanting had stopped, but there was a clash of arms as the Jewish captain shouted an order. At the side of the far building he could see a path leading out to the street. That was the way from which help might come, but probably too late for them to see it.

'Lock shields and wait for them.' It was a long time since Eros had done any drill and it surprised him to find how easily his own shield swung up to join that of Sextus and the sergeant, to form a wedge of metal before the doorway. Only five men against almost a hundred! In time that wedge was bound to break, but there would be a lot of bodies piled in front of it first.

'Here they come, boys.' The Roman sergeant's voice was completely calm as some of the guards, unable to contain themselves any longer, broke rank and charged. Eros felt the breath knocked out of his body as they met, and for an instant the sky seemed to grow dark. When it cleared, he saw that his sword was red and dead or dying things were lying on the ground. The first charge had been shattered like a handful of pebbles thrown against a rock, but there was no comfort in that. The point of the wedge was blunt now, and one of those bodies at his feet was the Roman sergeant.

Yes, the second attack might be the last. No four men could stand up to a disciplined charge, and that was what it would be. He watched Sextus take the sergeant's place while the Jewish captain moved his men into position. They had learned their lesson from that first wild rush and would come in disciplined formation.

So, that was that. He would never know the true story of the Nazarene. He would never help to destroy the disease which could rot the empire. He had been born in shame and failure and it appeared he would die the same way. Though Eros had no particular belief in the gods, he offered a quick prayer to Artemis whom his mother had worshipped, and watched death marching towards him.

And this time the Roman wedge was bound to give way. The guards were approaching in two parallel lines, and they were not a mob any more. The young captain headed one column and Malchus the other, and all Eros hoped for was that he might take one of them with him. As though it were happening to someone else, he watched them break into a charge, and then hope came. For somewhere over his head there was a strange hissing noise and Sextus shouted in triumph.

For the spearmen were falling. Their front ranks were going down in heaps, and the captain's face was red mash under his helmet. That uncanny noise came again, mingling with the screams of the wounded, and things like enormous hailstones fell from the aqueduct above.

The Jews were brave enough, but only heavily armoured troops could have resisted such an onslaught. For a count of five the remaining spearmen held their ground and then reeled back as the Balearic slingers delivered their third volley.

'We are not detaining you, my dear.' Eros turned from the window and smiled at Rachel. 'All the same, I think you will be wise to accept our hospitality for a time.'

That was true enough, he thought. The crowd before the citadel was vast. Well over a thousand people packed the square and all of them completely silent, staring at the Roman sentries as if hatred alone was strong enough to injure them.

They had reason enough to hate too. A priest struck down! Twelve guards killed or wounded! Temple property desecrated and a prisoner removed by force. Eros had dreaded what the Governor would have to say, but strangely enough Vinicius had been affability itself.

'Don't worry, my friends. These people need a lesson, and if there are any more disturbances, they'll get it.' He had insisted that they move into the citadel for safety's sake, and detailed two of his own servants to look after them.

Vinicius' attitude had been very strange. Eros had expected him to have raged, and threatened to report to the Emperor in person what had happened, but he had smiled to himself like a man who had just heard some very good news. He kept a deputation of priests waiting for an hour and then sent them away with a curt reminder that all Jewish troops were confined to quarters till further notice.

Yes, the Governor's reaction had certainly been odd, and Eros had had the feeling that some important event had taken place, and was being kept from him. Even the General did not complain about his lack of troops any more, but grinned hugely as he heard the story.

'So, my Majorcans climbed up on to the aqueduct and let them have it. Three well-aimed volleys and they broke. If there's any more trouble we'll show the blighters what it really means to face the Roman soldier.' He had distributed a gold piece to all the men involved, and three to the boy who had climbed through the window.

'Yes, it is far better that you remain with us, Rachel. You won't find many friends out there, I'm afraid.' Again Eros looked at the crowd. There was something uncanny in their set, glowering faces.

'I didn't have many friends before; only my adopted father, and they killed him.' Rachel sat on a couch beside Sextus. She had been completely calm during the fight in the prison, but had wept like a child when she told them about Lucius Timeus. The doctor had tried to resist when the guards came to arrest her, and they had hacked him to pieces in his doorway.

'I'm sorry, terribly sorry about that.' Sextus reached out and

took her hand. 'And in a way it was all my fault. If I hadn't gone
blundering into those ruins . . .'

'It was not your fault.' She shook her head and forced herself
to smile at him. 'You were wounded, Timeus was a doctor, and it
was his duty to help you. What happened afterwards was nothing
to do with you.'

'And that, I'm afraid, is untrue.' Eros pulled up a chair and
sat down facing them. 'Sextus Ennius and I are here for just one
reason; to obtain information about the Nazarene preacher who
called himself the Messiah. For that reason Sextus followed the
boy into the ruins and was attacked. For that reason you were
arrested by the Jews. If it had not been for Sextus' intervention,
you would have certainly been put to the torture and I would have
witnessed it.' Eros gave a slightly wolfish grin. They make a handsome couple, he thought, envying Sextus his youth and the girl her
beauty. Already he could sense that an attraction was springing up
between them. He himself was incapable of love or deep feeling.
He accepted that as a fact, like age and his small ugly body, but
somehow he begrudged it to other people. The department was
his obsession, and the knowledge shamed him.

'Now, my dear, let us get down to business. As I told you, you
are quite free to leave, but once past the sentries I am quite sure
that the mob will kill you. In return for our protection you will
have to answer one or two questions.'

'I will answer anything you want.' Her eyes were still red from
weeping over the doctor's death, but she was completely calm, and
Eros had the uncomfortable feeling that it was she, not he, who
was the strongest character in the room.

'Good,' he said. 'Let's begin then. You told us just now that you
could not be a Christian. Can you prove that?'

'Of course I can.' She looked away from him and turned Sextus'
hand palm upwards. The wound was healing well, but the mark
stood out sharp and clear in the new skin.

'Surely your own brain should give you the proof, Eros Dion.
If I wished to become a Christian, do you think they would accept
me? To them I am accursed because of my father's blood. Do you
know what the man, Simon, said about my father? He said that he
was the only living creature who would remain in hell for ever.'

'I can understand that.' Eros nodded. 'Your father betrayed Jesus to the priests, didn't he? Before that, he was one of his most intimate disciples, however, and he must have talked to you about his leader. I shall come to that later, but first I want to know more about your father himself.' There was a sudden flash of lightning followed by thunder, and Eros looked towards the window. Though it was still early evening, the sky was darkening in the north.

'Was he a revolutionary who wanted to overthrow our government by force?'

'My father a Zealot? Do you really think that?' Rachel's eyes crinkled with amusement. 'A nationalist who imagined Jesus planned to lead a military revolt? That old, silly story that he would bring down angels to fight your legions? That he felt himself betrayed when he discovered the truth and sold Jesus to the priests? I thought you were an intelligent man, Eros Dion.'

'But he did betray him?'

'Oh, yes, he betrayed him.' She still stared at the mark on Sextus' hand. 'He had a reason for it, though; the only possible reason.'

'Money!' Eros longed to break her composure, but she looked up smiling.

'You think that too? You imagine Judas Iscariot, who wasn't a fool, would destroy himself for a few silver pieces; just enough to buy a grave for his body.'

'Then why, woman? Tell us why.' As though her touch irritated him, Sextus got up and crossed to the window. Lightning was flashing over Calvary and rain had started to fall in the square.

'I will tell you, Sextus, but you may not believe me.' There was no bitterness in her voice, but her eyes suddenly looked dead and empty.

'Think of the other disciples for a moment. Eleven men who were not sure about their master. They thought he was a wise and holy man, a great prophet, but they were not certain what he really was. Remember what happened when the men came to arrest him. Simon the Fisherman tried to hold them off with a sword.'

'But your father did know what the Nazarene was.' Eros' words were drowned by another burst of thunder and it was really raining now. The water dropping straight out of the windless sky and bouncing off the pavements like a forest of spikes standing upright. To Eros its noise was a triumphant march, for at last he felt he was getting somewhere. Yes, this might be exactly what he wanted to hear. Somehow, Judas Iscariot, one of the Nazarene's most trusted followers, had found that he was an impostor.

'Your father discovered the truth at the end. He learned that the Nazarene was just a fraud – a man like himself. That was why he betrayed him to the priests.'

'I expected you would say that, Eros Dion.' With the lightning flickering over her face, Rachel looked completely ageless. A goddess who would live for ever and still remain a girl.

'You are wrong, though, completely wrong. The others may have loved Jesus, but they couldn't have been completely certain who he was. They didn't realize that the scriptures must always be fulfilled. But my father had no doubts at all.' She nodded and her cold smile widened.

'My father betrayed his master because he knew that he was the Son of God.'

Was it possible? Was there even a remote chance that she had spoken the truth? Thirteen men sitting in the room of an inn, breaking bread together, and two of them preparing for the ritual sacrifice of a god?

Eros stared out across the square. The crowd was still standing in the rain, silent, bitter and threatening, with their heads bowed on their breasts, and not one of them looked up as a party of horsemen clattered up the street from the right: five cavalry troopers and a sergeant. Their wet cloaks were clinging around them like shrouds and their horses had obviously been ridden hard for a long time. The sergeant shouted a password to the sentries and they trotted through the arch of the citadel.

And Rachel was probably right. Judas Iscariot had not discovered anything to discredit the Nazarene. On the contrary he was the only one with a firm belief. The true fanatic who imagined himself to be the instrument of divine will. Eros had spent some time studying Hebrew mythology and he knew most of the story.

The Messiah was a part-king, part-god who would one day send his angels to conquer the world and destroy his enemy whose name was Satan. Before that, however, he had to be sacrificed, so that human sin could be redeemed, and later he would rise again like the harvest. It was rather similar to the cult of the Egyptian Osiris whose images were planted each year in the mud of the Nile; hollow statuettes filled with seeds which germinated when the spring floods reached them and brought life back to the valley. A fertility symbol for simple people, but in this case a very dangerous one. Unlike Osiris, the Messiah would favour the poor and outcast when he set up his kingdom and humble the recognized rulers of the world.

That was a dangerous notion, and the Nazarene's promise of eternal life to his followers made it ten times more dangerous. Eros glanced back over his shoulder. Sextus and the girl had left him some time ago, and he was quite alone. All the same he had the uncomfortable sensation that eyes were watching him from every corner of the darkened room. He stretched out his hands into the rain and moistened his face. The lightning had passed now and was far away to the south over Bethlehem, but the rain was as heavy as ever and had filled the gutters like mountain streams.

Yes, it could have been like that. Thirteen men in the room of an inn, drinking wine and breaking bread together. Then their leader had looked at each of them and stated that the betrayer had already made his preparations. Eleven of them had been horrified and stared back at him and each other with quick denials: 'Not I, lord.' 'I could never betray you, master.' But the twelfth had simply nodded, because he knew, or imagined he knew, what his master was. A god who had to be betrayed and sacrificed before he could enter into his kingdom. He also knew that he himself was the chosen instrument of fate and Jesus had not merely made a statement, but confirmed an order.

What happened afterwards was logical enough too. Judas had demanded money from the priests to show himself a bona fide informer, and the way he had betrayed him made no sense unless one accepted Rachel's statement as the truth. No pointing hand and a simple 'There he is,' but a kiss of farewell. Then he had killed himself, because he was the 'Deodand', the instrument of destruction which, however innocent in itself, had to be returned to God, just as the stone knives of the Druids were ritually shattered immediately after the sacrifice.

No, there was no help from the story of Judas Iscariot, and the Jews themselves realized now that he was the most dangerous of the twelve. The true fanatic who had destroyed himself for his faith. Finding Rachel was merely another false hope that had come to nothing. She had only seen the Nazarene twice herself, and from what she had heard from her father, he had never mentioned his middle years to any of his followers, and none of them had dared to question him.

And yet he must have been somewhere! And not merely as a simple hermit, because he appeared to be a man of authority and worldly knowledge. His reply to the elders who questioned him about Caesar's image on a coin proved that. Just where had he been during those middle years of his life? Somewhere, in some spot on the earth, there must be people who knew the story.

Again Eros moistened his face with water, struggling to concentrate while another deep rumble of thunder echoed across the hills in the south. Again he had the feeling that eyes were watching him.

'Ah, there you are.' He swung round as the door opened and Vinicius and the General came striding across the room. Behind them was a slave bearing a jug and a tray of goblets.

'We apologize for disturbing your meditations, my friend, but we hope you will drink a toast with us.' Their smiles were ingratiating as well as merely friendly.

'Perhaps you have been wondering why I took that incident at the prison so calmly.'

'I did wonder, Your Excellency.' Eros nodded as he took a glass. 'I was also surprised at your attitude, Rufus Aquila. For once you did not complain of your lack of troops.'

'No, that didn't worry me, because soon I shall have plenty. I have already asked Syria and Egypt for reinforcements, and I think we will get them. You see . . . this afternoon . . .' The General was obviously longing to announce the news, but Vinicius broke in.

'Early this afternoon, while you were at the prison, Eros Dion, I received letters from Rome telling me that the Emperor was very ill and would certainly be dead by the time they reached me. I naturally wanted confirmation before making the news public, and it has just arrived.

'Tiberius collapsed in a villa near Misenium. Everybody thought he was dead and started to celebrate, when he was suddenly heard calling for wine. They all started to panic, but . . .'

'But only your friend, Macro, kept his head!' The Tribune, Marcus Cato, came lurching through the doorway. There was a wine skin in his hand and he was plainly drunk.

'Naevius Macro is a man all right. He went into the bedroom and did what was necessary.

'So, here's to us, my lords. To the end of oppression and meanness, and a powerful army again.' Cato raised the skin and squirted a jet of wine into his mouth.

'And here's another toast. To the boy I played with on the Rhine when I was a centurion. To the son of Germanicus, the best general a soldier ever followed. To Caligula, as he always liked to be called. To Gaius Augustus Germanicus Caesar and the happy times he will bring.' Cato almost capered in his glee and wine dribbled from his lips.

'The old goat is dead. Macro made the slaves smother him under his own bedclothes. Tiberius rots with the Shades and Little Boots is our Emperor now.'

# Three

Felix Plotius, officially a centurion of the Damascus garrison, was a very discontented man. For six months he had been engaged in rebuilding a fort far out on the borders of Cappadocia, and it had proved to be the most thankless task he had ever been made to undertake.

Normally the command would have consisted of a detail of legionaries, but owing to the economies of Tiberius, all Plotius had were a hundred Syrian irregulars, half of them raw recruits and not one of them a craftsman. For technical assistants he relied on two veterans; old, bitter fellows, constantly grumbling at being removed from their comfortable quarters and being forced to toil in the wilderness. The repairs to the fort progressed slowly and boredom made discipline a constant anxiety. The King of Armenia was known to pay his mercenaries well, and already one of Plotius' men had deserted.

The celebrations to mark Caligula's coronation had made matters worse too. The Syrians were entitled to three days holiday by imperial edict, but it was the fourth day now, and some of them had been clearly drunk when they appeared on parade, and a young recruit had grinned openly when Plotius rebuked him.

There was only one thing to do of course. The nearest Roman post was fifty miles distant and the slightest hesitation could turn discontent into open mutiny. Plotius had the boy tied to the whipping post and formed his men into a square to witness the punishment.

'You, Marcus. You give it to him.' Plotius' right shoulder was stiffened by an old arrow wound and he called one of the veterans from the ranks and handed him his cane. 'Twenty-five strokes and make sure that he feels them.

'What are you waiting for?' He frowned as Marcus took the cane but seemed to hesitate, and he suddenly regretted his decision. Until recently he had thought the man to be a steady enough soldier, but a month ago he had had a week's leave in Damascus and appeared strange ever since; very quiet and withdrawn and brooding. Even his usual flood of complaints had stopped.

'Didn't you hear me, fellow?' The cane had been splintered to increase its effect and Marcus was staring foolishly at the jagged tip apparently unable to understand its purpose. 'Twenty-five strokes and see that each of them marks him.'

'Please, Plotius. Please, lord, do not ask me to do this.' The man looked up at him and there was a hint of tears in his old rheumed eyes. 'Erestis there is my friend, and I have been forbidden to shed human blood.'

'You have been what?' Plotius could not have been more surprised if the walls of the fort had suddenly risen into the sky. 'You, the veteran of a legion, forbidden to shed blood! What nonsense is this?' He listened to a rambling, disjointed story of what had happened during that leave in Damascus. Some people outside a tavern had told Marcus about a strange god who demanded complete love and the brotherhood of mankind.

'You fool, Marcus. You poor, senile fool.' Plotius gripped his arm. 'What is any Jewish sect to us? We are soldiers of Rome: citizens whose only allegiance is to the Emperor and the senate. I have given you an order, so obey it.'

'Yes, I am a soldier, lord.' Marcus' voice was very low and the tears were clear in his eyes now. 'For thirty years I have followed the legions, and what have they given me? Blood on my hands, scars like yours on my body, and the marks of the cane as that boy will have soon. And finally I shall be thrown on the rubbish heap with nothing to look forward to.' As he spoke, Plotius could hear the men whispering together and he knew that his death or that of Marcus was very close.

'But this god does not only belong to the Jews as you have said, lord. He is open to every race of mankind and he has promised his followers life.'

'Listen to me carefully, fellow.' Plotius' grip tightened and his right hand was on the hilt of his sword. 'We will talk about this god later, but now you will obey me. Take the cane and do what I have ordered.

'I see,' he said at last, noting the complete refusal on the old man's face. 'You have forgotten your vows to the Emperor, to the senate and to the Roman people, and there is nothing more I can say to you.' He drew back and pulled his sword out of its scabbard.

Plotius was a merciful man and he hated to kill a lunatic. At the same time, he was the only officer in the camp and the faces of the Syrians told him what his duty was. Even the boy at the post was grinning at him. He flexed his arm and did what he had to do quickly. What surprised him even more than Marcus' insanity was the fact that he made no sound and offered no resistance. He just stood there, waiting for the sword to run him through.

The movement had ceased to be merely a Jewish sect and was starting to spread through the Empire as they feared. All the same, Eros had much more hope of destroying it now, because Naevius Macro sat at the Emperor's right hand and had sent him all the assistants he needed. It was merely a question of time before they found the evidence they required.

He kept a few of his agents in Jerusalem, poring over old texts relating to the story of the Messiah, interviewing witnesses, and sifting the reports of innumerable false leads. The majority travelled.

Some of them went south; down along the road past Sinai and into the cities of Egypt, Alexandria and Ramases and the ruined village which had once been Thebes the Golden. Others headed west and east; to Crete where Christian communities were said to be springing up, and far away over Ararat into the land of the Scythians whose heads were bald, but bodies so hairy that they went naked even in the dead of winter. The men posed as merchants and camel drivers and runaway slaves, and they asked searching questions of everybody they met, and they learned nothing. Only from the north came a glimmer of hope and a British barbarian found it.

Beric was a monster. Physically he was very tall, standing a full head above most men, but so broad that in the distance he appeared squat. Sometimes to amuse an audience, he would lift a grown man in either hand and hold them at a level with his shoulders. That trick won him great applause in the wine shops and people trusted him on sight. His face was like a dull, friendly child's and it took a very shrewd observer to see through it and recognize the cunning in his little twinkling eyes.

It was that appearance of innocence that had got him where

he was. He couldn't remember the name of the man he had first fought as a gladiator, but he was said to be a very good *retiarius*, and Beric had been entered against him as the substitute for a swordsman who was sick with fever. He'd heard his master talking to the overseer about his chances . . . 'The dumb fool will probably be killed after the first few feints, but he is scarcely worth the cost of feeding.' Beric would never forget that master and he had been reminded of him every day in Jerusalem, for Sextus Ennius could have been his double.

The crowd who watched the fight had thought he was a fool too. They had jeered and laughed while he stood there in the sand and then shuffled back before the small vicious figure with its net and trident, but their jeers showed him what he should do. As the net slipped over his shoulders he had pretended to cower in fear, and his legs started to buckle. He hadn't allowed the net to fall too far though and, as his knees touched the ground, the sword had gone up into his opponent's groin. He still smiled when he remembered the astonishment on the man's face as he saw the point appear from under his ribs.

Beric only fought once more in the arena and then deliverance came. He had been matched against a German named Catumer, who was a very great gladiator indeed, with twenty-seven victories to his credit and the promise of liberty when he reached thirty. He had looked contemptuous, almost bored, as Beric dropped his sword and cowered before him and glanced towards the Master of the Games. Then a huge hand had suddenly shot out, twisted the trident from his grasp and driven it into his throat.

That was Beric's last fight. His master was waiting for him in the disrobing room and his face was contorted with anger and disgust as he listened to the jeers of the crowd still ringing across the benches outside. Beric certainly hadn't expected praise, but he had not anticipated such anger. He was struck across the cheek, and told that he was a cowardly fool who had won purely by chance and brought disgrace to the Games. He was to be soundly flogged and then sold to the mines or the galleys, if anybody was stupid enough to buy him.

'How much, my lord Flavius?' As long as he lived Beric would remember how he had first heard that voice and seen the man standing in the doorway; a tall, stooping man with the pale face of a scribe, though his toga was very splendid. 'You wish to sell this boy, so how much do you want for him?'

'You would buy him, Naevius Macro?' Flavius was a member of one of the richest families in Rome, but his tone was cringing. 'He is a fool who has shamed me twice and I merely want to be rid of him.'

'I might buy him, but who knows?' The man had shrugged his shoulders and walked up to Beric.

'Well, fellow,' he said. 'Your master says you are a worthless fool, and you look like one.' Though he smiled, his eyes were deadly cold, and Beric knew it was important to stare back at them.

'All the same, last month you killed a very good fighter, and today you dispatched the best man I have ever owned. As I watched, it did look as if chance had come to the help of stupidity and brute force and cowardice, but now I am not sure.' He raised his hand and tilted Beric's face into the light, studying it like a jeweller examining a stone for hidden flaws.

'Tell me the truth, boy. Are you a fool?'

'I am a fool, my lord.' Beric suddenly realized that there was only one answer to satisfy this man and he replied in Greek. 'But I have heard it said that only a wise man knows he is a fool.'

'Good! Very good indeed.' Naevius Macro turned to Flavius. 'Ten gold pieces for your fool, my friend.' He smiled again as Flavius nodded, and motioned to the slave who bore his purse.

'Pay him, Cleon, and I don't think I shall regret the bargain. His – no – my fool is a British barbarian of nineteen years, yet he killed two seasoned fighters by cunning, he knows a little Greek too, and can quote Socrates.

'My thanks to you, Flavius.' He gave a formal bow and walked out with Beric and the purse-bearer behind him.

So, Beric became a Decator, a secret agent and informer of the Vigiles, and Naevius Macro never once regretted his purchase. In the taverns and market places, men looked tolerantly at the big, good-natured simpleton and spoke openly in front of him. And, though he smiled stupidly as if at nothing, his hidden active mind was recording everything they said and sorting out all that could be useful to the Department.

His ability for language was an asset too, and he had been in Gaul and Spain and Syria in his time; a simple-minded wanderer, begging for crusts and hearing the complaints of petty chiefs who imagined Rome had ruled long enough, and soldiers who fancied a change of general.

Women found his gigantic body attractive and confided in him, thinking he was incapable of remembering what had been said. Very well-to-do women, usually, who paid him with money as well as their favours.

'My bear, my great, stupid, lovely bear,' some of them had crooned as they lay beside him. 'This is for you, so go and spend the money and never imagine I can't afford it. My husband is a Treasury official,' or a senator, or a prefect. 'I have persuaded him to transfer certain sums for our own use.

'But you can't understand that, can you, my bear? Don't worry, though. Don't even think about it. Just buy what you like and now give me what I like in return.' Often there had been a little tinkling laugh at that point, but not one of them had laughed when the Vigiles made their arrest a day or two later.

And now the Department had sent him to Jerusalem, and Beric was to become a Christian. 'You may go wherever you wish,' Sextus had said, and, like his features, his voice reminded him of that hated master.

'Do not report back for six months or until you have something definite to tell us. But find what we want, Beric. Give us the information to discredit this self-styled god, and I will personally see that you receive your freedom. We are relying on you, because Macro has written that you are the best agent he has.'

'I will do my utmost, master. That is all I can promise.' Freedom meant little to Beric but he had flushed with pleasure and bowed deeply. After Caesar, Macro was the most powerful man in the world and he was his dog. The compliment delighted him.

He set out alone, with a parchment in his wallet which stated that he was a freedman whose master had died leaving him with no allegiance, and he worked his way north by casual labour. His enormous limbs kept him well-fed, and every employer regretted the day he moved on. Up through Mysia and Bithynia he went and then across the Hellespont into Thrace. Then at last, in a town called Neapolis, he found the people he was looking for; five men and two women standing before a platform on which an old bearded fellow was addressing a crowd about something he referred to as the 'One True God'. As soon as Beric heard that he pushed his way forward and sat down, staring up at the preacher with dog-like respect: an earnest seeker after truth who lacked the mental power to understand it fully.

Most of the crowd were Greeks, polite but cynical, and they listened to the preacher as though he were an indifferent actor to whom they gave a hearing out of good manners. But, to the right of the platform were a group of men who weren't polite at all. Like the preacher himself they were Jews, with long silky beards, and their fists were clenched within their flowing sleeves. Now and again they muttered angrily, and one of them, a young man with a very shrill and high-pitched voice, kept shouting 'Blasphemer'.

Beric prepared to enjoy himself in the cause of duty. It was clearly only a matter of time before trouble started and this might be his opportunity. He smiled inwardly as he listened to the sermon, and waited.

He didn't have to wait long. One of the Greeks asked a question, and as the old man started to reply, he suddenly staggered back before a shower of stones. The next moment, the Jews closed in around the platform and the fight began.

Beric didn't do anything at first. Really big men don't need to hurry, and he sat there quietly till one of the brawlers was within easy reach. Then his right hand shot out, grasped an ankle, and he stood up. The ankle belonged to the young man who had kept shouting 'Blasphemer', and his voice was even shriller as Beric swung him into his companions as a living club. Six of them were on the ground before he finally became silent.

'Thank you, my son. God bless you.' The two women had helped the preacher down from the platform and he held out his hands to Beric. The fight had only lasted a few moments, but the square was practically deserted. The Greeks had hurried away, shocked by such uncivilized behaviour, and the Jews were carrying off their wounded. Some of them turned to curse and shake their fists, but they obviously had no intention of risking another battle with the Titan who had taken their enemies' part.

'Yes, God will reward you, friend.' The man, who Beric later learned was called Micah, withdrew his hands and smiled up at him.

'We are very grateful for what you did, though perhaps your methods were a little rough.

'No, no, Ruth. This is an honourable wound and the Lord himself will heal it.' One of the women had torn a strip from her dress to bind a cut on his forehead, but he waved her aside. 'Now, brother, how are you called and why did you help us?'

'My name is Beric, and I was a slave to Pytheas of Alexandria. He freed me just before he died and now I am a masterless man.'

'Beric! That is a strange name. Where were you born, my son?'

'Far away in the north, but I was taken from there when I was a child.' In a dim corner of Beric's mind was the memory of a green country with little wooded hills, and streams that were full, summer and winter. 'I think the land is called Britain.'

'From Britain. A Samson come to help us from the edge of the world.' Micah smiled at his companions. 'But you haven't said why you helped us. Are you of our faith, perhaps?'

'No, lord. Pytheas was a devotee of Poseidon, and I naturally worshipped him too. Since Pytheas died, I have become nothing; a masterless man without the protection of any god, but with many fears.' Beric struggled to put exactly the right amount of self-pity into his voice.

'I am a fool as well, and I couldn't understand what you were saying on the platform. But something told me that you are the favourite of a great deity, and I had to protect you.' Genuine tears were pouring down Beric's face and very slowly, like an ox, he sank down on to his knees.

'Lord, take me as your servant. I have been a slave all my life, and freedom terrifies me. Let me call you "Master".'

'No, Beric, I cannot be your master.' Micah raised him to his feet. 'I am just a chattel myself – a servant of God – and under our law no human being may belong to another. All men and women must be brothers and sisters, equal under God and owing allegiance only to God. Can you understand that, my son?'

'I will try, lord.' Yes, Macro and Eros Dion were right, Beric thought grimly. These people really were dangerous. Though a public slave, he was well rewarded by the Department, with the use of a small villa near Herculaneum for his leisure moments. *Allegiance only to God!* There were three servants at that villa, and he would not like them to hear such poisonous talk.

'Not "lord", Beric. I am merely a man like you, and the only true Lord is a spirit, though once he lived amongst us on the earth. Would you like to hear about him, and learn how to serve him?' Micah smiled again as Beric nodded, and then turned to his companions.

'Shall we accept him, brothers and sisters? Shall we take this gift that the Master has sent us; a Samson from Britain?

'Good. You may kneel now, my friend.' He dipped his fingers in the blood on his forehead and touched Beric's face.

So, Beric became a Christian. But, though he was of great service to Micah and his band, he learned very little from them at the beginning.

They travelled slowly across Thrace, and then into Macedonia; through Philippi and Amphipolis and Appolonia; preaching in every town and village, and staying in any house that welcomed them, but often they slept in the open. Always their reception was the same; the Greeks polite but cynical, the Jews hostile, and a steady trickle of converts from slaves, and the lower orders. Though the Jews still heckled, there was no more violence. The sight of that huge figure standing in the group cowed them, and their only resort was to complain to the local Roman officials who appeared indifferent. Micah constantly referred to Beric as 'God's Sword' which had been sent to protect them.

Yes, Beric was a great advantage to the band, but he gained little from them. None of them had actually seen Jesus in person, and though they continually spoke of him and repeated stories they had been told, they either knew nothing of his early life, or refused to talk about it. Time and again Beric would question them, sitting by the cooking-fire with his big head propped against a fist, or trudging along the endless roads with half their baggage on his shoulders.

'What did the Master do before he appeared to John the Baptist, Micah? Where had he come from?'

'He was descended from kings, Beric. His mother belonged

to one of the noblest families of Israel and her husband was a poor carpenter from Nazareth. In that way our lord's background embraced all mankind.'

'I know that, Micah. You have told me that before. But what did he do after he left home as a boy?' Though Beric's face was full of pleading, the answer was always the same.

'I do not know, my son. The master never told his disciples and they did not presume to question him. Some thought that he had been with his father in heaven, and others that he was in some remote part of the earth preparing himself for his ministry. If he did not wish to say, it was not their right to pry into his past.

'Now, let us sit down for a little while, and I will tell you one of his stories. It is about a group of maidens whose duty it was to await a bridegroom . . .'

Time passed, the seasons altered, and Beric began to despair of learning anything useful. Like several other agents, he had been ordered to try to join a group of Christians, and listen to what they could tell him, but these people obviously knew nothing. His only hope was that one day they might meet up with others who knew more.

After Appolonia, they headed south. Down into Achai past the capes and islands where civilization had been born, and men spoke as though the heroes were still living amongst them; Perseus and Hercules and Achilles, the Cretan bull bellowing for its tribute of children, and the ships sliding out through the moonlight to Troy. The Christians ridiculed the legends and condemned them as blasphemous myths; the excrescences of a corrupt civilization which worshipped gods that did not exist. But, though Beric nodded in agreement, he grinned quietly to himself. Once Macro and Eros had the information they needed and the Department decided to take open action, these people would learn which gods were to be feared. The men were puny specimens who would provide poor sport in the arena, but Leah, the younger of the two women, was attractive enough. He felt his mouth grow suddenly dry as he watched her, half listening to Micah criticizing the morals of Hercules. Yes, it would be very pleasant to take Leah to some quiet spot and make her admit that her god had died on a cross.

At last, at a place called Pernina, they met the African. It was a small village, but obviously prosperous, with white houses dotted around a stone jetty and well-kept olive groves stretching up the hillside. The fishing boats were out, and apart from a few old men, Micah's audience consisted of women and children who regarded him as a welcome diversion. There were no Jews in the neighbourhood, so he got an uninterrupted hearing, though there was an incredulous murmur when he spoke of a god who allowed himself to be crucified like a slave. One of the women politely asked how such a person could be regarded as a hero, let alone a deity, and he had started to answer her when they heard the laughter; a deep, throaty, grumbling chuckle that sounded like water in a blow hole. At first Beric couldn't make out from where it was coming, and then a boy at his side pointed to one of the huts.

The man lounged in the doorway, and like his body, his tunic and sandals were as black as coal. He was a huge man; almost as big as Beric and in perfect condition. As he moved out into the sunlight Beric could see his muscles ripple under the gleaming skin.

'That is Cano the Wrestler.' The child's voice was full of awe. 'He travels all over the country showing his powers, and it is a great honour that he stayed in our village. Men say that he has never been defeated.'

'That might well be true.' Beric studied the knotted muscles as more laughter rumbled out. The African was obviously a very tough nut indeed, and there was an arrogance about him that suggested a long line of victories. He had never been beaten himself, but he wasn't sure if he would get the better of this Cano.

'I have said something to amuse you, brother?' The laughter was becoming intolerable, and Micah gave up trying to answer the woman's question.

'You amuse me, brother.' Cano gave a great lazy yawn. 'You say that you follow a certain prophet whom you never saw, but whose symbols were a fish and the fleece of a lamb. I came across that man once, and it is your description of him which amuses me.'

'You knew the Master, brother? You have seen Jesus from Galilee; the Son of God?'

'I never heard his real name or his country, fellow, and I am not your brother. But I have seen the man of the fish and the lamb, and, though he claimed to be a god, he was not as you describe

him. "Meek and gentle, the Son of Sorrow", you say. "The Great
One, the Lawgiver, the Man of Authority"; those were the names
we used for the bearer of the fish.'

'Yes, The Man of Authority. I have heard that he was called that
too.' Micah hurried across and stood dwarfed before the enormous
ebony figure. 'Where did you see him, friend? In Judaea or Galilee?'

'Not in Palestine or anywhere near it. Far to the south it was, in
a country few people visit, where the mountains of Sinai meet the
Arabian Sea.' Cano stopped laughing and closed his eyes as though
the sun was bothering them.

'Ten, twelve years ago, it must have been, when I saw this
prophet of yours, but I can still remember every detail. Very deep
and well hidden this valley was. Three streams ran down the gorge
and met before the village, and high above was a rock that made
music. Whenever the wind blew from the south there was a sound
exactly like women singing.'

'Tell us about him, friend.' All the Christians had crowded
around the man. 'Tell us how you came to know the Master.'

'If you wish.' A single red-veined eye opened and inspected
them. 'All the same it is a good story and worth a fee. Twenty
silver pieces you must pay to hear what happened to your God and
Rosetta, his woman.'

'We have no money, friend, but tell us for the love you must
have borne him.' Micah spread out his hands in supplication, and
the villagers joined him. 'Tell us the story, Cano.'

'Love? Who said I bore him love? Fear and awe was what that
tall man gave to his people. A healer of the sick, a bringer of good
fortune, but more terrible than Caesar.' Cano opened his other eye
and walked towards Beric like a dealer inspecting a slave.

'I give nothing without reward and must be paid for the story.
All the same, I need exercise and might tell it to a man who could
stretch me on the ground.' He raised his hand and felt Beric's
biceps.

'You have fought in the arena, big man?'

'In Rome itself.' Beric nodded and his eyes studied him. Ten to
twelve years ago, he thought, and this holy man, this healer, was
known by the signs of a fish and a lamb. The Man of Authority,
they called him, as people had done with the Nazarene. It must be

the same person, and this mention of a woman sounded promising. 'You have fought there too, Cano?'

'Not in Rome, but in Alexandria and Corinth and Athens. Thirty-five good men I killed before they gave me my staff of liberty, and I am master of every weapon. I have fought with the sword and the net and trident, I have fought blindfold, and I have fought with wild beasts. Now it is my pleasure to use only what you can see.' He spread out his legs and arms and his smile widened. The feet and hands were like clubs and the teeth were filed to sharp points.

'Will you face my weapons, white boy? Will you fight me in return for the story of the Man with the Fish?'

'I will fight you.' Beric started to remove his tunic. There was no other answer he could give because the Department had to have the information. But he wasn't sure if he would be a match for Cano. The fellow was a professional, and though older than himself, looked in far better condition.

'Shall we start, Cano?' He swung round as Micah gripped his arm.

'No, my son, though we all wish to hear the story, you must not do this thing. How many times have I to tell you that the Master condemned violence except in defence of the weak. I forbid you to fight with him.'

'You forbid me, old fool! You give me orders, Hebrew apostate!' The sneer on the African's face had infuriated him and Beric threw Micah aside, completely forgetting his role of servile simpleton. 'Let us get it over with, Cano.'

'As you wish.' The black man stooped and slipped the sandals from his board-like feet. 'This should be amusing, for it is a long time since I heard a giant plead for mercy.' Already the villagers were forming a circle, chattering with excitement at the promised spectacle.

'Let us fight in any style we like, and if I plead instead of you, I shall tell you what happened at the Valley of the Singing Rock. You agree?'

'It is a bargain.' Beric nodded and drew back to the edge of the circle. 'I have a great thirst, though, and would like to pause and drink after every five hundred counts.'

'Five hundred.' Cano's pointed teeth mocked him. 'I doubt if

both of us will be on our feet as long as that, but if it pleases you,
I agree.' He removed his tunic and stood naked apart from a loin-
cloth and a very broad leather belt. Above the belt, his body was
notched with the scars of a hundred other contests.

'You are ready? Good. Then start counting, women.' He flexed
his biceps for a moment, laughed again and charged.

It was like facing the rush of an animal, for Cano bounded
rather than ran across the ground, with his head low down and
both arms stretched out in front of him. Beric stood quite motionless and waited for the attack. He knew how it would be made,
he knew the defence against it, but he was badly out of condition
and didn't know if he would be quick enough. Cano was almost
up to him before he moved, twisting to one side to avoid the foot
that slashed at his groin, and then straightening so that the flat of
Cano's right hand missed his throat and landed harmlessly against
the shoulder. As it did so, his own hands caught the African's
arms and swung him round till he found a knee-lock against the
spine.

'Good, my friend. You are a professional and can really fight.'
Even in that terrible grip, the man still laughed. 'Perhaps you are
going to hear the story after all.' His body seemed to shrink and go
slack and the next moment he bent forward, throwing Beric over
his shoulders.

'No, not just yet, I think.' His hands were on Beric's throat
now and their faces pressed tightly together making an eye-gouge
impossible. Beric felt that there was blood instead of saliva in his
mouth and behind Cano's face the sun had turned a deep purple.
He was almost unconscious when he found the lock he wanted
and those terrible hands released him. Around them the counting women sounded as if they were taking part in some religious
ritual. 'Eighty-nine – ninety – ninety-one . . .'

The fight continued just like that. Always the African attacked
with skill and enormous strength and animal ferocity, and always
Beric somehow managed to break free at the last possible moment.

'Three hundred and ten – three hundred and eleven . . .' But
the point was that he couldn't hurt Cano. Every kick and slash
and squeeze might have been a caress for all the effect they had on
the man's stone body, and he laughed and mocked, though Beric

himself was tiring fast. Beric gasped with relief when the count finally reached five hundred and he could stagger back to the edge of the circle.

'Listen, lord. Do not speak, but listen very carefully.' Two women squatted beside him, one squirting vinegar into his bleeding mouth and the other massaging his shoulders. Her lips were almost touching his right ear.

'That black animal shamed me. He beat my husband and took me to his couch by force. I am his bitter enemy and I can tell you where his weakness lies. Will you trust me, lord?'

Beric nodded slightly. He had no choice but to trust her. Though he himself was completely worn out, Cano hadn't even bothered to sit down and was joking with the women opposite. Unless a miracle happened, the next round would see the end of the contest before the count reached one hundred.

'Go for his belt, lord.' Her lips were like fluttering moths against his ear. 'I cannot remember whether it is to the left or the right, but the belt hides his weakness.' She drew back into the circle and her companion followed.

Was it a trick? Was she Cano's lover, perhaps, who planned to shorten the fight by persuading him to attack leather instead of flesh and blood?

No, she was telling the truth, for he had hurt Cano once; only once in the whole fight. The counting started again, and as Beric stood up, he suddenly remembered. He had aimed a blow at the man's face and Cano had knocked it contemptuously down, so that it landed on his belt. It shouldn't have hurt him at all, but as the fist met the leather, Beric had heard him grunt as if in extreme agony.

That was strange, Beric thought, watching the African grin and flex his muscles for the next charge. One would have imagined the thick leather would have protected him from any fist. And why should he wear such a belt if it came to that? Hard, barkened ox hide, and so broad that the top pressed against his ribs.

But on which side had the blow fallen? The woman couldn't help him with that, and, if he made a mistake, Cano's hands would be around his throat, and this time he might be too weak to break free. He saw the man start to hurtle towards him, lowered his arms as if powerless to resist and heard the African shout in triumph. He stood swaying there, supported only by the fingers which kneaded into his throat and the filed teeth meeting in his shoulder, and then suddenly both his fists came thudding up with every scrap of his remaining strength behind them.

He had him! It was Beric who smiled now, because Cano had screamed and his hands went down to cover his waist. Not before another blow went home though, and, all at once, the skin wasn't shining ebony, but a flat, unhealthy brown. Beric slammed him again and again across the face, waiting for the moment when he would have to raise his hands, and then, one after the other, his knees shot upwards.

Yes, that was the way. The face, the throat, and then down to the waist again when punishment became intolerable and the hands were lifted. The man's body was damp with sweat and red stuff dribbled down over the loincloth.

'A hundred and eight – a hundred and nine . . .' Was it so short a time since the women began counting? Another stab at the waist and outstretched hands were far more effective than knees or fists. There was a softness behind the leather and he could feel his fingers run into it like knives.

'Beric, do not kill him.' It was the old man, Micah, who was shouting, of course, but his voice sounded strangely like that of Naevius Macro. 'I beg you not to kill him.'

But whoever it was, Micah, or the voice of Macro in his own mind, Beric could not obey. The Department needed Cano's story, it was his duty to spare him, but the lust to destroy was a roll of drums, the hoofs of a bolted horse drowning reason. On and on his hands beat against the belt, till blood suddenly spurted from Cano's mouth and he toppled to the ground. Only when he realized that the man was dead did Beric cease to strike him.

'A man whose signs were a fish and the fleece of a lamb. A miracle worker who was known as the "One of Authority". And he lived on Sinai ten or twelve years ago, in a village with three streams and a curious hill which makes a sound like singing women.' Eros Dion frowned at Beric standing forlornly before his desk.

'You animal, Beric. You stupid, bloodthirsty barbarian. That African was the first real lead we had. The only witness who claimed to have known the Nazarene during his middle life, and you killed him.'

'I am sorry, my lord. There was an old sword wound hidden below Cano's belt and my blows opened it. I know I should have spared him, but the pain from this had driven me out of my mind and I couldn't stop myself.' Beric pointed to the half-healed scar where the filed teeth had met in his shoulder.

'Let me try and make amends, Eros Dion. Send me to Sinai so I can discover the truth for you.'

'No, Beric, not you.' Eros suddenly smiled. 'You are forgiven because you are the first of our agents to come up with anything at all, but you are not the man to go to Sinai. I have heard that the people of the peninsula are small and nervous, and a giant like you might frighten them into silence.

'You have had a long journey, so go and get some rest. And do not worry about what happened to the African. When I next write to Rome I shall inform Naevius Macro that I am completely satisfied with your work.'

'Thank you, master.' The huge figure stooped and kissed his hand. 'And I would like you to remember one thing, Eros Dion. Whatever Fate holds in store for either of us, I will remain your servant.' Beric bowed and walked heavily out of the room.

'Well, my friend, is our luck starting to change at last?' Eros turned to Sextus as the door closed behind Beric. 'A miracle-worker on Sinai, a healer of the sick, and a bringer of good fortune whose symbols were a fish and a lamb. A person referred to as the "One of Authority". A man who was also mixed up with a woman named Rosetta. Was he our Nazarene?'

'It sounds likely, but you say "miracle worker" as though you accepted the possibility.' Sextus smiled back at him. 'I always thought that you were the complete cynic, Eros, who believed in nothing except order and reason.'

'You misjudged me badly then.' The Greek stood up and walked out on to the balcony. The summer was over and autumn in Palestine had started miserably. Cold and dank and dull with constant grey cloud over the little scrubby hills, and, now and then, days of fine soaking rain. The kind of weather he remembered from Britain and Northern Gaul.

'I believe that certain human beings may be possessed by super-natural powers, as is the Oracle at Delphi, but unless they can control them, it is a terrible thing to happen, because they injure not only themselves but all they come into contact with. "Whom the God wishes to destroy he first drives mad," in fact.

'This Jesus may have had such gifts, but that need not concern us now. What we have to do is to check on the Sinai story and find out exactly what happened there. The time factor is correct, the symbols and the physical description fit, but the character sounds quite different. His followers spoke of a mild, gentle creature preaching this absurd doctrine of human equality under the gods, but the African described a man who could inspire awe and obedi-ence.'

'It must have been the same person.' Sextus crossed to his side and scowled out over the city. 'It has to be, because he must have existed somewhere. We have searched for almost half a year, ques-tioned a thousand witnesses and followed a thousand false trails. We have found not a single clue to his whereabouts, and until today I was almost beginning to believe that the fellow really was a divine being who vanished from the earth before appearing to the Hermit, John the Baptist.

'But now this report of Beric's gives me hope again. Sinai is a desolate, little-travelled region; just the kind of place in which he might have hidden, and something tells me it was the same man.' As he spoke, all the months of frustration dropped from Sextus and he felt eager and excited again.

'Let me go to Sinai, Eros, and I know I will find what we are looking for: something petty, or dishonest, or wantonly cruel: the information to bring down his whole gospel in disgust and ridi-cule.'

'I hope so, but my anxiety is that we may not find it in time.' Eros leaned forward over the balustrade. Reinforcements had reached the city and the people were quiet enough: that was one slight comfort. Three reserve cohorts of veterans from Egypt were attached to the garrison now; worn-out men who constantly grumbled at being taken from their families and small-holdings near Alexandria. But they could relieve the regular forces for more active duties and all fears of a Jewish uprising had been lifted.

There were many other things to fear, however, because, though they had so far learned nothing about the Nazarene himself, his adherents were coming out into the open with a vengeance.

In the north, the man Saul, who for some reason now called himself Paulinus, was boasting of a sudden conversion to Jesus whom he referred to as 'Christ', the 'Anointed One', and had stated that the 'Kingdom of Heaven' was open to all races of mankind. In Asia Minor, the Fisherman, Simon Peter, was said to have worked countless miracles, and another of the man's original followers, named Philip, had been heard of as far south as Ethiopia.

Yes, the fire was starting to spread, the Christians were revealing themselves, and hardly a week passed without some provincial official demanding powers to act against them. But always the Department in Rome refused. Naevius Macro agreed completely with Eros that there were to be no more martyrs, no more examples of superhuman courage to attract imitators, till the time was ripe. Only when they had something to discredit the man himself, would action be taken. And, when they had it, news would go round every slum, every slave compound and sweat-shop in the Empire, and the flames would be blown out in a gust of ridicule and scorn.

'By all means go to Sinai yourself, Sextus,' he said. 'Find me a story to shame these people, and I think that Macro will give you any honour which is in his power to bestow.'

'That will not be necessary,' Sextus glanced at his scarred palm. 'Saul of Tarsus did this to me and he now appears to be the leader of the cult. Revenge on him and his followers is the reward I will treasure most.'

All the same, some public recognition would be pleasant, he thought, and suddenly life seemed very good indeed. Revenge on Saul, Pilate's wealth which would soon be his, and Rachel.

Rachel was hardly ever out of his thoughts these days, though their relationship was eccentric, to say the least: a stolid, unimaginative Roman officer and a woman who could change her personality from hour to hour. A gay, vital girl one moment, and the next a brooding creature with a single dream; to find proof that her father betrayed a divine master because he was ordered to. She had rejected all his physical advances, and once wept when he reminded her they had lain naked together, but she fascinated him more than any woman he had known. If he could only show her the truth, supply proof that the Nazarene was an impostor, he had no doubt that he could gain her love.

'Leave at dawn tomorrow, and I pray that you will return with the information we need.' Eros' voice cut into his thoughts.

'But should you fail, should it be a different man the African knew on Sinai, or the story contain nothing to discredit the Nazarene, there is still no cause to despair, because certain precautions are being taken against further failures.

'Come with me, and I will show you.' He let him out of the room and opened a door across the corridor. Beyond it two men were bent over a mass of documents on a table. They stood up as he entered.

'I am sorry to disturb you, my friends, but I want to acquaint Sextus Ennius with our scheme.

'You know my scribe, Publius, of course, Sextus, but I don't think you have met Uriah, the keeper of King Herod's library.' He bowed to the older of the two men, a bearded Sadducee with a thin humorous face and eyes that were as bright as a boy's.

'King Herod has been kind enough to place Uriah at our disposal, and I think we will find him a most useful ally. Though a pious Hebrew on the surface, he is very much like myself, and worships nothing except the pursuit of knowledge. Isn't that true, Uriah?'

'It is true up to a point, lord.' The youthful eyes twinkled back. 'As long as I am with Romans, I am a cynic. Outside your walls, however, I follow the faith of my fathers, and regard you as a blasphemous idolator! You are right in saying we are allies though. In one thing we will always be agreed.' He smiled at a roll of parchment in front of him. 'To both Roman and Jew, the threat is the same.'

'That is a fair enough answer.' Eros turned to the other man. 'It is going well, Publius?'

'Excellently, lord.' The scribe followed Uriah's smile at the parchment. 'We have already reached the twenty-fifth year of the man's life and I think you will find it interesting reading. Uriah here is providing the background and I am surprising myself with powers of sinister invention.'

'Good. But don't make it too sinister, Publius. What we want is ridicule and contempt. You will also make sure that all the witnesses you name are not only well-paid, but reliable too.

'Yes, it has come to that, I'm afraid, Sextus.' Eros motioned him to look at the scroll. 'As our search has been fruitless so far, I am having a fictional biography prepared. We won't use it unless we have to, but I want to know it is there. It should make interesting reading as well. Uriah has promised to see the background is authentic, and Publius is a very bright boy with a talent for describing the more sordid details of life. I am relying on him to see that the Nazarene's hidden years are very sordid indeed.'

'Letters, masters.' He turned as a slave appeared in the doorway, bowing deeply and handing them each a sealed roll of papyrus. 'They were delivered by a ship that reached Tyre last night.'

'Thank you, friend.' Eros had been a slave himself and was always polite to subordinates. 'Now we must leave you for a moment.' He nodded to Uriah and the scribe, and walked back to his own room, forcing himself to appear unhurried. Below the seal on his own letter was a tiny dot as though the wax had run; Macro's sign that its contents were urgent.

'Light me a taper please, Sextus.' He sat down and opened the scroll. Yes, the first sheet was a dupe, and Macro had been wise to take precautions, for the seal was broken all right and the join was clear to a trained eye. He read quickly through the customary greetings, the inquiries as to his work, and the news from Rome.

All goes well, Eros, and we are delighted with our boy Emperor. I thank the gods that I supported the claims of Caligula for he is indeed a son of Germanicus, the greatest of our generals. Everywhere people acclaim him as a demigod, for already his worth is proven . . .

Accounts of Caligula's talents followed; his charity in bringing exiles back to the city, the public buildings he had started to erect, the pensions he had promised to soldiers, a thorough reform of the legal system, a golden age beginning to dawn.

'No, tell me later.' Sextus had finished his own letter and was trying to talk about it, but Eros waved him aside, and held the

papyrus over the taper. A corner crinkled, then divided, and he
pulled away the false backing to show what Macro really wanted
him to read.

Yes, everywhere people hail Caligula, my friend. They speak
of him as a deliverer and, so far, they are right. The finances
of the city have never been better, and the shops are full. The
true picture is rather different, however.

When I decided to support Little Boots, I was fully aware of
his weaknesses; conceit, lust and those delusions of divinity
shared by many of his ancestors. At the same time I thought
he was a weakling whom the Department could control.
Now it is beginning to appear that I was wrong. Already
he resents my authority and it may not be long before he
attempts to discard me.

Be prepared, old friend, to hear grave news in the future,
because I have made a terrible mistake. From my private
interviews with Caligula it is becoming clear that we have
put not a man, but a wild animal, on the throne.

From Gaius Vinius, steward to Pontius Pilate, Procurator
of Judaea, to his new master, Sextus Marcellus Ennius, greetings and the blessings of all the gods . . .

Sextus considered his own letter as he turned his horse through
the Fountain Gate and out into the country.

Since you left us, my lord, your uncle's sickness grew
steadily worse and we would constantly hear him cry out
in his sleep. The mock trials, one of which you witnessed,
were performed almost every other day, and after them he
would scrub his hands with pumice till the flesh was raw and
bleeding.

Two mornings ago, on the second day before the Nones
of July, his valet, Eyrtus, a freedman devoted to our master,
found the door of his bedchamber bolted and was unable to
awake him.

My lord Sextus, it is a sad duty to inform you that your

uncle is with the dead. When we broke into the room we found that he had slashed both his wrists, and the body was already cold. For months I had endeavoured to deprive him of weapons but somehow he was able to conceal a dagger upon his person.

Master, for such I hope I may call you, it is with pleasure that I dictate the following. When we realized the strength of the Procurator's sickness, Eyrtus and I, wishing to serve the family interests, persuaded him to sign the will which he had prepared. It has already been dispatched to Rome and his estates are now yours. We, and all our fellow retainers, humbly await your instructions . . .

So, it had happened and he was a rich man. Though Sextus felt bitterly sorry for Pilate, he had hardly known him, and death was probably an escape into mercy. He muttered one final prayer to Pluto, and considered his new-found wealth as the horse trotted across the Valley of Kidron on the way to the little villa Rachel had inherited from the murdered doctor.

Estates in Italy, a farm in Egypt, two quarries in Sicily, and half a million gold pieces locked away in a Roman vault. Vinius and Eyrtus would be well rewarded for their work, and the world was his as soon as he had reached Rome and proved the will.

It would be pleasant to see Rome again too. Eros had promised him leave as soon as he had finished his business on Sinai and a fast ship should get him there before the end of the month. His bridle jingled pleasantly and he hummed to himself, considering the future. Though he was still curious, still eager for revenge on the people who had branded him, Vinius' news made the Cult of the Nazarene seem trivial and unimportant. Whatever Eros might say, it would only spread to the rabble, and soon die out of its own accord.

That letter from Macro was surely an exaggeration as well. Although there was bad blood in Caligula's family, and rumours of an unnatural relationship with his sisters, he had shown himself a good Emperor so far. Besides, nobody could be worse than Tiberius, and life had gone on normally enough during his reign. And even if Little Boots dreamed of absolute power in private, he would have to behave himself. Macro had given him the throne, Macro controlled both the Vigiles and the Praetorian Guard, and he couldn't afford to discard him.

And then there was Rachel. As soon as he had heard the news he had made up his mind, and at every movement of the saddle his decision grew firmer. Apart from a single act of compassion when he was barely conscious, they had had no physical relations at all, but he suddenly knew that he loved her. As Eros had said, a Jewess obsessed with the dream of justifying her father would make a most unsatisfactory wife for a Roman nobleman, but he would ask her to marry him all the same.

'A foul evening, my lord.' The road to the villa passed a check-point, and Sextus reined as a grizzled veteran raised his lantern.

'Have you any news for us yet, lord? Have you heard any talk of us being sent home?' Sextus was a frequent visitor at the post and the questions were always the same.

'Only a few weeks they said we'd be stuck here, and it's over three months already. I don't know what'll be happening to the farm without me. Just a Nubian my old woman is, with no idea of running things.'

'I shouldn't think it will be long now, sergeant. I did hear that reinforcements were coming from Italy to relieve you.' That was a lie, but there was no harm in giving the veterans something to hope for.

'Did you, my lord? That is good news, and I'm sure it's true, because Caesar isn't the man to let us old chaps rot here for ever.' The wrinkled face beamed up at him. 'As I said to the centurion only yesterday, "The Emperor is the best friend the army has. No, our boy, the son of Germanicus won't forget us. He'll see that we get our rights."'

'I'm certain that's correct, sergeant.' Sextus smiled back and then rode on up the slope. Whatever Macro might write, the common soldiers had no fears of Caligula.

There were the lights of the villa now. He slowed his horse to a walk at the crest of the hill. The descent was rough and the sky already dark.

Yes, it would be pleasant to take Rachel with him to Rome. To take her anywhere, as long as it was far away from this wretched country with its constant memories of her father. Her mother had died when she was a young child, and her feelings for Judas had been much stronger than normal. If only she could forget the whole horrible story, she might begin to love him. 'Let the Dead bury their Dead.' That was one saying of the Nazarene's with which Sextus agreed. If her father could be driven from her memory, Rachel might begin to live.

'Whoah, boy. Steady, boy.' The horse had smelled the stable and fodder and he checked him sharply. 'Don't you go and break a leg now.' The road was just a narrow track between boulders, and Rachel's villa the only building in sight. He hated the thought of her living there, but she had refused all offers of Roman hospitality, and it was probably safer for her than Jerusalem itself.

'Thank you, Simeon.' An old freedman of the doctor took the horse's head, and Sextus dismounted and hurried across to the house, wondering what he would find; a gay, laughing girl, or a brooding figure staring silently out towards the salt lake they called the Dead Sea.

But it was all right. The moment he entered the room he could see that she was pleased he had come, and her eyes shone with happiness as she poured him wine. He sipped at it for a moment and then without a word handed her Vinius' letter.

'Poor man – poor, poor, old man.' Her smile turned to a look of sympathy as she read of Pilate's death. 'Once he did a terrible thing, but nobody should have to suffer as much as that.

'This means that you are rich at last, Sextus. I am happy for you.'

'I will be as rich as any human being needs to be.' He sat down on the couch beside her and took her hand. 'There is one more job for me to do here, and then I am going to Rome to claim the estates. I came here this evening to ask you to go with me.'

'I don't understand.' The parchment fell from her fingers and drifted on to the floor. 'You want me to go to Rome; to leave Palestine? Why, Sextus?'

'Because I love you, Rachel.' He smiled to himself as he considered their future. A house in Rome, on the Capitoline hill, a villa by the sea, wealth and honour and ease for the rest of their lives. 'I want you to marry me, my dear.'

'No, that is impossible.' She pulled away her hand and turned her face from him.

'Oh, I am flattered, Sextus. I even think I could love you in time, but I am not free. Till the truth is revealed, I am bound to him.'

'Bound to your father!' Sextus fought back a curse. 'Judas Iscariot is dead, Rachel. He betrayed an evil man and there is nothing you can do for him. Let him rest in peace.'

'Let him rot, you mean.' She stared out of the window as if fascinated by the shadows creeping across the hill. 'Let the name of Judas stink and foul men's minds for eternity. No, I said I was flattered, I said I might be able to love you if I were free, and I wish you every happiness. But I am chained to my father's memory and I can belong to no one else till I have absolved him.'

'You fool.' Sextus gripped her shoulders and pulled her towards him with love and anger fighting each other in his mind.

'You hope to prove the Nazarene was a god who ordered your father to betray him.' She struggled in his arms and Sextus' grip tightened. He suddenly knew what he had to do, and with the knowledge came a feeling of certainty. Jesus of Nazareth was not merely a threat to the Empire, the dream of a group of men who had tortured and shamed him, but a personal enemy whom he was bound to destroy. When he did so, Rachel must be there to witness it.

'Listen to me, woman. I told you I had one more job to do before I returned to Rome, and you can help me with it. You wish to know the truth about the Nazarene and I shall give you that truth.' She had ceased to struggle and was staring wide-eyed at him.

'Tomorrow I am leaving for the south and you will come with me. The journey will be long and hard, but there is a story at the end of it; a story of your imagined god, my dear.' He stood up and tightened his tunic and he felt like a giant, a colossus who could achieve anything.

'I will call for you at first light and we will go to the Mountains of Sinai where the story took place. It will be the story of a man, Rachel; I know that as surely as I can distinguish night from day. Just a man – a man who died.'

They travelled down the coast at first, past Ascalon and Gaza, the old cities of the Philistines, along the main road to Egypt, a level, well-engineered highway running beside the sea and thick with traffic; chained galley slaves on their way to Caesarea, camel trains, merchants riding in litters and chariots, a squadron of irregular cavalry transferring to Syria. The route of the conquerors that Alexander had taken, and Antony, and the demi-god Julius; outside Italy the busiest road in the world, and at every mile-post Sextus wondered if it would lead them to the first definite piece of information.

'By all means take the girl with you,' Eros had said. 'I think you are insane to wish to marry her, but that is your business. All I know is that to gain her love, you must first destroy her absurd belief in the Nazarene, and something tells me you will find the means on Sinai.' He had smiled and kept fondling the hilt of his dagger as he spoke.

'The African mentioned a woman, didn't he, Sextus? A woman named Rosetta, and that interests me very much indeed. Go with the gods, my friend, and bring back the information we need so badly.'

Eros was right of course. From the moment he had told her they would go together, Rachel had been like a child setting out on some miraculous adventure, though her expectations were very different from his. She believed implicitly that they would find proof of the man's divinity in the peninsula, and her eyes gleamed with excitement as the long road carried them on to the south and west.

Behind her, the man whom Eros had detailed to accompany them lolled rather than rode, and only a tuneless dirge which he constantly hummed proved him awake. His name was Thassi, a Jew born at Alexandria who had served the Department since he was a boy, and was regarded as one of Macro's most trusted agents. Thassi admitted that it was fifteen years since he had visited Sinai but though Sextus would have preferred someone who knew the country better, Eros had insisted on him.

'We are dealing with a Jewish story,' he had said. 'And, though Thassi has cast off his religion long ago, his understanding will be much clearer than ours. Besides, the fellow has a gift which is far more precious than any knowledge of local topography. He can make people talk without the use of fear or pain. Trust Thassi, my friend, rely on him completely, and if there is a story to be found, he will dig it out for you.' Well, perhaps Eros was right, but Sextus could see nothing impressive about Thassi so far. An old, stout man, recognizable as a Jew by the Star of David pressed tightly against the dewlapped folds of his throat, who looked as though he could hardly survive the journey. Behind him, the pack mule occasionally lifted its head and gave a hideous blare, as if in protest at the continual humming.

They left the sea and the road at a promontory called Mount Cassius and wound south between enormous sand dunes resembling the Pyramids of Egypt. Beyond the dunes lay the Paran Wilderness; the country over which Moses and the Israelites had wandered, preparing themselves for the conquest of Palestine. Wilderness was a good name for it, Sextus thought. Not so much a desert, because there was vegetation and now and then flocks of small, dispirited-looking sheep, as in a decayed country. Ridges of rock covered with edible lichen, the legendary manna of the Hebrews, jutted out of the plain; scrubby bushes had been bent into fantastic shapes by the wind, and the ground rang hollowly under their horses' hoofs, like the roof of Hades. As the miles passed and a cairn finally told them they had left the Empire and entered Arabia, Sextus had the odd feeling they were crossing a land that resented their presence and in which every grain of dust was an enemy.

The weather was strange too. A warm south-westerly wind blew most of the time, but occasionally it would veer round and bring sudden flurries of rain. In front of them a dark line started to appear on the horizon and slowly grew into a ridge of foot-hills with jagged peaks behind; the sacred, rose-red mountains of the Moon God. Sextus and Rachel kept staring hopefully towards them, but Thassi still slouched over his horse's neck, apparently disinterested, and only spoke when they stopped to eat or make camp for the night. It took them three days to reach the hills, and not a mile passed without Sextus asking himself if they really were following the steps of the Nazarene or bent on another fools' errand.

Village was too grand a name for the first settlement they came to. A dozen mean huts of undressed stone clinging to the side of a gorge and inhabited by small dark people clad in goatskins, who might have been the children of Pan himself. They were shy and timid at first, but became friendly as soon as Thassi spoke to them, and offered a nauseous-looking dish of crushed locusts and mead which proved both pleasant and powerful.

But where information was concerned, they appeared useless. 'A village with three streams, and a hill over which the wind makes a noise like Singing Women? A tall, pale man from the north and a woman named Rosetta? My lord, when the rains come there are streams everywhere and many hermits live on the holy mountains of the south. But we have never heard of such a place or the people you describe.'

'For the first time, I am starting to think Beric's story may be of interest.' The track had become rough and very steep after leaving the settlement and Thassi let go the reins and held on to his pommel for support. 'You naturally realized that those people were lying.'

'Why do you say that?' Sextus frowned back at him. The red hills were closing in on all sides and in the distance towered jagged peaks which looked as high as Etna.

'Because I am trained to know such things, lord.' Thassi nodded smugly and then clutched the reins and brought his horse to a halt.

'They lied all right, and now they are telling their neighbours to lie also.

'Look for yourselves.' He pointed to a cliff down the valley. Puffs of smoke were rising up from it and drifting away in the breeze.

'An invention of my ancestors which was copied by the Greeks and the Babylonians. When Moses crossed Paran, he sent guides ahead to show that the way was clear. During daylight they signalled with smoke like that and at night they used fire.' Thassi shielded his eyes and squinted at the tiny grey clouds.

'It is a long time since I have read such signals, but I think I can make out the gist of what is being said. "Three men on horses . . ." They cannot express differences of sex, my lady. "Three strangers seek news of a place which is accursed."'

'Accursed!' Sextus felt a wave of hope as the last cloud dispersed

in the air. 'That could not have been the village, though. It doesn't
fit the description at all.'

'No, that was not the place. All the same, the headman lied and
has warned his neighbours of our presence. I want to know why
he lied, because I am interested in hidden things, as I think you are,
my lady.'

'Only in one thing, Thassi.' Rachel rode on, turning her horse to
avoid a boulder. 'Because the people lied, you think there is such
a village?'

'I think it existed once, but I am not sure about the present.'
Thassi shrugged his plump shoulders.

'In my opinion, there is a story or legend about such a place
which these people have vowed not to repeat to strangers. It is
obviously discreditable or frightening, but who knows when it
happened? Perhaps generations ago, and the tale has been handed
down by countless parents to their children. Yes, perhaps long ago
and the village has vanished. After all, this is not a very permanent
landscape.' He nodded across the valley. Cedars grew on its slopes,
but here and there, huge swathes had been cut through them by
rock falls from the cliffs above.

'All I know is that the headman lied and we must discover why.'

The days passed and they moved towards the south. All the
people of the peninsula were friendly and hospitable, offering
them food and shelter in flea-infested huts, because they worshipped a deity named Abbadon, the brother of the Moon God,
who demanded courtesy to strangers.

He was obviously a debased form of Jove, this Abbadon, and
he lived on the great summit of Sinai itself, punishing offenders
with shafts of lightning. Every village kept a little fire burning day
and night through the whole year to show they were under his
protection.

But, however friendly the people might be, they were all reti-
cent and gave the same answers to Thassi's questions. 'Many villages lie by three streams and all are surrounded by hills over which
the wind sings. We have never heard of a man with a fish, though
Rosetta is a common name in these mountains. Often black men
from the south cross our country, but we know of no one called
Cano.' Thassi might have had the knack of making people talk, but

his talents seemed to have deserted him, and no plea or bribe could break through the polite denials.

'We have nothing to tell you, strangers, so eat your fill and then leave us in peace.' After a week Sextus had started to lose hope and even Rachel was less confident. Only Thassi remained assured of success, and every set-back increased his spirits. Though the Jew looked soft and out of condition, he appeared incapable of fatigue, and took the lead now, urging them up the gorges and down the valleys that led to the south. On the eighth day his confidence was rewarded.

They had just left one of the settlements; a place even smaller and meaner than the others, with fleas that were unusually hungry, and had stopped by a spring to try and get rid of them, when a woman suddenly appeared from behind a boulder; a thin, unkempt figure with a face that belonged to a young girl, but had been worn and wrinkled by toil and poverty.

She ignored the men and threw herself down before Rachel, kissing her feet and staring up at a bracelet on her wrist; a pretty thing of silver and polished glass, though of no great value.

'Queen, Great Queen, give me the jewels. Give them to me and I will tell you what you want to know; the way to the village where sin was released.' Grimy hands reached out and fondled the beads.

'And why shouldn't I tell you? It all happened a long time ago and the shame was not ours. Our people had no part in it, and the guilt belongs to the Children of Golab; such of them as are still alive. Why should we hide them any longer?'

'You know about the village then? Its name is Golab?' Rachel slipped off the bracelet and held it out of her reach. 'You can take us there?'

'No, I would not dare to take you, but I can show you the way. The place of the three streams and the singing rock. The Valley of Golab which has to die because of the shameful thing that happened there. Give me the jewels, Queen, and I will tell you how to find it.'

'Tell me first.' Rachel held up the bracelet, and the beads glittered in the sunlight. 'Then I will give you this.'

'As you say.' A goat moved across the hillside and the girl looked nervously around, obviously terrified of being seen by any of her people. 'The men would beat me if they knew what I was doing, though it happened when I was only a child and the sin is not ours.' She gave another glance over her shoulder.

'The village is less than half a day's journey from here. You must follow this track over the pass and go down into the next valley where it divides. Take the left fork over the far ridge and then turn left again as soon as you can see the sea.

'Now, give me the jewels as you promised.' She suddenly snatched the bracelet from Rachel and bounded away down the slope.

So, the place did exist. Sextus and Rachel smiled at each other as they rode on to their different hopes. The story of a risen god, or an incident in the life of an impostor whose gospel threatened the world. A shame and a sin, the girl had kept mentioning, and Sextus felt sure they were on the right road at last. Who had made these Children of Golab commit a crime which caused their neighbours to conceal their whereabouts? Why had their village to die? Something cruel, something criminal, something ludicrous. That was what Eros wanted to find in the Nazarene's past and the story might lie a few hours' journey away. Sextus loosened his tunic because it was getting hot now. A soft wind had blown up and the sky was clear apart from a little drifting cloud and hawks and eagles for ever wheeling over the cliffs.

The girl's directions were easy to follow. In the next valley, by the mouth of a disused copper mine which had probably been worked by the Egyptians centuries ago, the track divided, the left-hand branch climbing towards a further ridge. From then on the route lay beside a dried-up stream and was far too steep and rough for them to ride, so they dismounted and tugged their horses around boulders and across scree. Only the mule and Thassi found the going easy. The fat man dripped with sweat, but he quickly outpaced Sextus and Rachel, and was sitting on a rock with a wine skin in his hand when they finally reached the summit.

'I'm afraid our informant appears to have deceived us, my lady,' he said. 'I only hope that your bangle was of no great value.'

'Only to me, and I suppose to her.' Rachel looked at the track. It ran down the hillside to a plain which ended in blue water. The Arabian Sea that Augustus had ordained to be one of the limits of his Empire. There was a hint of villages along the shore, but none of them could have fitted the African's description.

'There might have been a fork once, I think, but it obviously doesn't lead anywhere now.' Thassi got up and pointed to the left. For a few paces the track appeared to branch and then ended before a bank of thorn bushes and unpruned olive trees. In the far south they could see that a gale was blowing up and the water was flecked with foam.

'I'm sorry, my dear.' Rachel smiled sadly at Sextus. 'What a fool I was to let her take the bracelet. We should have made her lead us there herself.' The mule suddenly drowned Rachel's words with a hideous bellow and when it stopped she and Thassi stood staring speechless towards the bushes, while Sextus had drawn his sword and started to hack a way through them. From somewhere far below came a soft crooning sound, which an imaginative person might easily describe as women singing.

It took them a long time to get down the hillside and at first the going was hard. Thorns clutched and tore at them, briars ripped their feet, and more often than not, the branches were too thick to cut and they had to climb over or around them. The mountain fell away to the right, and split into a narrow gorge riddled with caves that might have been inhabited by giants. At every turn, Sextus half expected to find Polyphemus regarding them malevolently with his single glaring eye.

But, though nobody could have come this way for years, there had been a track once, and it appeared to be taking them to the place Cano described. From far below they heard the murmur of several streams and straight ahead the cliff face broke into jagged pinnacles.

'There it is again.' Another gust of wind sprang up and they realized the crooning sound came from a gash in the furthest summit. Sextus slashed through more branches. A waterfall gushed out of a spring in the right-hand cliff and the going should be easier now, because the track followed the side of its stream, and though still steep and narrow, no bushes grew amongst the piled boulders.

'The Place of the Singing Rock.' Thassi grinned and wiped the sweat from his forehead. Further down he could see another

stream and the gorge was opening up into a valley with level
ground at the end of it. By local standards, it looked a lush place
and, though low at the moment, the streams would probably be
torrents after heavy rain.

'Your bracelet was well-spent after all, my lady. All we need
hope for now is that the African's story concerns the same man.'

'It must do. The man must have been the Master.' Rachel's eyes
were bright in the glare of the sun, though a belt of cloud was
drifting in from the sea. 'The fish and the lamb were his symbols.
Soon you will know the truth, Sextus, and we will worship him
together.

'And look there.' She gripped his hand and pointed down-
wards as the path swung around a boulder and the whole valley
lay spread out before them to the sea. A third stream ran in from
the north to join the others and just beyond the meeting of the
waters stood a village. In comparison to the rest of the settlements
they had visited it was huge, almost a town, with at least fifty huts
forming a square.

'Yes, this can only be the place Beric heard described.' Sextus
felt a purely boyish excitement as they hurried on down, and then
frowned.

'All the same, I think we may have arrived too late – many years
too late.' Their pace had become steadily faster as the angle of the
hillside lessened and shale and gravel took the place of rocks, and
at every step the details below grew clearer.

The village looked as if it had died a long time ago. Once a
bridge of cedar logs had spanned the main stream, but some flood
had washed it away and only a single spar remained in position.
Most of the huts had been pulled down or allowed to decay into
heaps of rubble, and the rest were overgrown by bushes, while
cultivated olive groves had rioted into a wilderness. The wind was
starting to veer round slightly, and instead of making that pleasant
singing sound, it brought a stench of offal and rotting fish from
the sea.

At least there was animal life, however. Little brown goats were
grazing on the lower slopes, and an old, shaggy donkey stood
completely motionless by the side of the track as they passed. The
belt of cloud had finally obscured the sun and the ruined village

appeared immensely sinister in the sudden gloom. Beyond it, fire-blackened posts stood out of the water like decayed teeth to show that there had once been a jetty.

'Not entirely dead.' Sextus pointed towards a gap between the huts. A group of people were standing in the square beyond, and their manner was quite different from that of the other villagers. They didn't look shy or suspicious or frightened so much as stunned; standing close together for protection and staring at the two men and the woman as if unable to believe their eyes.

'But there are no children.' Rachel's hand tightened around Sextus'. They were very close now, and she could see that every one of the staring faces was wrinkled and old.

'There are no young or middle-aged people at all.' Sextus withdrew his hand and laid it on the hilt of his sword. Was this a trap, he wondered. Were those old people the bait to lure them into the square where the warriors were waiting? He was on the point of warning Thassi, but the Jew appeared incapable of fear as well as of fatigue, and was already past the line of huts and had raised his arm in gesture of friendship. Sextus shrugged his shoulders and followed.

'Why have you come here, strangers, and what do you want of us?' One of the old men took a single pace forward and returned Thassi's salute. 'Do you not know that this is the Village of Golab, the Valley of the Singing Rock, and no men may enter here without sharing the curse of the gods?'

'We come in peace, father.' Thassi bowed and spread out his hands to show they held no weapon while Sextus let go the sword. 'We are travellers who crave your hospitality.'

'Hospitality! From the Children of Golab!' The headman gave a thin, bitter smile and the people behind him muttered their disbelief.

'Very well. Food you may have, and then you will leave us.' He nodded to a crone and she hobbled away to one of the huts. 'You will eat and then go back by the way you came; the road which was barred so that the guilt would not spread to our neighbours.'

'Why was that done, father?' Rachel glanced around the valley. All the streams entered by waterfalls and the cliffs were almost vertical. The path they had used was the only possible exit.

'I am not your father, girl. We have no children and merely wait for death.' There was a sudden hint of hope on the wrinkled face.

'But why have you come? Are you messengers sent to release us at last? Has the sin finally been paid for and we may die among our fellows?'

'It is possible, if you tell us the exact truth.' The woman had returned with a platter of dried dates and Thassi squatted beside it. Guilt and sin and shame, he thought. Those were the words the girl had used to describe these people, and their story was obviously very horrible. He reached out towards the dates and then, as if finding them not to his taste, moved his hand and started to trace something in the dust.

'We wish to hear of the man who brought the curse,' he said. 'The miracle worker from the north, the "One of Authority", who settled with you. We are indeed messengers from beyond the mountains who can give you release, but only if you confess all the sin to us.' He drew back to show what he had drawn.

'Tell me about your miracle worker and Rosetta, his woman.'

'The signs; the marks on his arm and the walls of the cave; the signs of Abbadon's enemy.' Thassi had hoped for a strong reaction and he got it. The man looked as if he were terrified and the rest of the villagers drew back whimpering.

'Yes, the fish and the lamb of God, as he told us. But they lack something.' The headman obviously had to force himself to kneel beside Thassi and slowly join the two forms together with a 'T' shape.

'This was also a mark of our shame.'

'The "Tau" cross or a carpenter's square.' The conversation was taking place in Aramaic which Sextus found difficult to follow, but as he looked at the tracings he knew that their journey had not been in vain. The Nazarene must have been there, because the three symbols of his cult were staring up at him from the dust.

'And you are the servants of the Mighty One, lord? You really have come to forgive us and say that the sin is forgiven at last?' One of the women threw herself down before Thassi and her tears fell on to his sandals.

'Surely we have been punished enough now? They took all our young people, saying that children could not be held responsible, and they burned the jetty and pulled down most of the huts. They planted briars across the path so that we, the old, must remain in the valley till death, and they told us that no one should ever enter here to be contaminated by our sin.'

'Tell me that it is over at last, lord. Say that the Fire Bringer is appeased at last.'

'That depends, woman.' Thassi stood up and glanced around the square. In its centre was one of the little stone hearths sacred to Abbadon, such as he had seen in the other settlements, but this was cold and had obviously been unlit for years, for rain had washed away all traces of soot. 'If all is confessed, you may be forgiven. If not, the punishment will be increased even more.

'Come on, fellow, are you going to start.' He pulled the headman towards him and stared into his face. 'Repeat every detail of your sin, and we will decide if you can be released from it.'

'Very well, master.' The man's eyes kept flicking nervously away from Thassi's towards Mount Sinai, towering over the northwest horizon.

'It is hard for us, though. We are a simple and foolish people who acted out of ignorance. All the same, the sin was so great that we never mention it even amongst ourselves.' His face was ravaged by age and fear and misery, but Thassi could still see the tiny expression of hope.

'As you, his messengers, must know, we deserted our god for an evil man.'

The man had appeared as if from nowhere, in the middle of winter, and the first sign of his arrival was smoke before one of the caves on the hillside. The villagers were a friendly people, but they resented anybody settling in the valley without permission, and Berca, the headman, led a party of elders up the gorge to investigate.

They found the man squatting on a rock before the cave. There was an old pack donkey tethered beside him, and he was staring out across the hills as if in a deep trance. Berca was about to go up to him when one of the elders suddenly gripped his arm and said, 'I'm frightened. Look at his face.'

Berca did so, and then drew back hurriedly. Though the man

was in deep shadow, his face shone with a strange metallic light of its own, and they all realized they were in the presence of some deep mystery. They returned to the village and that night a goat was sacrificed to Abbadon the God, and prayers asked for his protection.

For weeks nobody went near the cave, and then the children's fears were overcome by curiosity and they used to hide and watch the stranger from the bushes. At first he appeared unaware of their presence, sitting cross-legged for hours at a time and staring rigidly at the hills, till they imagined he was blind. Then one day he turned and smiled at them, and from that moment the children knew he was their friend. He motioned them to approach, and they sat around him in a circle while he told wonderful stories of the gods and what happened to the men and women who offended them.

In time the adults grew to accept him as well, and now and then he would come down to the village and share their food. They never saw his face shine again, but something told them he had the favour of a great deity and they would beg for advice, never daring to ask his real name, but simply referring to him as 'Our Hermit' with a good deal of pride.

'There is a dispute between these women, Our Hermit. Hear their stories and judge who is in the right.' 'This child has been crippled from birth. What can I do to make him grow straight, Our Hermit?'

And the village prospered with his presence. The fishing-nets were always full that year and the crops were the heaviest that the oldest men could remember. But better still, the pirates' tribute went unpaid.

Every summer, between June and August, an Arabian galley packed with armed men tied up at the jetty, and in return for peace the villagers handed over six children to her captain. That year she left empty-handed. Fear had left the people and they were ready and waiting. There were no slaves for the Arabians, but slinged stones and arrows met them as the prow slid alongside the jetty, and red hot sand burned their feet as they tried to fight their way forward. The pirates fled in complete disorder, and 'Our Hermit', who had planned the resistance, became 'The Lawgiver', 'The Man of Authority', 'The Holy One of Golab'.

'He taught you war?' Thassi broke in, frowning as he considered the other accounts of the Nazarene. 'What did he look like, Berca?'

'He taught us to fight, lord, but only to protect ourselves. He said we must live at peace with our neighbours, and obey him in everything. If we did that, the people of the peninsula would one day become the greatest nation on earth.

'As to his appearance . . .' Berca frowned too, struggling to bring back memories, and then looked at Sextus. 'He was tall; even taller than you, and his face was as pale as the moonlight and grim like a metal mask. Yes, such a face he had! I have never seen another like it and I do not wish to. Once we were fitting a new support to the jetty. There was a wind blowing and the stream was full. The spar was heavy too, and we were about to abandon the job for another day, when we saw him watching from the opposite bank and took courage. Somehow we all felt that that dead piece of timber wouldn't dare to fall out of position unless he willed it.'

Authority! Supernatural power! Wise counsel! Sextus and Rachel and Thassi considered the man's attributes as they listened and each of them was disturbed. Sextus and the Jew because there was nothing discreditable in the story so far, and Rachel because there was little of the Man of Love and Sorrow. But the fish and the lamb were joined by a 'Tau' cross. It must have been the same person, though Berca's account contained no comfort for any of them.

So the months went by and the other inhabitants of the country heard of his fame. Parties of headmen and elders would come down over the pass to seek counsel and pay their respects to the Holy One, and women would bring their children to be blessed by him. Sometimes he would be in a trance and not even see them, but now and again he spoke, and gave advice and foretold the future. Only faith was demanded, he said, and the land would grow rich and powerful. He told of cities and temples and palaces springing up in the valleys and a great wise people who would be the envy of the earth. Then he would point to the symbols carved before his cave and stare up at the sky, and everybody would bow down before them.

Strangers came to Golab too; merchants who had made a

detour over the mountains, and a band of brigands much feared in the south who entered the valley like supplicants, loaded with gifts. Berca described their leaders in detail and Cano was clearly recognizable.

'But what of the woman, Rosetta?' Fear and hope were almost equally balanced in Rachel's thoughts. 'Let the sin and guilt be something which was done to him,' she prayed. A rejection like that of her own people, a sacrifice to worldly pride, a refusal to defend him against evil. The Good Shepherd who laid down his life for the sheep. God who is rejected by men, but triumphs in the spirit.

'Rosetta?' The cloud had passed and Berca lowered his eyes before the glare of the sun. 'Poor, crazy Rosetta with her demon. She brought the punishment upon us. She made our neighbours take away the young people and leave us to rot. But she was also the instrument of the god sent to reveal his truth.

'Rosetta had a demon, strangers. Tall and straight and lovely she was while he slept, but when he awoke, it was a terrible thing to see. First her mouth would twitch, then her whole face, and white foam would appear at the lips, and the body start to dance like a bear being trained with hot coals under its paws. Louder than the singing rock she would scream and, when the demon returned to rest, she would fall on the ground and lie senseless for half a day. Rosetta was the most desirable girl in the village but not one man dared to take her for his wife and risk the anger of that demon.'

'I have heard of the condition.' Thassi nodded. The Evil of the Conquerors, it was called, because the strong and ambitious were its usual favourites. Hercules was supposed to have suffered in such a way, and Alexander, and the demi-god Julius.

'And your hermit fought with the demon?'

'He fought him, lord, and that was the beginning of our sin.' Berca was becoming tired, and one of the women brought him a gourd of water from the stream.

'Rosetta had begged him to help her and at the next full moon he promised to drive away the demon. So crowded the valley was that night. The brigands were still with us and from all over the mountains people had come to witness the spectacle.

'We formed a circle and Rosetta stood there by Abbadon's

sacred fire which had never been allowed to die in living memory. For a long time we waited there, and then, when the big moon had climbed over the valley, the hermit joined us, all naked apart from a loin-cloth and the glittering thing on his arm. Tall and gaunt and terrible he looked in the silver light, and as he approached Rosetta, we heard the demon awake. Like a man screaming it was, and Rosetta's body twisted and writhed and danced till I thought her limbs would be torn asunder.

'But the hermit just stood looking at her and he smiled; it was the only time I ever saw him smile. "Come to me," he said at last. "Come to me, girl", and that tortured, screaming figure came dancing towards him as though cords were dragging it. His fists were clenched like a boxer's and he brought them up, holding the face towards his own, and stared down into the open mouth.

' "Leave her," he said, so quietly that I could hardly hear him. "I, your master, command you to come out of her." Twice he gave the order, and Rosetta's mouth opened wider and wider to release the demon.

'We are a simple people, my lord. That was our weakness, but we all saw it. A small black shape appeared at her lips, seemed to glance around for an instant, and then dropped to the earth and scurried away.'

'The cure worked?' There was sudden triumph in Sextus' voice, and he grinned at Thassi. Though he hadn't made out everything Berca had said, he had heard enough. Yes, that was it: an impostor using conjuring tricks to awe gullible people. A mask treated with some luminous substance and a clenched fist hiding some small animal or insect. This was exactly the kind of story they needed. The way to destroy the cult with ridicule and mirth. His pleasure was only slightly dimmed as he looked at Rachel. She also had understood, and her face was drained and wretched. After a while she would accept the truth though, and begin to live.

'We never discovered that, lord, but it seemed so at the time.' Berca took up the story again. 'At the moment that thing left her, Rosetta became still and quiet like a wild horse that has finally been broken.

'She went down on her knees before the hermit, but he raised her up and led her to Abbadon's fire. "Well, my people," he said, staring down at the flickering hearth. "Have I proved my powers enough now? Do you realize who I am and what you must do to please me?"

'That was how sin came, strangers. The children and the young people could be forgiven because they knew no better, but we, the old . . .' Berca stared at the little rain-washed hearth in the centre of the square while high above, the rocks started to sing again.

'And I was the worst of them all. I and my wife, and two of the elders who are dead now, went to the sacred fire of Abbadon, and poured water on it, and trampled the steaming embers into the earth. Then we all knelt down before the Man of the Fish, and worshipped him as a greater deity than Jove, or Abbadon, or the Sun God of Persia.'

'How did you discover he was not?' There was no hope in Rachel's face, but a slight flicker of defiance.

'He himself showed us, woman. Up he got on to the cold hearth which had burned since our forefathers first settled in the valley, and he made Rosetta stand beside him. Then he talked about the future and a new religion which would spread across the earth and tolerate no god except himself. Great cities and temples were to be built in his honour and armies and fleets were to go out to punish all who refused to worship him. He was insane of course, possessed with a demon as Rosetta had been, but there was a great power in him, and we believed every word that was said.'

'Go on, man. Finish your story.' Berca had broken off as if too weary or ashamed to continue the story, and Thassi gripped his arm. 'What happened next?'

'He destroyed himself, lord. He put his arm around Rosetta and said that he loved her and would take her as his wife. She would be the Queen of Heaven sharing his kingdom, and we must reverence her as a goddess.

'One by one we started to stand up then, all realizing the truth, and all horrified by what we had done. A god may couple with a woman, may cause a woman to have children, but to love her! To marry her! To make her an equal of himself. I can still see my people's faces as they closed in on him with the steam of Abbadon's fire drifting before them, and hear their cries of shame and anger. "Not a god, but a man. A man who can die."'

'But he didn't die.' Sextus was shouting in his eagerness. 'Tell me that you didn't kill him, fellow. You let him live so that he could deceive others.'

'We gave him to Dagon, the Sea God, my lord, and all I can tell you is that he was indeed a man. He cursed and fought like a man when we dragged him from the hearth, and a man's body ran with blood as we scourged him. It was a man who begged for mercy while we tied him and Rosetta to a raft of logs and let them float out to sea.'

'So, he could have lived?' Thassi stood up almost capering. 'The fellow survived the sea and returned to preach his hideous gospel in Palestine.' This was exactly the kind of story they needed to discredit his followers, and there would be a rich reward for those who produced it. Thassi had two great longings in his soul; the life of a certain enemy and a villa outside Alexandria belonging to that enemy. He had little doubt that Naevius Macro would give him both. All they needed now was some piece of material evidence and the matter was finished.

'His belongings, Berca? The things he must have had in the cave? Where are they?'

'We burned them, lord, and what would not burn we threw to Dagon. Only this I keep with me as a reminder of my shame.' He reached inside his ragged tunic and something glinted like gold. 'His amulet with the carved symbols which he always wore.'

'Yes, this is enough, Sextus Ennius, quite enough.' Thassi's fingers fondled the polished brass and the marks cut into it. 'A fish and a lamb joined together by a "Tau" cross or a carpenter's square.'

'Let me look for myself.' When the old man produced the amulet, Sextus had felt a tiny stab of anxiety and now as he studied it, anxiety was replaced by the certainty of failure.

'You do not know what this is?' He pulled out his dagger as Thassi shook his head, and pressed the blade against the metal. The carved boss opened like an oyster, showing a cavity and a scrap of parchment. He studied the faded writing for a moment and then nodded to Rachel.

'Your Nazarene is not defeated yet, my dear. This was a person of authority all right, a man who could command, but his power came from my people, not yours.' He held the circlet out to her, grinning to hide the frustration he felt.

'A certain type of fish, isn't it, Rachel, and the fleece of the lamb has been drawn with much more detail than the rest of its body. And this is not a cross or a square, but a simple "T"; the initial of the Goddess, Thetis.

'Jesus stole details of other religions, as we know. The plunging dolphin sacred to Apollo, and the golden fleece of the Sun. Two symbols of divinity, but joined together by the letter "T", they have a more earthly significance.' He turned to Thassi and shook his head.

'You were born in Egypt, I think, and I am surprised at your loss of memory. Surely you should recognize the crest of the Third Legion which is based at Nicopolis.'

'Thank you, Sextus, and you too, Rachel, my dear. Even though it does not help me at all, that was a most entertaining story, and I am pleased that you returned by way of Egypt to verify the details.' Eros' eyes twinkled with amusement.

'A standard-bearer named Balbus Clodius who became smitten by religious mania, deserted his legion, and for a short space of time fulfilled his divine claims. A man of authority indeed! And who knows? If the fellow hadn't loved a woman, he might still be worshipped on Sinai.'

'Don't smile, Eros.' Sextus scowled at him. 'Every trail we have followed has led to a dead end and I am beginning to feel that the Fates are playing with us. The man's years are still hidden and all the time his movement is gaining ground.'

'That is true enough.' The Greek looked at the documents littering his desk. An account of something called a 'love feast' at which men and women vowed eternal fellowship. Reports of people in Greece and Asia Minor who proclaimed that the Kingdom of Heaven was open to all who acknowledged the Nazarene as the sole god and creator of mankind, and hell waiting for those who fought against him.

Hell: that was a terrible notion. Eros felt waves of disgust as he considered it. Baits of bliss for the faithful, and everlasting punishment for those who denied. The Gehenna of the Maccabees transformed into a place of retribution to over-awe cowards. The idea sickened him.

The demand for a single object of worship was hideous too. Every educated person realized that there was only one god, of course; Jupiter, Jove, or whatever you chose to call him. But the point was that he had countless different forms for every situation and type of human being. A god of nations, and cities, and trades; timeless, self-sufficient, but always varied, and revealing only those aspects of his personality which separate individuals could recognize and appreciate. The concept which made Rome acknowledge the deities of her subject people, and kept the Empire secure. Osiris, the god of the Nile, was an Egyptian because Egyptians worshipped him, but he was also Father Tiber and countless other river gods: all images of the multi-faced creator appearing to different men. Civilization was based on such religious tolerance, and the claim that God might only be worshipped in one form was the road to civil war, anarchy and ruin. Children turning against their parents, and brother against brother because of a presumptuous blasphemy that one man's image of God must be accepted by his neighbour. Eros' early fears of Christianity had been political, but under the tuition of King Herod's librarian he was well versed in the religious ethic, and that seemed even more dangerous.

The movement was spreading fast too. All the documents before him confirmed that. Acts of insubordination among soldiers, a slave who had openly refused to venerate his master's family gods, constant discord in the Jewish communities outside Palestine.

His latest news from Rome was equally disturbing. The Vigiles were the only organization which could destroy the movement, and as long as Naevius Macro commanded them, the fight would go on. Today's letter made it clear that Macro's position was tenuous, to say the least.

Gaius Caligula had been the obvious choice for Emperor. Little Boots, the Darling of the Army, who had paraded with the legionaries when he was a child and been used as a symbol to crush the Rhine mutiny. The boy hero whom the people hailed as The Saviour of his Country. Well, if Macro was right, that boy had grown into a monster who resented all authority except his own. At any day now someone else might control the Department, and it could be a man with no fears of the Nazarene cult who would let the danger spread unchecked.

'And what now, Eros Dion?' Rachel interrupted his thoughts. 'You have searched and searched and discovered nothing, because the Master did not wish his middle years to be revealed. Aren't you beginning to feel defeat at last? To realize that you are fighting against the Messiah, the Son of God?'

'The Messiah! A Hebrew folk tale!' There was something bleak and sad in Eros' smile. 'I feel frustration, girl, fear of the man's teaching, but nothing else. You see, I know that there is bound to be means to destroy him, and that knowledge keeps me strong.

'You are so obsessed with the hope of exonerating your father, Rachel, that you cannot appreciate what is happening. An impostor foisted upon mankind as the divine deliverer with a promise of eternal life to all who follow him. And there is another promise too. Our Hades, the Abode of the Dead, is a place of rest and shadow. But the Christians threaten the ignorant with the promise of everlasting pain. Two offers with a single purpose behind them; the destruction of every civilized institution that raises men from the animals.

'No, it isn't the myth which frightens me, but the teaching. That fear of the Nazarene's hell destroyed your uncle, Sextus, but it won't touch the son of a Greek harlot. I shall fight this thing till my dying day, if necessary.'

'Then how do we go about it?' Sextus studied his face. Eros had aged since he had last seen him. The leathery skin was sagging, and the smile forced and uncertain.

'We have wasted two weeks going to Sinai and drawn another blank and, as you admit, the Movement is gathering strength every day. It really seems as though the man's past had been screened by some supernatural force, and I would like to know what our next move is.'

'You shall know, Sextus. I think it was Ovid who wrote that a gentle wind gives life to the flames, but a stronger destroys them. I shall show you our wind which will blow out this fire from Nazareth like a candle.' He crooked a finger and his scribe who had been sitting beside Uriah at the far table got up and handed him two rolls of parchment.

'Thank you, Publius. Tell our colleagues that we will soon be ready to receive them.' He watched the man go out through a door on the right. Beric stood on guard beside it, his towering head almost on a level with the lintel.

'Before you left for Sinai, Sextus, I told you that Publius and Uriah here were preparing a fictitious biography of Jesus. I did not wish to use such a story then, because I was positive we would manage to unearth an incident in the man's middle years which could be used to discredit him and his teaching.

'Well, I am still certain that such an incident exists, but the news from Rome is very disturbing and we may not be given time to dig it out. What we have discovered, however, are certain facts about the man's execution and supposed resurrection. The chapter is not quite complete as yet, but I would like you to read our fictitious preface.' He handed the rolls to Sextus and Rachel and leaned back in his chair, grinning at Beric.

'But I don't understand. This tells us nothing.' Sextus frowned as he read quickly down the parchment. The account that Uriah and Publius had concocted was dull, to say the least.

The story told of a boy with a compelling personality, delusions of religious power, and a deep hatred of all human authority. On being apprenticed to the Jewish elder, he had run away from his parents and served as a carpenter's mate on a Phoenician galley. During his travels he had encountered the faiths of many different races and their symbols had been incorporated in his mind; the Fish of Apollo, the Fleece of the Sun God, and the shepherds who greeted the birth of Mithras. At the age of twenty he returned to Palestine, completely obsessed with dreams of personal divinity, and withdrew into the Wilderness of Judaea to prepare for his ministry. Then ten years later, he felt the time was ripe to reveal himself and appeared to John the Baptist.

'This is pure invention, and it contains nothing to discredit the fellow either.'

'You do not approve.' Eros' eyes mocked them. 'I am sorry if it makes dull reading. Publius and Uriah concocted a large number of hair-raising incidents, but I had them cut out.'

'The personality is wrong too; quite wrong.' Rachel saw the mockery in his face, but she couldn't understand the reason for it, which worried her slightly.

'You describe Jesus as a simple man with only this religious faith to strengthen him. From all accounts, he wasn't like that at all.'

'From the accounts of his adherents, you mean. But what about the physical description, my dear?' His smile flickered across to Beric and the big man smiled back. 'Would you say that was fairly accurate?'

'In as far as it goes: tall and thin, with a very pale face and compelling eyes. Compelling is far too weak a word. I only saw him twice, but there was something about his personality which I would always recognize.'

'Good! Excellent, in fact.' Eros might have been complimenting a clever child. 'Bear with the simplicity for the sake of argument, and we are agreed. A simple man of distinctive physical presence, a compelling personality, and a burning religious faith.' Eros paused for a moment as Publius came back into the room and returned to his table.

'Well, this fanatic gathers together a band of followers who, with the exception of your father, Rachel, appear to be very simple men themselves and who were all drawn from the lower orders. Men who could be impressed by conjuring tricks and awed by promises of bliss or retribution.

'But, one day, they meet somebody who wasn't simple at all; the rich and influential merchant, Joseph of Arimathaea. A man with a deep hatred of both the Jewish hierarchy and the Roman Peace. Will you tell us about him, Uriah?'

'The little I know, lord.' The librarian leaned forward, his long black sleeves spread out on the table like the wings of a dead bird. 'As you say, Joseph was a bitter man. He believed in the destiny of our nation to become the law-givers of the world.

'And so do I, my masters, but I think the race must be purified first, and the event will not take place for many generations.' Uriah gave a boyish smile and shrugged his shoulders.

'Joseph wanted our kingdom to start in his lifetime. He hated seeing Rome's occupation of the land of Jehovah's Chosen People, and he also hated the elders and priests whom he considered your slaves. I do not think he ever contemplated a military uprising against you, but he hit on a much more dangerous scheme. The whole nation must be united by a single religious revelation, and passive resistance and civil disobedience would drive you out.

'Yes, that was what Joseph planned. The Messiah must appear to his people and be shown as a risen god. Fortunately for him, a candidate for the role was available.'

'This is all supposition. You admit it here.' Sextus had come to the end of the roll while the librarian was talking. 'And you finish like that, Eros? The Nazarene riding into Jerusalem with his followers to attend the Passover. Apart from the theory about Joseph, the story is almost the same as the Christians tell it themselves.'

'So it is, because it suits our purpose and also happens to be true. The final chapter is not transcribed yet, but let me give you a verbal sketch.

'Fetch me a cup of wine first, Beric. This building was never intended for cold weather.' As the man handed him the cup Eros leaned up and whispered something in his ear.

'We leave the Nazarene, this simple fanatic, riding into Jerusalem to be hailed as a deliverer by the people. He is completely under the influence of Joseph of Arimathaea by now, and obsessed with delusions of his own divinity.

'After that the story becomes stranger. In the room of a tavern, Jesus informs his twelve closest followers that he is the Messiah who must suffer death on the cross. He also orders Judas Iscariot to betray him to the Temple authorities.

'Yes, Rachel, I am quite certain that your father merely obeyed orders, but whose orders were they? Who persuaded Jesus to seek such a death and what did he hope to gain by it?

'Anyway, he is arrested, and handed over to the civil authorities from whom he demands sentence. By refusing to deny that he is a king and a rival to Caesar, he ensures that Pilate has no choice but to condemn him to death.'

'But what proof can we give?' Sextus stood up and paced across the room. 'This argument has been considered before. The man was a lunatic, deluded by Joseph into thinking he was the Messiah who would rise from the dead. But the story goes that he did so rise, and we have found nothing to discredit it.'

'I am not trying to discredit it, Sextus, but please bear with me a little longer.' Eros took another sip of wine, lifting the cup very slowly, as though he feared his hand might shake and spill its contents.

'Jesus was duly sentenced by your uncle and another character appears. A certain Marcellus Pollius, the officer in command of the execution duty. Pollius died some years ago, which is a pity. I would very much have liked to interrogate him.

'The Nazarene and two other malefactors were taken up to Calvary, but he was treated differently from his companions. Instead of roping him to the cross as is the custom, the soldiers used nails, so that he died quickly. Though it is also the custom to certify death by breaking a thigh-bone and severing the artery, this was not done in his case. We will never know how much Pollius was paid for his services, but I wonder who paid him. The elders, fearing a disturbance if the Apostate was alive when the Passover started, or the merchant, Joseph, who bought the body and placed it in his own tomb?'

'That lie has already been tried.' Rachel laughed aloud. 'Your priests invented it, didn't they, Uriah? They claimed that the Master was persuaded by Joseph of Arimathaea to demand the cross and was killed quickly before pain could break his spirit and make him cry out the truth. Afterwards a physical double was paid to impersonate him and then smuggled out of the country. You could prove nothing at the time, Uriah, so why are you bringing the notion up again now?'

'Who said we were, woman?' Uriah smiled around the room as if he, and Eros, and Beric and the scribe were sharing a private joke.

'At the time we did not have the power of Rome to help us, but that is different now. Let Eros Dion finish his story and I think even you may be impressed.'

'Thank you, Uriah.' Eros bowed back at him. 'I have no wish to impress Rachel, but I hope we may disturb her.

'And it is a disturbing story. Jesus was seen to have died on Calvary, removed from the cross and buried in Joseph's tomb. For some time afterwards his followers were broken men, and at least one of them denied him publicly. They had expected an army of angels to appear and save him at the last moment, and their hopes were proved false. They had no leader, no assurance, and very little faith. The cult should have withered away, but something happened which restored their courage and made them come out into the open.

'According to those men and women, the strangest thing of all happened: their master returned to life. The boulder had been removed from the tomb, the body was missing, and certain women thought they saw the man alive and walking. Then, later, he appeared to the disciples at a village called Emmaus and they recognized him clearly. The Messiah had fulfilled the prophecies, in fact. God had conquered the grave and proved that life may be eternal.

'Well, is there any other explanation, my friends? How else can you account for a group of frightened people who are suddenly given the courage to speak openly and face persecution, torture and death? Was Jesus of Nazareth a deity who returned to life?'

'He was not merely a deity, but the Son of God who can conquer everything.' There was a great flush of pride and joy on Rachel's face. 'And unless you cease to fight against him, he will conquer you too, Eros Dion.'

'If I can't destroy him first, my dear.' Eros turned to Sextus. 'But what about you? Do you think the Nazarene died and rose again?'

'No, that is impossible.' Sextus tried to sound confident but he felt trapped in a nightmare world he could never understand. 'The whole thing must have been the invention of his followers.'

'I see. The invention of a group of very simple and frightened men. I think you give them too much credit, Sextus.' He nodded towards the door and Beric laid his hand on the knob.

'Those people saw something, and I wonder what it was. A figment of the mind, brought on by drugs or self-imposed starvation perhaps; a risen god; or something entirely different? What do you imagine they saw, Beric?'

'I imagine nothing, my lord. I know what they saw and it was this.' He pulled open the door and stood aside. Thin sunlight entered the adjoining room to show what it contained and Rachel screamed. Two men were standing looking at them. One was Cinna the garrison doctor, and the other was tall and gaunt and completely naked apart from bandages on both hands and feet. The marks of a whip laced his shoulders and the forehead bore scratches which might have been made by thorns.

'Well, my friend; well, Master . . .' Eros walked slowly towards him and bowed. 'Who are you, and how are you called?'

'My name is . . . is . . . No, I cannot remember.' The almost bloodless face wrinkled in concentration, and then the man suddenly smiled.

'My name is Jesus . . . Jesus of Nazareth . . . the King of the Jews.'

## Four

When she was a girl, the lady Julia Valeria Flavia had been regarded as a very great beauty. Even now, at eighty-three, her wonderful bone structure gave her a remarkably youthful look, if you didn't stare too hard and the sun wasn't too bright.

She was also a happy woman, though her neighbours often wondered why. Her husband was dead, her two daughters were married to men she despised, and her son had been hacked to pieces during a fruitless foray across the Rhine.

Julia was happy because shortly after her son's death she had discovered religion, and her dead had been returned to her. Both husband and son were safe on Olympus, trusted servants of the gods, and whenever their duties permitted, they would come and visit her. Each night, after her maid had gone, she would lie expectantly on the couch, and more often than not she would hear the shutters open and see Plautius or Marcellus come towards her with faces that shone like the divine beings they were. In her heart, she knew that this was just a dream of course, but it still gave her great comfort.

For human companionship she relied on her slaves whom she regarded almost as friends; children, who needed to be chided only when it became really necessary. Her meals might be poorly prepared, the house not quite as clean as other mistresses demanded, but such trivia never bothered Julia. The sole thing that could cause her anger was any lack of respect to the gods.

It was therefore with some surprise that she saw her maid, Artemesia, give an almost insolent curtsy to the statue of Capitoline Jove after morning prayers.

Artemesia was an old, trusted servant, and for a time Julia thought she must have become insane. The woman not only admitted her insolence, but appeared to glory in it, and repeated a story she had heard in the market place. The tale of a new god who had arisen in the east, to whom the gods of Greece and Rome were only shadows. This god had promised eternal life to those

who gave him their loyalty, and would free slaves because he
regarded all men and women as equals.

Julia slapped her face of course, and reminded her that she
could be put to death for such insolence. But the slap hadn't been
very hard, and soon her threats and rebukes stopped, and she made
Artemesia tell her more about this strange deity.

That night, she risked a tiny prayer to him, and when she awoke
in the morning, she knew that she had not been dreaming, and
the Jewish god did exist. Across the marble floor were two lines of
dusty footprints to prove that her dead were alive.

The world smelled. It smelled of anger and fear, and worst of
all, the knowledge of defeat. The smell hung over Jerusalem like a
cloud, screening the wind and drifting down into the city to merge
with the normal odours of spices and animals and humanity. It
was far, far stronger than the stench of garbage from the Valley
of Hinnon.

But defeat was a visible thing too. Sextus saw it in the crowded
streets, and the faces of the sentries before the citadel, and every
face he passed in the corridors. It was clearest on a soldier's polished shield which reflected a face he hardly recognized. Three
days had gone by since Eros had revealed his plan, but the memory
of that tortured thing repeating its well-learned message still sickened him.

'Do not kneel, girl.' Eros had laughed as she had fallen down
before the bandaged feet. 'This is not the Nazarene. The real Jesus
died, but not quite when he was supposed to have done. He was
alive when they took him down from the cross and this is how
his disciples saw him. He probably died later when his wounds
festered, or was killed by the said Joseph of Arimathaea, so that
a dead man could tell no tales. A clever fellow, Joseph. He has my
deep respect.' Eros held out his cup for Beric to refill it.

'I am very grateful to you, Rachel. You thought you recognized the man, so the physical resemblance appears to be satisfactory.'

'But who is he then?' She stared at the tall motionless figure. Its
eyes were closed as though in deep sleep.

'He is my weapon – the sword Marcellus Cinna has forged for

me. Show them the rest of your work, Doctor.' He nodded and
Cinna unwound a bandage. The hand beneath it was crooked like
a talon, and through the palm was a jagged, half-healed rent.

'In himself this creature was nothing; a half-witted slave employed in the naval dockyard. One of my men noted his resemblance to the descriptions of the Nazarene, however, and he has
become the means to save the Empire.' Eros reached out and tilted
the pallid face into the light. 'Tell me your story, master. Where
have you been hiding all these years?'

'In a place called Kereth; a village in the Wilderness of Judaea.'
The voice had no expression at all. 'They had to think I had died
and risen, and I was hidden there, so that nobody would ever know
the truth.'

'Excellent, Doctor; really excellent.' Eros beamed at him. 'You
understand it all now, Sextus? In time those wounds will heal and
appear old, but the answers will never change. Cinna has treated
the mind too, and he cannot remember anything except the words
we have put there. Not even torture would change them.'

'You could do that!' The rest of the bandages had been removed
and Rachel stared at the mutilated hands and feet. 'You could do
that to another human being?'

'I could do it, Rachel, but the man was hardly a human being
to start with. I would do anything to save the Empire, and this is
the obvious way. Let the wounds heal, so that he can be shown in
public, and the Nazarene will wipe out his own cult.' Eros laughed
as she suddenly turned and rushed out of the room without a
glance at any of them.

'Do not follow her, Sextus. That is an order.' He gripped his
arm and Beric moved towards the outer door as if in support.

'And do not look so shocked either, my friend. We didn't hurt
the fellow too much. Doctor Cinna is a merciful man and his
patient was heavily drugged during the operations.'

'It is not that which worries me. It is the fact that we have lost
– that you admit defeat.' Sextus stared at the door in the hope that
Rachel might return.

'You have failed to discover anything against the man by fair
means, so you produced this obscenity. I think I am beginning to
despise you, Eros.'

'Do what you like. Despise or even hate me. It makes no differ-
ence at all. All I am concerned about is destroying this evil in our
midst, and I shall use any means I think fit.' Eros returned to his
desk and smiled almost affectionately at the imbecile.

'Well, master,' he said. 'Who are you and what is your name?'
Like a door catch falling, like grass bending before wind, like
everything that is mindless and automatic, the shoulders straightened and the reply came.

'Jesus . . . Jesus of Nazareth . . . the King of the Jews.'

'You still do not like the idea?' Eros looked up from his desk.
Though three days had passed, Sextus had the ridiculous feeling
that the Greek had been sitting in exactly the same position since
he had left him. 'You still feel about it as your Jewish girl does?'

'I don't know how she feels.' Sextus remembered the look on
Rachel's face as she had run out of the room without a single
glance in his direction. 'I haven't seen Rachel for three days. She
didn't go back to her villa, and I imagine she is hiding from me.'
He tried to conceal the pain in his voice and the emptiness he felt.

'You're right in saying that I still disapprove of the idea, though.
To me it appears horribly cheap. Oh, I agree that the cult must be
broken up, but not this way. You propose to take that creature to
Rome and parade him as the Nazarene; a fool who was persuaded
to undergo a mock execution and became completely deranged by
his suffering. Surely we should go on searching for the truth about
him. What you intend to do is obscene and . . .'

'And dishonourable, Sextus.' Eros grinned across at Beric who
leaned against the far wall. Like his master he might have been
standing there since their last meeting.

'You are a typical Roman nobleman who values honour and
likes to keep his hands clean. Well, Beric and I are not noblemen,
I'm afraid, and our hands are dirty. They have been covered with
filth since we were children and we don't mind soiling them a little
more.' He held his own hands towards the window, watching the
sunlight mottle them.

'You and I have been over six months in this country and we
have discovered nothing. I feel as if a great barrier had been placed
between the man and myself; the wall of Plato's cave which only

reveals shadows, and I have given up trying to bore my way through it.

'Yes, half a year wasted, and time is running out. I intend to take open action now, and attack those people with every weapon I can find.' There was a little nervous tic on the left side of Eros' face, and Sextus realized he was studying his hands to see if they were shaking.

'But let me congratulate you on your news from Rome, Sextus. I hear that your lawyers have settled Pilate's estate and you are a rich man. I wonder how long you will be allowed to enjoy those riches.'

Eros broke off, considering his own news from Macro. Everywhere the general populace still hailed Caligula as a deliverer, and the Empire was said to have entered another golden age. And on the surface it appeared to be true. Men exiled by Tiberius had been recalled to the city, enormous public works had been started, and the legal system was to be completely reformed. With a fine display of filial devotion the Emperor had gone to Pandeteria and brought back the ashes of his mother and brother, burying them in the Mausoleum with his own hands. He had also given proof of his moral standards and courage. Male prostitutes were to be banished from Rome, and he walked in the streets without a bodyguard, claiming that he could do nothing which would make anyone hate him.

But behind the scenes, matters were very different. Within that tall, youthful figure striding unprotected through the crowd, was a mind that had been sick from birth and was rotting quickly under the influence of absolute power. Macro wrote of hideous practical jokes, claims to divinity, and plans to replace the statues of the gods with images of himself.

'And I thought we could control him, Eros.' Like the other private missives, the sheet had been hidden in the backing of the scroll, but this one was in Macro's own hand.

I thought Little Boots was a weakling who would obey us, but I was wrong. Some days ago, he boasted openly that he had committed incest with his sisters, Julia and Drusilla, and when I reproved him, he laughed and then suddenly flicked

out his hand and killed a fly which was crawling on the table.
I asked if I had said something amusing and he looked across
at the German guards by the door.

'No, Naevius,' he said, giggling like a child. 'You haven't
said anything to amuse me, but I have thought of something
very funny indeed.

'I have suddenly realized that I have only to nod my head
and yours will be cut from your shoulders.'

And he will do it, Eros. That same day I lost command of
the Praetorians, and this morning I was dismissed from the
Vigiles. I am now detained at my villa and it is merely a question of time before Caesar gives that nod.

But regarding the matter of the Nazarene. Caligula will
bring great suffering to the Empire, but one day he will die
and become nothing but a bad memory. That sect will not
die, however, unless we can destroy it, and the responsibility
is yours alone now. All I can give you is my blessing, because
I am just a broken man waiting for the end. I pray it will be
as merciful as the death I gave Tiberius.

'Yes, my friend,' Eros said. 'Macro is probably dead, and the
time is running out for all of us. Soon Caligula will remove all the
powers of the Department, but before he does, I intend to use my
single weapon and come out into the open against the adherents
of that carpenter from Nazareth. I intend to show up his Kingdom
of Heaven for the lie it is.'

'Provided that it really is a lie.' Sextus had to bring his thoughts
to the surface. 'You realize that if the barrier you mentioned does
exist, you may be fighting a god?'

'I realize that, Sextus, but it doesn't worry me.' Eros nodded
and the tic in his forehead was much more pronounced. 'God or
impostor, I shall fight him, and it doesn't matter if he destroys me
personally. His teachings threaten everything I believe in, and I am
not just a man, but a guardian of the law and the future of civilization.' Eros swung round as the door suddenly burst open.

'Oh, it's you, Tribune.' He nodded as Marcus Cato stomped
heavily towards them. 'What's the matter, though? You look as if
you've seen a ghost.'

'Perhaps I have.' The man's face was white and puffy and, though on duty, he went straight to the table and poured himself a cup of wine.

'You obviously haven't heard the news, my lords. I didn't believe my ears when the general told me just now.' Cato emptied the cup in a single movement.

'Yes, I thought he was joking. "Not our boy," I said to him. "The son of our old master, Germanicus! The lad who drilled with us on the Rhine." No, I didn't believe he could have given such orders.'

'Orders, Tribune?' Eros reached out and refilled the cup. 'Please tell us what the Emperor has done.'

'He's gone mad, apparently.' Cato stared gloomily out of the window. 'He is an educated man and must realize what these people are like where their religion is concerned.

'Just look at them. They're peaceful enough now, aren't they?' He pointed down into the crowded square. Shopping women, loungers, priests walking together in deep conversation, and men going about their normal business. 'Not one incident there's been in a month, and we've sent back the reinforcements to Egypt. They won't stay peaceful for long, though. Not when they hear about the present Caesar has sent 'em.'

'What present, Cato? You still haven't told us the news.'

'I'll tell you, Eros Dion. A merchant ship accompanied by two war galleys, reached Caesarea last night. The cargo was too valuable to travel without an escort, you see, and there was a company of Praetorian guards thrown in for good measure. Their officer is with the general now.

'You'll be able to laugh, Ennius. I've heard you're off to Italy soon. When you get there, spare a thought for us poor chaps who have to stay behind.' He took another swig of wine and scowled at Beric. 'You're a big fellow, barbarian, but you'll die along with the rest of us just the same.

'The Holy of Holies they call it, don't they? The inner room in the temple where their god lives. The place which is so sacred that only the priests may enter.' Cato suddenly flung his empty cup against the wall.

'Well, old Jehovah is in for a shock. Bumping along from the coast at this moment is a great big marble statue of Little Boots, and it's going into that same Holy of Holies to keep him company. You can imagine what will happen, I suppose?'

'I can imagine.' It wouldn't have mattered with any other race, Sextus thought. Italians or Spaniards would shrug their shoulders, Greeks smile cynically at such human presumption, and Germans laugh over their beer, considering the thing a huge joke.

But the Jews! The Chosen People, whose god was the only being worthy of homage. No, they wouldn't shrug, or smile or laugh. The whole pack of them would come out in open revolt. 'When is the statue to be placed there?'

'In five weeks' time, to honour the birthday of his sister.' The Tribune gave Sextus a bitter grin. 'I don't think we'll have to wait so long, though. Once the people know what's intended, the whole country will be up in arms, and the safest spot in this building will be down in the dungeons with your Jewish girl.'

'What? What did you say?' Sextus drew his sword and swung around, glaring at Eros. 'Rachel is in the dungeons?'

'Yes, that is true, Sextus.' The Greek smiled back, as though oblivious of his anger. 'I needed Rachel to tell me if our mock Nazarene resembled the original, and she was arrested the moment she stepped out of this room.

'Try and understand, my friend. If we'd let her go, she would have talked about our plan. She would have ruined everything. We had to lock her up.'

'And you didn't tell me.' The sword was under Eros' chin now, but he still showed no sign of fear. 'I loved her, you knew that, but you threw her into the dungeons without a word.'

'I knew you were infatuated by her, Sextus, and that is why you were not told. You are my only friend and I didn't want you to suffer. The girl has to die; even you must realize that, but I hoped to keep it from you.

'But because Cato has forgotten his promise of secrecy, you do know. Rachel has to die, but you will get over it. After all, what does one Hebrew slut matter? You will soon forget her.'

'I love her, Eros. She matters much more to me than you, or your obsession with the threat to the Empire, or even my own life.

'Stand back, Beric.' Out of the corner of his eye, Sextus saw the man creeping forward. 'Take one more step and I will rip him open.

'Now, Eros, listen very carefully.' The point of the sword had
started to go home and blood was trickling down Eros Dion's
throat. 'You will give me your promise that Rachel is released
unharmed. If not, we will walk out on to the balcony together,
and with you standing in front of me, I shall shout the news of
your plan to the people.'

'Well, well, well. And what have we here, General?' Sextus
turned as he heard the voice. It was soft and girlish, and its owner
was the same, a stout young man in a flowing toga of green silk.
Rufus Aquila was at his side and behind them was an officer of the
Praetorians and two guardsmen.

'Please do not kill him, my friend. That would be most annoy-
ing, because I have come a long way to see the fellow.' The young
man moved with a gait that was similar to that of Pilate's major-
domo; smooth and oily as if wheels were hidden under the toga.

'Ah, that is better.' He smiled as Sextus finally lowered the
sword. 'My name is Florius Vibius, third secretary to Caesar, and
your very humble servant.

'And you, I presume, are Eros Dion, once representative of the
Department of Vigilance in this town.'

'I am Dion.' Eros returned his low sweeping bow with a curt
nod. 'And I do represent the Vigiles here.'

'No more, my lord. I have come to tell you that your days of
exile are finally over.' Vibius smiled again and Sextus saw that his
lips were painted. 'My orders are to see that Caesar's statue is delivered safely, and also to take you back to Rome to receive proof of
his imperial favour. Yes, the Emperor wishes to reward you for
your proven loyalty. Doesn't that please you, man?'

'Of course it pleases me, but there is no need for any reward.
My loyalty to Caesar is automatic.' Eros could see his death in
those mocking eyes, but he kept up the pretence of nonchalance.

'Good! Very good indeed. Spoken more like a Roman than the
spawn of a Greek harlot.' A furred tongue ran across the rouged
lips. 'But Caesar was not referring to your loyalty to himself, but
to a piece of carrion named Naevius Macro, a fool who failed to
destroy certain diaries before he killed himself.' Vibius nodded
and the soldiers stepped forward. One of them carried a pair of
manacles.

'Eros Dion, your master is dead and his treachery has been established. For you it is a sad thing that I arrived in time to stop this young man slitting your gullet.' He reached out and took the sword from Sextus.

'But do not despair, Dion. The Emperor is all merciful and he has allowed you a choice. If you do not wish to face him in person, use this now.' Vibius handed him the sword and drew back still smiling. 'I would strongly advise you to do so.'

'No, I will face Caesar.' There were many ways of dying, Eros thought, and a cross, a stake, or a fire was not the worst of them. But he didn't hesitate. Something told him that he would come through this. He had to come through it, because there was work to be done, and death would not touch him till it was finished. He raised the sword and hurled it across the room in a purely theatrical gesture. The point thudded into the panelling, and it remained there quivering.

'Take me to Rome, Vibius, but grant me one personal favour. I have heard that Caesar is interested in strange gods, and I have a god to show him. Give that god passage to the Emperor and I will be your debtor till my dying day.'

'Your dying day!' Vibius giggled. 'Not a far distant date, I imagine. All the same, Caesar is interested in outlandish religions, and you may have your wish.'

'Thank you.' Eros bowed and then very slowly turned to Sextus. Even the tan seemed to have left his face and its pallor contrasted with the dribble of blood on his throat.

'So, you command here, my friend. You are the master now and I implore you . . .' He suddenly went down on his knees before him.

'I beg you to remember your duty, Sextus. I am sorry for what I planned to do to the girl, but I had no choice. This thing must be destroyed whatever it costs us personally.' A stammer made his words almost inaudible and his left cheek twitched convulsively.

'Whatever you think of me, carry on the fight, Sextus. Curse my memory, if you wish, but please continue the work on the story. Your journey to Sinai, Hanno's story and the woman who killed him were false trails and they might have been set by some great power to deceive us. But the battle must go on. Even if the

Nazarene's past is hidden, even if he was a deity which can vanish from the earth, we must go on fighting. He is to be resisted or the poison of his gospel will rot our world.' Like a corpse dragging itself out of the grave, he stood up, and held out his wrists for the chains.

At least Rachel had been well-treated in the dungeons, though she was pale from lack of sunlight, and there were hard lines under her eyes.

'Well, my lord, what do you want with me?' She came into the room with Beric and gave Sextus a mocking curtsy. 'Am I to be shown another monster, perhaps?'

'Please don't talk like that, Rachel. What happened was not of my doing, and I didn't know where you were. Eros told me nothing.' He came towards her, but she drew back beside Beric as if for protection.

'No, Sextus, do not touch me. I have had a lot of time to think in the cell and I know who the real enemies are now. The very sight of a Roman disgusts me.' She smiled at the flash of pain in his face.

'But why have you had me brought here? Eros Dion made it quite clear that I would die as soon as the Governor signed the warrant, and I was prepared for death. What am I to look at now? Another poor mutilated creature? Another doll for your puppet show?'

'You are here because I wanted to apologize to you personally, Rachel. Also to tell you that you are free to go. You can walk out of this building and nobody will try to stop you.'

'My lord, that is impossible.' Beric shook his head. 'Our last orders from Eros Dion were that the girl was to be executed. That may be unnecessary, but we must hold her here for the time being at least.'

'Are you deaf and blind, Beric?' Sextus flushed with anger and sat down behind the desk. 'Eros Dion has been arrested for treason and the Emperor's secretary is taking him to Rome. I command the Vigiles here.'

'Is that true?' Though the news could give her life, Rachel's face only showed curiosity, and she looked at Beric for confirmation. 'Has Dion really been arrested, or is this another Roman trick?'

'It is true, woman.' The big man nodded. 'Somehow Eros Dion has caused the Emperor displeasure, and is under arrest. Until further orders are received, Sextus Ennius automatically commands our group in Palestine.' Beric felt sure that those orders would not be long in coming, and there was an open smile on his face. Like Eros he was a professional who had reached his position by proven worth. But, unlike Eros, he had taken care to offend nobody in authority. He regarded Sextus as an amateur who had been accepted in the Department through influence, and was sure he would soon be replaced. He didn't really care who took command after that; himself or Thassi, or somebody sent out from Rome, but he hated working under an amateur. He also had a very personal reason for disliking Sextus; his hatred of that face which constantly reminded him of his former master.

'So, it is true.' Rachel's laugh rang across the room. 'Poor Eros. His plans have gone astray. And poor Sextus, too, if it comes to that. Do you think you can control the puppet strings, my dear? Even with men like these to help you?' She glanced at Thassi who lounged by the window, apparently oblivious of the proceedings.

'I will control them, Rachel.' Sextus hadn't thought about it till that moment. However much he disliked Eros' plan, however great his doubts about the Nazarene, there was a job to be done. The revolt of the Sicilian slaves and the war with Spartacus were still stories to frighten children; murder and rape and pillage; old men forced to fight as gladiators while the rabble jeered, women violated by their own servants, senators' bodies hung from hooks in the meat shops, temples and villas burned down for the mere joy of destruction. If Eros had been right, the next Spartacus might have a god fighting beside him.

'Now, listen to me, my dear. As I have said, you are free to walk out of this building. All I need is a promise that you will repeat nothing you have seen or heard here.'

'Do not be a fool, my lord Sextus.' Thassi turned from the window and Beric had stopped smiling. 'Though Dion is under arrest he may still regain Caesar's favour, and you are only in temporary command. We do not know what your successor's views will be and it would be insane to release the woman till the position is clear.'

'I agree with Thassi, lord.' Beric's eyes were very small and a pale yellow. They looked like amber beads screwed into the huge slab of his face.

'Whatever happens to Eros Dion, our duty must come first. We are to discredit the cult of the Nazarene, and the girl knows some of our plans. It is essential that she remain in custody, whatever our personal feelings may be.'

'Shut your mouth, fellow.' Beric's tone was openly insolent, and Sextus got up and pulled his sword from the panelling where Eros had hurled it.

What they said was correct of course. Soon another man would come from Rome to replace him, and it was his clear duty to see that Rachel repeated nothing, whatever he felt about her.

And yet . . . and yet. The word kept running through his head like water dripping on to a stone. He loved Rachel; perhaps he could trust her. Also the memory of that crazed, mutilated figure repeating its parrot phrases still shocked him deeply. These were clear and obvious thoughts, but there was something else which he hardly dared to admit to himself. An odd, uncomfortable feeling that allegiance to Rome might not be the most important loyalty in life.

'Rachel,' he said. 'Will you give me that promise? Will you swear to repeat nothing you have learned from us? Once you have done that, you are free to leave.'

'I swear it, Sextus.' Her face was completely blank, and once again Beric broke in.

'No, that is not enough. The girl has not the slightest intention of keeping such a promise. Look at her expression and see for yourself.' He grasped Rachel's chin and tilted her face into the light.

'Take your hand off her, Beric.' As Sextus spoke, a strange noise started to come through the window. A soft, whistling moan, like wind stirring a forest, and behind it, very faint and far away in the distance, there were snatches of some tuneless chant which might have been made by rowers struggling against the tide.

'I said let her go, Beric.'

'Lord, you must not do this thing.' Beric's hand remained where it was. 'All of us here have risked our lives for Eros Dion, and his plan is still in operation. We cannot let this girl ruin it now.'

'Eros is not here, Beric. He is on his way to Rome to stand trial, and I am your master.' For the second time that day, Sextus raised his sword. 'Do you still refuse to obey me?'

'No, I have to obey you.' Beric grinned at the sword, as though it were a child's toy.

'But I will promise you something, Sextus Ennius. The moment you are relieved of your command we will go into this matter again. Bring a sword and a shield, and ride a horse if you like, and I shall be unarmed. All the same, I will kill you with these.' He released Rachel and stood aside, flexing his fingers like the talons of a monstrous bird.

'Very well, Rachel, you are free to go.' Sextus stared at her longing for some flicker of gratitude or affection, but her face remained dead and cold.

'Thank you, Sextus.' She gave him a brief nod. 'And goodbye, my dear. I don't suppose we will meet again, and I am very sorry. Once I thought I could have loved you, but what Eros showed me has destroyed all that.' Without another word, she turned and walked out into the corridor.

'How very strange!' Now that the matter was settled, though against his advice, Thassi had returned to the window. 'Yes, very odd indeed. A few minutes ago the street was crowded, but now there is nobody in sight except for the sentries.

'And listen to that.' Again they heard the low crooning moan, and behind it another snatch of tuneless chanting.

'My lord, Sextus Ennius, will you come with me, please?' One of Vinicius' secretaries bowed to him from the doorway. 'The Governor wishes to see you immediately.'

'Of course.' Sextus followed him, glad to be rid of the glare of hatred on Beric's face. As they hurried down the corridors to the other side of the building, the chant grew in volume and they could make out the beat of a big drum leading it.

'The Governor is on the balcony, lord.' The secretary opened a door and stood aside. The room beyond was vast, but crowded almost to overflowing. More secretaries sat at tables, groups of officers were talking excitedly together, and along one wall stood a line of men who looked like beggars. They wore dirty sackcloth robes, and though their heads were bowed, Sextus saw that their faces were smeared with ash. It took him a moment to realize that they were members of the Sanhedrim dressed in mourning.

'Ah, there you are, Ennius.' The Governor nodded as he stepped out on to the balcony. At his side was another Jewish elder and the Praetorian officer who had accompanied Florius Vibius. 'I understand that since Dion's arrest you represent the Department of Vigilance in Jerusalem.

'Good. Then I hope you will join with me and the military authorities. We intend to write to the Emperor protesting about his intended action.'

'A protest, Your Excellency! A protest to Caesar!' The Praetorian broke in, frowning. Though dressed as a tribune, he couldn't have held the rank for long. Sextus had known all their senior officers and the face was unfamiliar to him.

'If you value your lives, my lords, I advise you to do no such thing. It has been ordained that every major place of worship throughout the Empire shall house a statue of Caesar and the temple of this Jehovah is no exception. I am here to ensure that those orders are carried out.' He nodded towards the approaching noise; a soft wailing from the shuttered windows opposite, and the thud of the drum followed by meaningless words. 'Ulla – ho – ho . . . Hum – ha – ho . . .'

'In thirty-five days' time, to honour the birthday of Caesar's sister, the Lady Julia, his statue is to be placed in their so-called Holy of Holies. I intend to see that this is done with fitting dignity and I shall expect your full co-operation.'

'You will be here in person, Tribune?' The Governor gave him a little bitter smile. 'That at least pleases me. We shall all die together, then. Our few troops will not last long against a whole nation in revolt.'

'You won't have to wait five weeks either, my lords.' The Jewish elder had to raise his voice to make himself heard. 'To place a heathen statue in the temple is unspeakable, but it is blasphemy even to bring such a thing into the city. Our people will revolt on that account alone.

'I want peace, Your Excellency. My master, King Herod, wants peace and he will try to hold the people back, in the hope that your Emperor may change his mind. We won't be able to hold them for long, though.' He leaned over the balustrade as a white dome appeared behind the far line of buildings and came jerking forward. The chant was deafening now, and lines of men were rounding the corner of the square; galley slaves from Caesarea following a chariot on which the drum was mounted. Hundreds of them; the complements of several warships. Apparently the thing they pulled was too precious to be entrusted to animals.

'Do not worry, Governor.' The Praetorian smiled as the last line of slaves came into view. The cart behind them was enormous, and it needed to be, for the statue it carried was as high as a two-storied house, and constructed of marble. A throned Apollo with laurels on his brow and a lyre in his hands. Beneath the laurel crown, Caligula's face grinned triumphantly as if already mocking his rival, the God of the Jews.

'Should there be any insult to his person, the Emperor has promised that he will lead an army to this country and turn it into a desert.'

'Thank you. That consoles me a great deal.' Vinicius looked at the Jewish elder again. 'Tell me, Samuel. How long can King Herod hold your people back?'

'Two weeks easily.' His old voice was barely audible against the thunderous chant of the slaves struggling uphill. 'Three weeks, probably. A month, perhaps.'

'There is one problem though.' The Tribune looked at the statue and then frowned across the city. 'It is too large, and we didn't imagine their miserable temple would be so small.' He grinned, suddenly discovering the solution, and Sextus knew he was as mad as his master must be.

'Yes, that is what must be done, of course. As Jehovah's temple is a hovel, we will remove the roof and the inner walls till it becomes large enough to contain Caesar's image.' Below them the drum beat on, the huge white figure swayed past, and the voices of the slaves made further speech impossible. 'Ulla – hi – ho . . . Hum – ha – ho . . .'

It was a long, hard voyage home, with the wind constant against them, so that the heavily oared war galley made slower progress than a laden merchant ship would have done under normal weather conditions. At times the sea was so rough that rowing became impossible, and they lay pitching for whole days and nights. Vibius kept constantly staring at the hour-glass and noting each sunrise on a wax tablet. Apparently the Emperor had given him a strict schedule to keep, and time was running out.

Eros was treated well enough. His chains had been removed as soon as they cleared harbour and he was allowed a free run of the ship. He passed some of the time with the sailing-master, a Greek like himself, who had a fund of tales about old wrecks and men who had sailed out across the western sea, searching for the great kingdoms that were known to lie there, but never returned, and what happened to those who caused the sea god's anger. But mainly he merely leaned over the rail, listening to the waves and the wind and the thresh of the oars, or discussed their charge with Cinna, who had accompanied him. The imbecile's wounds were healing cleanly, apart from the left hand which was inflamed and causing Cinna some anxiety. But even Eros, the originator of the scheme, had sudden spasms of nausea, as he watched the mutilated figure lying in the dim light of the lower deck and heard his voice endlessly repeating the message they had given him. 'Jesus . . . of Nazareth . . . King of the Jews . . .'

The sailing-master had become more and more taciturn and worried as the weather continued foul. Ahead lay the Straits of Messina with Scylla and Charybdis, the rock and whirlpool placed by the gods to destroy presumptuous seafarers, and he had advised the commander to set a course for Tarentum, when the wind suddenly changed. A fair breeze from the east replaced the westerly gale and it was of just the right force for sail and oars to be used together. Mist and cloud fled with its coming and the omens of good fortune took their place; the friends of the sailor, Apollo's beak-nosed dolphins, leaping and dancing and diving at the bows to guide them home. Though the breeze was taking him into great danger, Eros' eyes sparkled as those beasts of the god pointed their way through the blue water, the straits opened harmlessly to receive them, and the hills of Italy stretched out in welcome. Perhaps it was the sea air, but his stammer had gone, the tic no longer troubled him and he felt as healthy as a boy.

They were only a few miles from Ostia when he knew that his

earlier premonition was correct and he wouldn't die. The sound of
the oars, the scream of the gulls surrounding the ship, and the surge
of the wind was like the voice of a god reassuring him. If he had
been intended to die, it would have happened before; in Britain, or
on the Rhine, or when he was a slave. One day death would come
of course, as it did to all men, but not before his mission was com-
pleted. Macro was dead because he had been a fool who rebuked
Caligula instead of preying on his vanity and using him. Well, he,
Eros Dion, was no fool, and somehow he would find a way to
make those Little Boots march at his bidding. He was smiling to
himself when at last they entered the harbour and, with a slightly
apologetic air, Vibius ordered his wrists to be chained.

Ostia was very different from when he had last seen it. Most of
the ships in the harbour looked smarter and more brightly painted,
legionaries were at work extending the mole, and everywhere
new buildings were springing up. Whatever Caligula might do in
private, he obviously had a passion for public works.

The people seemed different too. As the chariot rattled along
the road to Rome, Eros sensed a jollity in the air which he had
never known under the reign of Tiberius. Even the escort of cavalry troopers was light-hearted, though discipline was relaxed to a
dangerous extent. The officer made no attempt to check his men
when they whistled at girls, or cat-called at a group of eunuch
priests who giggled hugely and made obscene gestures with their
plump beringed hands.

And gaiety was in the city as well. The temples had been
cleaned and sparkled in the sunlight, and the shops and stalls were
bursting with goods. In his constant efforts to swell the Treasury,
Tiberius had taxed merchants almost out of existence, but apparently his successor possessed no such ambitions. On the street up
to the Capitoline hill, the statues were garlanded, and placards
announced public games.

'Wait for me here.' The chariots and their escort clattered to
a halt in the palace courtyard, and Vinius went on ahead with a
major-domo. Eros glanced around him. Yes, as was to be expected,
a lot of work had been done here, and probably Macro's money
would help to pay for it. Though the old Emperor sated himself
with luxury at Capri, he had paraded poverty in Rome, and the

palace had been a gloomy place with a quite inadequate staff. Now the pillars and outer walls shone like mountain snow, and contingents of smartly dressed slaves moved in droves across the courtyard. Only one thing was disordered; the statues of the gods lacked heads. Eros grinned as he looked at them, knowing full well whose head would provide the replacements. Surely he could get the better of a man who would do that.

'Come now.' Vibius had returned and led him through the portico. 'And I want to tell you something, Eros Dion. I have no personal quarrel with you, so take my advice. You are going to die, that is quite certain, but you may be able to earn an easy death. Cringe before Caesar. Pay him every compliment you can think of, and admit that you plotted with Macro against him. Say that you are now filled with such shame that you no longer wish to live and beg him to kill you. If you do that there is a slight chance that your death may be merciful.'

'I am grateful to you, Florius Vibius.' Eros thanked him out of politeness, but he had no intention of taking any advice. As the brass doors swung open, the final details of his plan clicked into position, and he knew it would work.

'This way, fellow, and do not let your chains clank unless you wish to face wild beasts in the arena. The Emperor is concentrating.' The major-domo led him forward across the hall, his feet making no more noise than fingers drumming gently on a table.

Caligula sat on a canopied throne mounted above a dais. He was big and tall, and long spindly legs were stretched out in front of him. His face was boyish and extremely handsome, though blotched by dissipation, and he was smiling pleasantly at an old man in senator's robes at the foot of the dais. On either side of the throne, two women, whom Eros recognized as the Emperor's sisters, Julia and Drusilla, lolled on couches with their eyes closed as if bored with the proceedings. Behind them stood a line of German guards, naked from the waist up.

'But naturally I am worried about the health of our good friend, Asinus Balba.' The Emperor's eyes were soft with compassion. 'How long did you say the poor fellow had been ill?'

'Three months, Caesar.' The old senator bowed. 'Asinus is far from well, but your kind inquiries are bound to cheer him, and his physicians are confident of making a permanent cure very soon. All he needs is a further extension of sick leave. As you know, his duties as Quaestor are very arduous.'

'Of course, of course.' Caligula nodded sympathetically, but Eros thought he saw laughter in his eyes.

'Naturally Balba must have his sick leave. Caesar is ever merciful, and what are a few months' salary to Rome? As you know, Balba was a friend of my father, and I often stayed at his house when I was a child. I remember that once he took a dagger away from me. He said that I would get up to some devilment with it, but of course, he was only worried that I might injure myself. Such a very good old man.' Though she had appeared half asleep, one of the women looked up sharply.

'But I am a little concerned about the treatment they have been giving him. His symptoms are headaches, vomiting and cold sweats at night, and he has been taking massive doses of hellebore.' Caligula shook his head and frowned.

'Hellebore is no remedy for Balba's condition. Let us think what must be done.' His frown deepened in concentration and then he suddenly smiled and motioned one of the German guards to step forward.

'I think I have it. A man who has not responded to such a long course of hellebore needs drastic treatment. He must be bled. Yes, bleeding is what Balba needs and my own physician here shall attend to it.' His fingers fondled the German's spear.

'Go and bleed the old pig, Hermann. Bleed him soundly, but be slow and gentle too. Strike so that he may feel he is dying.' A gust of laughter burst from the Emperor's mouth, and apart from the senator everybody joined him, the women cackling like hens, the Germans roaring; even the slaves lining the walls laughed.

But Eros laughed louder than any of them. He threw back his head, forcing tears into his eyes, and his whole body shook, making the manacles jingle like bells. He went on laughing after all the others had stopped, as if unable to control himself.

'Who is that thing?' Caligula listened to the major-domo for a moment and then crooked his little finger. Eros was still laughing when he halted before the throne.

'Well, fellow. You find something funny? I have amused you?'

'You have amused me more than anybody has ever done before, Caesar. Your voice . . . the way you said it. "Bleeding is what Balba needs . . . He must be bled."' Eros studied him through his streaming eyes.

'"Bleed the old pig, Hermann. Strike so that he may feel he is dying."' He broke off in another spasm of mirth and saw that the first part of his plan was working. There was a slight flush of gratified vanity on the blotched face.

'Good. I am delighted that you have enjoyed yourself. I will try to arrange an entertaining death for you too.

'But why are you here, Eros Dion? As I told my secretary, you are nothing; just the dog of the dead traitor, Macro, who should be allowed an easy death. Why didn't you accept mercy and kill yourself while you had the chance?'

'Because I am a dog, Great One, and I have returned to my master.' Eros stopped laughing and he looked Caligula straight in the eyes.

'Yes, I am your dog, Caesar, and whatever Naevius Macro may have done, your person is my charge. Give me any death you like, but do not ask me to betray my trust. I could not die without warning you of a terrible danger that is coming from the east.'

'What? What do you say?' The Emperor's head jerked back as though Eros had struck him. 'Are they plotting against me in the east too? Who is it, man? The legions? The Governor of Syria?'

'No, do not tell me yet.' He stood up, swaying like a crane on his long spindly legs, and screamed across the hall.

'Out – all of you, get out.' One by one, bowing low and retreating backwards, they moved to the door till he and Eros were alone.

'They hate me, fellow. They all hate me.' There was no flush on Caligula's face now and his forehead was damp with sweat. 'The senate, the army, even my own family.' He glanced at Eros' wrists to make sure the chains were secure.

'The people as well. I do everything to earn their love; tax reforms, pensions paid on time, spectacles in the Circus which beggar me, but all they give in return is hatred. When my best net and trident man was killed yesterday, they laughed and cheered, and I knew they wished that it was my body lying there in the sand.'

'I think you are wrong, Lord. I think the people love you, but what does it matter anyway?' Eros shrugged. 'What does Caesar care for the rabble's opinion? Remember the maxim of Cicero and let them hate you, as long as they fear you.'

'Good. Yes, that is true, as long as they fear me.' Caligula nodded and sat down.

'Now, tell me about this danger. Who are concerned in the plot and who are their friends in Rome?'

'Nobody is plotting against you, Great One, and as I have said, you have nothing to fear from any human being, as long as they fear you more.' Eros saw Little Boots give a slight frown of irritation, his right hand fondling the hilt of his dagger.

'No, I am not wasting your time, Caesar. The danger I spoke of is much more terrible than the hatred of Man. A god who intends to destroy you has arisen in the east.'

'Only a god has the power to harm a god. That, of course, is obvious.' Eros had been talking for a full hour and till now, the Emperor had sat completely silent, sometimes playing with his dagger or a tassel of his robe.

'Your story interests me, but is it true? That is what I want to know.' His immense long right arm shot out and he pulled Eros closer to him by the manacles.

'How do I know if you are to be trusted, fellow? How can I be sure that the whole thing is not an invention to worm your way into my favour?'

'There is no need for you to trust me, Caesar. You will soon discover for yourself if this cult is dangerous.' Eros shrugged his shoulders.

'At the moment the movement is small and harmless, and only gathers adherents from slaves and the rabble. Allow it time, though, and you will see the spread. The mustard seed which the Nazarene spoke of, growing into a tree that will overshadow our world.' Eros studied Caligula's face, as he spoke, and he saw that Macro had been right. There was religious mania and sickness behind the pale mottled skin.

So this is the master of Rome, he thought. A destructive boy with a talent for practical jokes – a madman with delusions of divine power – a weak, terrified creature who pandered to his people out of fear. The ruler of the earth.

Well, he was going to find the way to rule Caligula, and every glint and twitch of the man's face made it clearer. In one letter Macro had mentioned that he appeared to resent the fame of his father, Germanicus, and hinted that there was some deep mystery surrounding his own birth. That might be the first stepping stone, but he would have to tread very carefully, working with hints and suggestions. Any direct statement could bring that dagger across his throat.

'But why shouldn't you trust me, Caesar?' he said. 'Whatever men say, I never plotted against you, and I came here of my own free will. I knew that you were displeased with Macro long before your secretary arrived in Jerusalem, and it would have been easy for me to escape. I have certain talents, and I think the Kings of Armenia or Parthia might have employed them.'

'That does sound like the truth.' A bird had flown in through one of the windows, and Caligula's eyes followed it across the ceiling.

'Sit down at my feet, Eros, and tell me this. Could the man have been a god, as he claimed?'

'No, not a god, Caesar. That is impossible. The son of a Jewish carpenter who died like a slave! All the same, if our information is correct; if those stories are connected and concern the same man; then I think he must have had some miraculous powers and the protection of a god.'

'I see. Just a man with divine favour. But the carpenter was not his real father, was he, Eros? Remember that. And the story is so close . . . so very close . . .' The Emperor frowned and shut his eyes for a moment.

'He claimed that he was the son of a virgin, and his real father was Jehovah, which is clearly another name for Jove. Then at an early age he preached to wise men in the temple and they acknowledged him to be their master. After that he wandered in exile preparing himself for the time when he would return as the saviour of his people. And, when he did, they first hailed him as divine and then destroyed him.

'Doesn't that remind you of other deities, Eros? The bull god who is sacrificed? Osiris buried in the Nile mud? Our own harvest goddess who must return each year to Hades? All divinities who show themselves to men and then are cut down.'

'Perhaps, Great One.' Eros permitted himself a slight smile. 'But I hope I have not made a convert of Caesar.'

'Do not be impertinent, fellow.' Caligula leaned forward and slapped him across the face. 'I have not yet decided what I shall do with you.

'All the same the story is interesting. Born of a virgin, proved himself a great leader as a boy, wandered alone to prepare for his ministry, and was finally betrayed by the people he wished to save. Doesn't that make you think of another story, Eros?'

'It is beginning to, Caesar.' Eros stared at him. It was happening too fast. The seed had taken root too quickly and Caligula's face was flushed with excitement. What crazy notions were flitting behind it, he wondered. 'But the person I have in my mind is divine, while the Nazarene was merely a charlatan.'

'Yes, that is true, but the stories are so similar, aren't they?' Caligula's eyes followed the flight of the trapped bird. 'The virgin birth, the wise men who recognized a boy as their master, and the saviour who was betrayed.'

'Please try and help me, Caesar.' Eros stared up at him with a look of pleading. 'Teach me to understand what you mean. Though I don't think I am a fool, it is very hard for mortal men to comprehend great truths.'

'Of course it is hard, Eros. No ordinary man can ever fathom the ways of a god. The gods are not merely stranger than you think, but stranger than any human mind can think.' He smiled benevolently and patted Eros on the shoulder.

'Now, fetch me a cup of wine and I will try to explain some of the mystery to you.'

'Of course, Caesar.' Eros hurried across to a table. His chains made the filling of the cup a difficult operation, and the nervous tic had returned. He could feel it trembling in his cheek.

But was it possible? he thought. Could Caligula have taken his bait so readily? The time factors themselves made the notion completely ludicrous. Was Little Boots crazy enough to have swallowed the hook in a little over an hour?

'Good.' The Emperor sipped his wine thoughtfully. 'Sit down again, Eros, and I will tell you a story which must never be divulged to anybody. When you have heard it I shall decide whether or not to cut your throat.' His finger nails were painted green and they ran up and down the case of his dagger.

'Listen very carefully. The Nazarene, as you call him, claimed to be the son of a virgin. Well, did you ever suspect that Germanicus was not my father?'

'Suspect is too strong a word, Great One. All the same . . .' Eros fought back a smile of triumph. The seed had fallen on really fertile ground, the arrow was in the centre of the target, and a new god was about to be revealed. But it would be the disciple who wrote his gospel.

'Shall I say that when I first saw your face I felt that there must be some deep mystery surrounding your birth.'

'Yes, that is the only answer I could hope for. You cannot understand, but you sense things like an animal.' Little Boots nodded.

'And, because you are incapable of understanding, you must rely on blind faith, Eros. The faith that can move mountains.' Caligula had looked as if he were barely listening while Eros recounted the Nazarene's doctrine, but apparently he had not missed a word.

'No, my father was not Germanicus, but someone far, far greater. And like this Jesus, I grew into a boy who confounded wise men. When the Rhine legions revolted and were preparing to march on Rome, neither Germanicus or anybody else could control them. Then what happened, Eros? A little child stood up, and those tough, rebellious legionaries returned to the standards.'

'All the world knows the story, Caesar.' Eros had heard from an eye-witness that Caligula had struggled in terror when he heard the plan and had been heavily drugged before his mother, Agrippina, took him out to the mutineers.

'Yes, the world knows. But do they know why those soldiers suddenly became as meek as lambs? The light they saw in that boy's face to remind them of their duty.

'And after that came the wilderness. The exile, the wandering among strangers, and the humiliations. That pig I sentenced just now struck me when he stole the dagger. He slapped my cheek as though I were a slave.

'What is the matter, fellow? Why don't you look at me?' The Greek had bowed his head and was staring at the floor.

'Forgive me, Great One. Somehow your face hurts my eyes. It is like watching a bright sun which blinds me.'

'Yes, that is understandable.' Caligula finished his wine and threw the cup over his shoulder. 'You are the first person to whom I have revealed my true identity, and it is hard for human eyes to look on a god. Keep your face down, then, but listen carefully.

'Like the Nazarene, I travelled the wilderness, Eros. I had to flatter Tiberius, to watch his filthy debaucheries at Capri, and take second place to his son at the Games while he insulted me. He once said that I was a monster who "had been educated for the destruction of the Roman People".

'And then, deliverance came; freedom like that.' He pointed upwards. The bird had at last found an open window and fluttered out into the sunlight.

'How the rabble cheered me after the old goat died. As with this Jesus, they spread garlands in my path and hailed me as their deliverer. Are you beginning to see the connection between his story and mine at last?'

'I am starting to, Caesar, but it is the end of his story that troubles me.' Eros concentrated hard. His plan was working too well. He had wanted Caligula to feel that the Nazarene was a rival to his own divinity, but a far madder notion appeared to be lodged in his mind.

'Jesus was rejected by the people, Great One. He died horribly like a common criminal.'

'Of course he did.' Out of the corner of his eye, Eros saw a pitying smile. 'God is always rejected and cursed, because men are evil and cannot accept the love he bears them. Every day and hour they turn against him.' Once again he recounted how the crowd had cheered when his favourite gladiator was killed in the arena.

'But, though God is cut down like the corn, he always rises again and returns to his people, however unworthy they may be.

'What are you doing though?' The master of Rome screamed in terror and pulled out the dagger. Eros was clutching his feet and his tears were pouring on to the sandals.

'Pardon me, Caesar. Please forgive me, Master. I did not know till this moment.' Had he gone too far, Eros wondered. If he had, death was as close as the dagger in that shaking, green-nailed hand.

'I have worked against you, Master. I feared your teachings, and tried to shame and discredit you; to prove to the world that you were an impostor. I was too blind to see the truth, to realize that all gods are one and you are he: the creator who rose from the dead and now has returned to rule the world.'

'Stand up, Eros.' He need not have worried, for Caligula smiled and helped him to his feet.

'You could not have known, and my mercy is infinite. You are the first disciple, the only one to whom I have revealed myself, and I shall reward you for your faith.

'But now, we have work to do.' He stood up and paced across the dais with a busy frown on his face. 'Those false teachers, those people who preach that I only made one short appearance after my death and then returned to heaven. The fools who cannot realize that I am not merely the Jewish Messiah, but Mithras, and Jove, and Dionysius, and all the others revealed as a single person.

'They must be punished, Eros. My provincial governors can start rounding them up immediately, and put them where they cannot spread their poisonous doctrines any further. That fisherman, as he calls himself, shall pull an oar in the galleys, and we will find some useful employment for the maker of tents too.' He walked down towards a gong at the foot of the steps.

'Master, listen to me.' Eros hurried after him. 'I do not presume to advise, but please listen.

'It has gone too far for that. These people are fanatics who will stand any amount of punishment. They will even deny your godhead under torture and there is only one way to put a stop to their evil teachings. Discredit the cult by pretending that the Nazarene was just a man whose execution was a mockery. Then, when that has been done, reveal yourself to the world in all your glory.'

'Mock myself! Discredit God!' Caligula stuck out his lower lip like a petulant child that has been deprived of a toy.

'I know that is hard, Master, but believe me, it is necessary and there is an easy way it can be done. I came prepared, you see, and the means to destroy this cult is already in Rome. Let me tell you my plan, Caesar.' As if they were not alone, Eros leaned forward and whispered in his ear.

'Good. Yes, excellent, Eros.' Caligula had listened attentively and then struck the gong and given his orders to the major-domo.

'Very good indeed.' The bloated body shook with amusement and his voice was a shrill cackle. 'And the fellow keeps repeating that? That is all he can say? "Jesus of Nazareth . . . King of the Jews." Even if we put him on the rack, he couldn't say anything else.' For the moment at least, God had left his mind and a practical joker was in sole occupation.

'We'll exhibit him in the city first, and then in every place where these Christian communities are springing up. And he will shout his message to the crowds, because it is the only one he knows. "Jesus . . . the King of the Jews."

'Oh, if you weren't such an ugly old crab, I could kiss you, Eros.' Caligula leaned towards him grinning. His breath was a revolting mixture of scented mouthwash and corruption, and Eros had to struggle to hide disgust.

'But there is one more thing that still worries me, Master,' he said. 'Your statue which is to be erected in Jerusalem. I do not think that is wise.'

'Why not?' Mirth stopped and God entered the brain once more. 'All temples are to contain my image. Why should Jerusalem be an exception?'

'Because I know the Jews, Master. In Italy, or any other place, you are right to reveal yourself, but not in Palestine.' Though Caligula frowned, Eros felt no fear. The man was his tool now, and could be made to do anything he wanted.

'The Jews are insane where their religion is concerned, and your image will be mocked secretly, though they pay it lip service. Do not allow that, Great One. For your disciple's sake, countermand the orders.'

'Very well, Eros. I will do it for you, though later I will lead an army into that country and see if they mock me then.' The doors opened and he watched the men coming towards him; Vibius mincing as usual, the major-domo cringing, and Cinna supporting the tall figure that limped on its maimed feet.

'So this is your puppet. Let me see if I can pull his strings.' Caesar crooked his finger for them to draw nearer.

'Who are you, master? What is your name?' He listened attentively to the mindless repetitions and giggled.

'No, not bad, my friend. Not at all bad. The fellow is shorter than I am, and naturally lacks my nobility, but he will serve our purpose.' He took a ring from his finger and handed it to Eros. 'I said I would reward your faith, and now I do.

'Have the orders prepared at once, Vibius. From this moment, Eros Dion commands both the Praetorians and the Vigiles.'

'A great deal of money must have been paid, but we never knew by whom.' The man's name was Bannio, a veteran from one of the smallholdings north of the City. Quite by chance one of Eros' informers had discovered that he had been stationed in Palestine and it was his cohort which supplied the execution party for the Nazarene. Eros had sent for him immediately.

'The majority of our lads thought the Jewish priests were responsible for what happened. The fellow we took charge of had been considered a great teacher by many of the people, and they didn't want him alive during the Passover. It was mostly chatter, though. Our centurion, Marcellus Pollius, was a man who could keep a secret and we were all split up a few days afterwards.'

'What do you mean?' Eros handed the old man a cup of wine and stared hard at him. Bannio was the sole Roman eye-witness they had managed to discover, and his evidence could be vital. 'The whole detail was disbanded?'

'Correct, my lord. That's why I said a lot of money must have been involved.' The man sipped the rich Falernian appreciatively.

'About a week later Pollius gave us our new orders and I'd never heard anything like them. We weren't legionaries based on one province for the whole term of service, of course, but just part of a second-class cohort. All the same, to split eleven men up into as many separate commands must have taken a bit of doing. Some went to Syria and Egypt and others as far away as Numidia. I was the lucky one, getting a posting home to Italy, and I didn't complain, however much I wondered why.'

'I'm sure you didn't.' Eros tucked the information neatly away in his head. 'And the centurion himself left Jerusalem?'

'That he did, my lord, and was killed some months later at a training barracks outside Alexandria: an accident, they said.

'It seems he was taking sword drill without wearing armour – dead against regulations, that – and dropped his guard. The lad he was instructing couldn't pull back in time and ran him through the guts. Poor old Pollius! He must have got a tidy sum for fixing that crucifixion, and he only had another year to go before he could retire and enjoy it. Not that I think he would have done; even if he'd lived. All shaken up by that execution, Pollius was; like a man who knows the Fates have turned against him.'

'I see.' So there could have been a third suicide to join Pilate and Judas Iscariot, Eros thought. Another mind driven insane because its owner had aided the Nazarene's crucifixion.

'But tell me about the execution itself, Bannio. Remember everything you can and you will be well rewarded.' There were two doors in the opposite wall of the office and each of them hid a different payment. Behind the one on the right was a bag of gold, and the other concealed a man with a knife. Bannio's evidence would decide the door by which he left.

'As you wish, though it's not a memory I'm fond of. Ah, that's kind of you.' He beamed as Eros pushed the wine jug towards him. 'It's not often that I get the chance to taste stuff like this.'

'Three chaps had been sentenced that day. Two brigands, and this preacher fellow who had annoyed the priests by claiming he was some sort of deity they call the Messiah. Our detail was to be in charge of him, and the first thing which surprised me was Pollius coming out of the guard house and saying he would go along with us.

'I ask you, my lord! A senior centurion taking command of ten men on a purely routine assignment!'

'Yes, very strange, but that was only the beginning, wasn't it? The manner of the preacher's death was unusual?'

'Indeed it was. Pollius told us that he must be supported by nails instead of ropes and the cross would be without a sedile. One of the lads started to ask why, and he shouted him down as if he'd insulted Caesar in public.

'Well, we marched round to the barracks to collect our prisoner, and the moment I saw him, I almost felt that his divine claims might have a bit of truth in them. Very weak, he was, having been knocked about quite a bit, and when we started to climb the hill, he kept falling down under his cross till Pollius made a bystander carry it. A weak, sick man, my lord, but there was something uncanny about him all the same; a sense of authority I've never known in any other person.' An old, gnarled hand refilled the glass and Bannio drank deeply.

'The road up to Golgotha was packed tight with spectators, most of them just louts who jeered at all three prisoners, but many were real fanatics only interested in our man. There'd been a story that some divine beings would appear to save him at the last moment, and they mocked him about it and spat in his path. I think there were some of his own followers about too, but they kept very quiet and I didn't hear one voice raised in his favour.

'No, our preacher had no active friends, my lord, but though it sounds crazy, I don't believe he needed any. Once, as we rounded a bend, he looked me full in the face, and I remember thinking that if he wanted to, that chap could walk out through the ranks and not one of us would dare to stop him.'

'It does sound crazy, Bannio.' Eros winced as another spasm trembled beneath his arm. 'You'd been drinking, of course?'

'We'd had a drop or two: one always does for that kind of job, but not enough to affect my imagination. There really was something strange about the man and I felt frightened till I knew he was dead.'

'How did you know he was dead, my friend?' Eros leaned forward. They were getting to the crux of the business now, and not only Bannio's life, but his own hopes depended on the answer. 'I understand that death was not certified by breaking a thigh, which is the usual practice.'

'That is true, my lord. But before I finish the story, do I have your promise that it will remain a secret between the two of us?

'Thank you.' He watched Eros nod and took another swig of wine. 'Well, we got up to the top of the hill; Calvary, the place was called, and the men detailed as executioners did what Pollius told them. Heavy iron nails they used instead of cords and the cross had no sedile. When we raised it up, he hung between the other two like a dead bird on a farm fence, though now and again he cried out to the people who were watching. I never learned Aramaic, so I couldn't understand what he said, but it affected them all right. Some of them cursed and shook their fists, one or two wept, and Pollius who was standing beside me suddenly turned and walked away.'

'He left his post before the man was seen to die?' Eros frowned. That must be wrong. The centurion had been well bribed for his trouble. Surely he would have stayed there till the job was done and that broken, but still living body had been taken down from its cross and handed over to the people who'd paid for it?

'That he did, lord. He walked right away to the far side of the hill and I saw him kneel down and stare out towards the city. I told you something happened to Pollius that day.

'A foul day it was as well. The sky grew very dark suddenly, there was a sudden flicker of lightning in the east, and then rain started to come down in sheets. Most of the crowd began to drift off after the first hour and soon there were only about a score of people left with us. Two of them belonged to the "Providers of Ease", pious women who distribute drugs to dying criminals, and they asked me to give the preacher a sponge full of myrrh. I held it out to him on my spear, but he shook his head, though he must have been in agony.

'With Pollius out of the way, I was the senior chap in charge, and there was no point in the rest of the lads getting soaked. I sent them off to shelter behind some rocks till the man died, and they passed their time playing dice for his few belongings.

'It was so cold up there, my lord. The details in charge of the other prisoners had marched back to barracks, but we had been ordered to stay with ours because there'd been some talk that his followers might try to rescue him. I can still see those women staring up at the dying face while the wind tugged my sodden robe like a sail.'

'And you were in charge all the time, Bannio?' Eros could almost share his memories of the scene. 'The centurion never came back to relieve you?'

'At the end he did, lord. After the man was dead, I went over to Pollius and he returned to supervise the lowering of the cross and the removal of the corpse.'

'A corpse or a living man, fellow. How can you be sure that he was dead?' Eros grinned, feeling the rewards of triumph at last. Pollius had betrayed his trust. He had sold himself to Joseph of Arimathaea and did not wish to show the guilt in his face. But he had to return at the end for the final deception.

'He returned and ordered you not to break the thigh bone.'

'That's correct. We did not break any bone, because there was no need for it, you see. The man was dead and I know that better than anyone.' Bannio started as Eros gripped his arm and his cup tilted, spilling a few drops of blood-red wine on to the couch.

'You have promised that this matter will go no further, Eros Dion, and I shall tell you exactly how he died.

'Yes, so wild that day was. The thunder and lightning spreading across each horizon, those women staring up at the dying man, and the rain soaking everything. I thought of our warm quarters, and food and drink and dry clothes, and then I looked up at that tortured face and I suddenly saw that he was dead, though every cold line and feature of it was the same as before, strong and confident and full of authority.'

'You only thought he was dead, fellow.' Eros' grip tightened. 'You told Pollius he had died and allowed the deception to go through.'

'That's not true, my lord. I'll admit that I wanted to get back to barracks. I'll admit that I was frightened of a corpse and wanted no part in breaking the thigh. But I was still a soldier who knew his duty and I made sure the execution had taken place.' The old man pulled away his arm and stood up.

'Jesus of Nazareth died on the cross and there's no doubt about that. You see, I ran my spear though his heart to prove it.'

'Thank you, Bannio. Your testimony will be most useful, and you may leave me now.

'No, not that way.' Eros raised his voice as the old man moved towards the door on the right. 'My secretary is in there and will pay you for your trouble.' He watched him go out through the left-hand door, heard a muffled scream as it closed behind him, and turned to his scribe.

'Give me what you have written, and then go and tell Doctor

Cinna that I wish to see him.' He read briefly through the transcript of their conversation and tore the parchment to shreds. Bannio's evidence would never be made public.

But the man had died on his cross. A spear was run through the heart as he hung there. And then later he had returned to his followers. Whatever they did, however hard they searched, the story remained unbroken.

'You,' Eros said aloud to the empty room. 'Whoever you are, God or impostor, listen to me. It is not I who am fighting against you, but the law. There is nothing personal in this, but I have to destroy you and your gospel that can taint the world.' The mirror on the wall reflected a face he hardly recognized: old and wrinkled and sick, with the left cheek twitching convulsively.

'Listen to me, Jesus-bar-Joseph. Even if you are divine, I shall defeat you. Even though you did return from the dead, I shall erase your memory . . .' He broke off as a door opened.

'You said something, Eros Dion?' Cinna came towards him with a frown of concern on his face.

'No, Doctor. I was merely thinking aloud. I wanted to inquire about your patient, as we may need him soon. Is his hand healing at last?'

'It is much better.' Cinna nodded. 'The infection has gone and it is only a question of days before all the scars appear old. I am using certain ointments to speed the process, and in about a month, he should pass any inspection.'

'But do you still think the deception will work, my friend?'

'It has to work. There is no other way,' Eros snapped at him. Why couldn't he control his temper, he wondered? Why did he bark and shout at the slightest irritation, and why did that twitch rack his body? He had all the powers he needed. Command of the Vigiles and the Praetorian Guard, and the favour of the Emperor. The imbecile was almost ready to be shown in public, and the plan was flawless.

So, what was he frightened of? Why couldn't he sleep, and why was he suspicious of everybody he came into contact with?

Was it associating with Caligula perhaps? The feasts and drinking bouts that always turned into obscene orgies, with a stench of vomit drowning the perfume: a mad face grinning like a child's as it plotted some malevolent joke, and then suddenly bursting into tears of self-pity.

'Only you realize the truth, Eros.' The Emperor had said that morning, staring up from a pillow which was damp with tears and sweat, and holding out his hand to be kissed.

'Only you had the faith and power to see that I was indeed the Anointed One, and you will stand by my side for ever, though all the rest of the world mock me.' He had broken off in a fit of maudlin weeping and buried his face in the pillow.

No, Caligula had nothing to do with his sickness. Normally curiosity would have been far stronger than disgust, and he would have watched Little Boots and his companions as a trainer studies a cage of wild animals who must be mastered by cunning and the whip.

What was it then? His fear of the Christians? The latest reports were disturbing enough, it was true; little groups springing up everywhere. But it was not them. He had boundless confidence in his plan, and ridicule would soon destroy the sect.

Not Caligula, not the Christians, not even the Nazarene himself. Again the thing twitched under his arm, and he frowned at Cinna, wanting to confide in him, but fearing to do so. Was he possessed by some demon which was taking over his mind?

'Our plan must work, Doctor, because it is the only one we have. Just see that our Nazarene's wounds look convincing, and people will accept him all right.'

'Oh, the wounds will heal. Also the brain has been well conditioned and he is incapable of repeating anything except the words I have put there.' Cinna gave a slightly smug smile and then frowned.

'But you are the person I am worried about, Eros Dion. You are the one person who can ruin the plan, because you are sick.

'Please don't try to deny it. I can see that you are ill, and I would like to know how ill. Would you allow me to examine you?'

'If you wish.' Eros slipped off his robe and followed him across to the light from the window. Perhaps Cinna could help. In any case he had to talk to somebody about his condition.

'You have been sleeping badly, haven't you?' The doctor peered into his left eye. 'How long has that been going on?'

'I haven't slept for over a week. One of the Emperor's own physicians gave me an opium draught to take, but it doesn't help.

When I am just about to drop off, there seem to be cords attached
to my body which jerk me awake.' Eros sat down on a couch and
told him everything; the fears, the constant suspicion that people
were plotting against him, and the strange feeling that some alien
creature was lodged in his skull.

'That must be most unpleasant.' Cinna gave a brief smile. 'An
orthodox physician would say that your basic fluids were out of
balance and you had a surplus of black bile.

'I belong to the school of Euryton of Alexandria, however,
and my diagnosis is different. Because of the Egyptian skill of
embalming, bodies are readily obtainable there and dissection has
become an art. Euryton discovered that other things control our
bodies. Tiny cords which run from the brain and pass its orders to
the limbs, just as you have described. Let us see if your limbs are
receiving the correct orders.

'Now sit up and cross your legs. Thank you.' He lifted an ebony
ruler and tapped him under the knee cap.

'No, not so good, I'm afraid.' Cinna frowned as the leg remained
motionless. 'I understand that you are an abstemious man, both
with women and wine.'

'I have been drinking more than I used to, but still in modera-
tion, and sex does not interest me. My mother was a prostitute and
I saw enough of it when I was a child.'

'Lie down again, please.' The doctor's hand ran under his left
armpit, feeling the thing pulsing beneath the skin. 'I suppose you
never knew who your father was.'

'Naturally not. He might have been any one of her customers.
But can you do anything to help me, Cinna? Would massage stop
this shaking? Is there a stronger draught than opium to make me
sleep?'

'I shall make you sleep, all right. But massage would be of no
use at all. You see, there is nothing wrong with your body. The
weakness lies in here.' He stood up and tapped his own forehead.

'And without knowing something about your father, there is
very little I can do to help. There is a great deal you can do to help
yourself, however.'

'You mean that you need to know my father's horoscope; the
stars he was born under, which gods he especially venerated?'

'No, I am not an astrologer.' Cinna shook his head. 'What I meant was that I would have to know your father's ailments, before I can diagnose your own. Did his face and side ever twitch, for instance? Did his leg remain motionless when tapped under the knee cap?' The doctor went to a table and started to write out a prescription.

'You remember Uriah, the librarian of King Herod. He told me that the Jews have a saying which goes something like this: "The sins of the fathers are visited upon their children." The meaning is supposed to be moral, but I think it is good medicine too. What weakness did your father hand down to you?'

'That we will never know.' Eros closed his eyes for a moment, letting the past slide behind them. Merchants, soldiers, workmen, scribes. Young men of good family visiting the brothel for adventure, and old men hoping to cure their impotence. The drunken laughter, the wet lips glistening in the lamplight, and the sound of the Beast with Two Backs behind a curtain.

'But what can I do to help myself, Cinna?'

'You can stop imitating that poor puppet we have made.' The doctor had finished the prescription and he stood up.

'We chose him for two reasons, didn't we? He resembled the descriptions of the Nazarene, and there was a weakness in his brain, an empty place which we could fill. Remember how I did it. For many days he was shut in a dark room, and from a grille above a relay of voices repeated the same message. Your name is Jesus, and so on. In time, those words were lodged in his empty mind and became all he knew or remembered.'

'You think my brain is empty too, Doctor?' Eros smiled bitterly. 'I may be sick, but I assure you I am not an imbecile.'

'I never said you were, my friend. All the same, I think that your life has been very empty, and a creature has entered your mind which you are feeding too well.

'This campaign against the Christians has become a personal battle, hasn't it? And it also gives you pleasure, because you have something definite to hate. There was little love in your nature before, and now there is none at all. Am I correct?'

'No, not entirely.' Eros stammered as he replied. 'You are right about my having a personal war against the Nazarene, but there is no pleasure in it. I fear him, Cinna. I know what he can do; the ruin and destruction that his gospel can bring. Oh, yes, hatred is there, but the terror is far, far greater.'

'You fear *him*, Eros Dion?' Cinna raised his eyebrows. 'You are terrified of a man who died like a slave? A Jewish fanatic who was executed years ago? I thought it was the movement we were supposed to destroy, and its founder had been disposed of. Are you starting to believe in him, perhaps? Do you think that he really did rise from dead?'

'Don't say that, Cinna. Don't even think it.' Eros gripped the sides of the couch to stop his body shaking. 'The man is dead. The Resurrection was a lie invented by his followers. But the fact that we could discover nothing about his middle years obsesses me. Sometimes I seem to see his face mocking me. Is there nothing that can stop me dreaming of him?'

'At night that will be easy.' The doctor handed him the prescription. 'Get an apothecary to make this up for you, and drink six drops mixed with a cup of wine before you go to your couch. I promise that you will sleep like a child; a happy contented child, not a frightened little boy in a brothel.

'But, in the daytime, I cannot help you. Only you can cure yourself, and you must stop hating, Eros. The cult of the Nazarene has to be wiped out, but try to regard it as a routine assignment, not a personal war. The man is dead. He died a long time ago, and there is nothing left of him to hate or fear. All you have to do is to discredit the myth which his followers invented.'

'And if I cannot stop regarding it as a personal war?' Eros got up and started to replace his robe. 'If this hatred and fear continues, what then?'

'Who knows?' Cinna shrugged his shoulders. 'Your body is very strong, but no mind can exist under really great tension for long. Unless you can control your emotions, I think you may become as deranged as that poor creature with the parrot cries I gave him.

'Will you try to help yourself, my friend?'

'I will try, Doctor. Only the gods know how hard I shall try.' Even as he spoke, Eros felt sanity returning, and the twitch become weaker.

'Thank you, Cinna. You have given me hope, and I will be in

your debt for a very long time.' He gripped his hand, and then turned as a slave appeared in the doorway.

'Master, this arrived by a ship from Palestine.' The man bowed and handed him a sealed roll. 'I did not like to disturb you, but it is marked urgent.'

'I can see that for myself, boy.' He ripped open the seals. The letter was addressed to whoever commanded the Vigiles, and dictated by Beric and Thassi, who could not have known that he had regained Caligula's favour. They started with formal greetings to their new master, whoever he might be, and followed with an abject request that the Emperor might be persuaded to remove his statue from Jerusalem, as a full scale uprising appeared imminent.

Well, they didn't need to bother about that any more, Eros thought. Little Boots had signed the orders and they were on their way to Palestine already.

'With regard to our former superior, Eros Dion . . .' He smiled as he read on. Beric and Thassi were loyal men, and brave too. They stated that, to the best of their knowledge, he had played no part in Macro's treason, and constantly expressed his devotion to the Emperor. He would see that they were well rewarded.

'Now, my lord, touching the superstition of the Nazarene, which keeps us in this city . . .'

What was this? As he read the next paragraph, the writing blurred and his twitch returned, jerking his arm, and he flushed with rage.

'He let her go after all I said to him.' The words came gasping out between his clenched teeth. 'Sextus let the Jewish girl go free, and she will tell everyone of our plans. I knew he was a fool, I knew he was angry, but I still thought I could trust him.

'No, you are wrong, Doctor. This is a personal battle. Sextus was the only person I ever regarded as a friend, and that dead Apostate has possessed him.

'You there.' He swung round to the slave. 'Run and fetch a scribe and be quick about it.' The saliva in his mouth had been replaced by stuff which burned.

'The ship that takes my letter to Palestine will bring them back. If that girl has talked . . . if the Christians know of my plan . . .'

The room was spinning, and the marble floor had become as red as blood.

'If they have talked, I will show Sextus how a traitor dies.' The redness turned to purple and black, the spinning walls closed in, and he pitched forward unconscious.

# Five

'Hail, Caesar. We who are about to die salute thee.' Marcus Cato grinned sardonically at the huge statue towering over the square. A battery of light catapults stood in front of it, and beyond them, the dead and wounded were lying.

'They fought well, didn't they?'

'They fought like men who had a cause to die for.' Sextus pushed back his helmet and wiped the sweat from his forehead. Jerusalem had been a dead city since Caligula's image arrived, and this first outburst of violence was almost a relief. It had been a mild, windless afternoon, and the soldiers were leaning against their engines half asleep when the attack came. A roar of voices growing louder and louder, and then the mob had come pouring into the square.

A few of them carried spears, a very few swords, but the majority were armed with clubs and agricultural implements, or sharp stones, and they'd never had a chance. The nets of the catapults were loaded, and a thousand lead bolts had ripped through their ranks like hail on a corn field. They'd still come on, though. Even the wounded had crawled forward towards the thing that desecrated their city. One man armed with a scythe had even managed to cut his way through to the statue and aim a single blow at its marble thigh before he was struck down. Then, a squadron of cavalry had trotted out of the citadel, cutting off their retreat, and the matter was finished.

'So, King Herod's secretary lied in saying that he could hold his people back for three weeks.'

'He didn't lie, Tribune.' Thassi was walking between their horses and he shook his head. 'This was not the start of the revolt, but an isolated attack by Zealots; fanatics who had become crazed by self-inflicted starvation. Look at that fellow, for instance.' He pointed to a body on their right. The face was ravaged by hunger, and even in death, the eyes glared up at them.

'The real revolt will not start for some days. Our latest intelligence is quite definite about that. And when it does start, you won't have just a few hundred madmen against you, but the whole nation.'

With the new emergency, the Vigiles' representatives in Palestine had put themselves at the disposal of the military, and the information they had brought in from outside the city was disquieting in the extreme. Scythes and reaping hooks sharpened, men and boys drilling in the village streets, and every smithy turned into an armourer's shop. Even the brigands had given up their trade, and come out of the hills and deserts to form a hard core for the rebellion.

'Don't worry, Thassi.' Sextus scowled at the statue which was still on its cart, ready to be drawn into the temple on the Lady Julia's birthday. 'Remember that we shall be revenged, because Caesar is all merciful. He has promised that should any disrespect be shown to his image, he will personally lead an army into this country and turn it into a desert.'

'That is a great comfort. That makes death worthwhile, doesn't it?' Cato acknowledged a salute from the centurion in charge of the catapults.

'Good man, Festus. Your lads did very well, but see they're kept on their toes in future.'

'And if our lord and master does bring an army, he'll have more than Jews to fight against. The Parthians and Armenians have been quiet enough lately, but a full-scale rising in Palestine will bring them down like wolves on a sheepfold.' With Jerusalem approaching a state of siege, Rome seemed a long way off, and Cato spoke openly against the Emperor.

'How long do you think we can hold out, once the revolt does start?' The question was faintly academic, for Sextus felt as dead as that huge marble face smiling above them. He had lost everything; the fight against the Nazarene had been abandoned now, Rachel had left him for ever, and his honour was gone. Whatever he felt for Rachel, Beric and Thassi were right, and he had betrayed his trust when he released her.

Even Pilate's fortune would evade him. Caligula was obviously a fool and Eros Dion would soon win his favour. Should he manage to leave Palestine alive, he had no doubts that Eros would settle the score against him.

'How long can we hold them?' Cato spat over his horse's shoulder. 'That depends how intelligently they attack. The General thinks about a month, which sounds a reasonable enough estimate. After that, they're bound to swamp us, unless Syria or Egypt manage to send a full legion.'

'We've brought in all the provincial garrisons now, that's one comfort, and we've got those.' He smiled paternally at the engines mounted on the citadel. They were huge things, far, far bigger than the catapults which had broken the mob, and should any resolute attackers penetrate under their range Greek Fire and red-hot sand were waiting for them. On the surface the position looked impregnable, but Cato knew that its foundations were rotten and crumbling. If the Jews found another Joshua to lead them, and drove a mine through the rock, the walls would topple, and they could pour in as they had done at Jericho centuries before.

'The General's plan is to hold this section of the city for as long as possible, and then sweat it out inside. We might last a month, as he says, but I wouldn't wager on that. As you know, we managed to disarm most of the Temple guards, but who knows what they'll collect in the provinces. That cohort which came in last night had to leave half its baggage train behind.

'See that you don't miss any, lads.' The Tribune raised his voice. All over the square men were busy collecting the missiles from the catapults. The dead and badly wounded could be left to lie, but those cast-lead bolts were irreplaceable.

'You're right in saying these chaps are fanatics.' He reined before a group of prisoners huddled on the ground, between Syrian guards. All of them were young, all of them were wounded, but each one of them stared up at their conquerors with hatred and contempt and not a trace of fear.

'Yes, you can pass along some water, Juba, but don't waste any food on them.' Cato nodded to the sergeant in charge. 'At dawn tomorrow they're to be hung on the Moriah walls as an example to their compatriots.

'What are you up to, though? We won't get any information from this lot.' He frowned as Sextus dismounted and walked along the line.

'There's something I want to examine.' Sextus stopped before one of the prisoners, a boy of about sixteen whose right hand had been caught by a bolt. The broken knuckles showed through the clotting blood, but that wasn't what interested him. Around the wrist was a thin circle of metal.

'Where did you get this?' Sextus lifted his arm and there was no doubt at all. It was the bracelet he had given Rachel to replace the one she had parted with on Sinai.

'I said where did you get it?' He slapped the boy across the face, but there was no change in his expression. Either he couldn't understand Sextus' faulty Aramaic, or was refusing to listen.

'Let me try.' Thassi repeated the question with the same result and he looked up at the Tribune. 'You said they were all to be hung on the walls, my lord, but will you make one exception in this case?'

'Thank you.' The Jew smiled and squatted down beside their prisoner. He spoke too quickly for the Romans to understand him, but the effect of what he said was obvious. The set, bitter mask melted into the face of a terrified child and he whimpered and cringed before Thassi.

'That is rather interesting, my lords.' Thassi's smile widened as the boy grovelled at his feet. 'This fellow would face your racks and crosses without complaint, but there is one death that terrifies him; an unclean animal. I told him that he would be forcibly fed with pork and sewn alive in a pig's skin.'

'But what about the bracelet?' Cato was laughing uproariously, but Sextus shouted in his impatience. 'Did he say where he got it?'

'He says that a lady gave it to him. She paid him to take it to a certain Roman nobleman as a sign of good faith. He was then supposed to lead this Roman to her.' Thassi's voice was outwardly respectful, but he sneered with his eyes.

'Now, let us hear a little more.' He asked another string of questions and smiled again.

'Yes, it is as I thought. The woman paid him well, but he discovered she was an apostate, and decided not to honour his side of the bargain. He bought a spear with the money and joined these other poor fools.

'Your girl appears to be rather careless, to say the least, my lord.'

'But where is she, Thassi? That is what I want to know.' For the first time in weeks, Sextus felt there was a purpose in living again. 'Where was he to take me?'

'Not very far, lord. To a village called Gethsemane. It is just outside the east wall, but I think it might as well be a thousand leagues away.

'Am I right, Tribune?'

'You are perfectly right, Thassi.' Marcus Cato was becoming impatient. He had a lot of work to attend to, and the whereabouts of one Jewess did not interest him in the slightest.

'Today's attack may have been an isolated incident, but our lads are sticking together from now on. I'm not sending any patrol out to look for your woman, Ennius.'

'You don't have to, Tribune.' Sextus turned to the prisoner. 'Stand up, fellow, and listen to me.' Though his Aramaic was poor, he spoke slowly and the boy obeyed him.

'If you take me to the lady, I shall set you free. If not, you will have the death my friend promised.' Sextus remounted and untied the cord of his tunic.

'No, Cato, don't try to stop me. Though my credentials are signed by Naevius Macro, they remain valid till fresh orders arrive. Don't worry about your men either, because I shall go alone.

'Now, come here and give me your left hand, fellow.' He started to tie the boy's wrist to his stirrup leather.

'You really are a fool, Ennius.' Cato gentled his horse which was pawing the cobbles. 'I suspected as much, but now you have proved it.

'Very well, go and die for your Hebrew slut, if you like, but don't expect me to shed any tears over you.'

'I only expect one thing from you, Tribune; the password for the sentries.' Sextus smiled at him with complete good humour. Death might be waiting outside the walls, but at least the life which was left had a meaning.

'The password is "The Ever-Protecting Goddess", and as far as you are concerned, I think she will have to work very hard.' Cato gave another wolfish grin.

'And what about you, Thassi? Are you following your master or staying here?'

'I will stay with you, if I may, my lord.' Thassi bowed low. 'I do not think Sextus Ennius would have remained my master for long, and I have no desire to die in the service of his lust.' For a long count of three his eyes flashed contempt at Sextus, and he turned and followed Cato back towards the citadel.

The men at the gate were lightly armed frontier guards brought in from the west and they looked completely bewildered as Sextus told them to let him pass.

'You surely don't mean that, Master; not after what happened this afternoon. The village is deserted now; we saw the lot of them going away up the far hill less than an hour ago; men and women and kids. Probably they imagine we'll send a punitive expedition out against them.' The sergeant was a fatherly man and showed genuine concern at Sextus' wishes.

'The men will be back though, as soon as it's dark. That's the terrible thing about the Jews. However much punishment you give 'em, they always come back for more.

'No, you stay with your own kind, my lord. We've seen what those Sicarii devils do to prisoners, and it's not pleasant.' Sextus had to curse him before the gate was finally opened, and he and the boy moved out into the valley.

It was a fine, clear evening and, though the country was dead and brown, Sextus sensed nature waiting for the spring. Soon crops would burst through the soil and cover the slopes like a tapestry unrolled on a stone floor.

But, if nature still lived, mankind appeared to have deserted the land. There was no smoke from the huts dotting the far side of the valley, and apart from goats, not a living creature in sight. Sextus' feelings were composed of excitement, and hope and dread as he turned his horse down the rough road to Gethsemane. Though it could be taking him to Rachel, the sergeant was right. As soon as darkness came, the Knifemen would probably return.

Darkness was coming quickly too. The sun was almost behind Jerusalem and long shadows were creeping over the slopes of the Mount of Olives. He glanced down to see that his prisoner's cord was secure and felt the handle of his sword. If he was attacked, his own body would receive the blade. He had little faith in his ability to withstand torture, and he knew a great deal about the defences of the city. The least he could do for his country was to die in silence.

'This is Gethsemane, fellow. In which house was the lady stay- ing?' The village was clearly deserted, but he might find some clue to tell him where Rachel had gone.

'Further on, master, but you must leave your horse. There are steps up the hillside and a wall.'

'As you say.' Sextus dismounted and removed the cord from the stirrup leather. Then he tied the boy's wrists together. Any sudden move towards freedom would open his wounded hand and bring him to a halt.

'Now, take me there.' He followed him up through the little mean village. The slope grew steeper and, after a time, the track was replaced by steps cut in the rock. At every step the sun sank lower behind Jerusalem and the sky darkened, though the moon was starting to rise, with Venus above him. Somehow her presence seemed a good omen.

But was this another trick? Why should Rachel wish to see him? Her face had shown complete rejection when she walked out of the room in the citadel. Had the bracelet been stolen and used as a bait to trap him again? The scar on his hand burned and itched as he hurried after his guide, and he drew his sword. At the first sign of ambush, he would fall on it.

Here was the wall at last: a rough, dry-stone structure to keep out animals, with a wicket gate leading into an olive grove. The trees were incredibly bent and gnarled and could have been old before Romulus laid the first foundations of Rome.

Gethsemane! Yes, of course, this was where the Nazarene had been betrayed; where Judas Iscariot led the Temple guards to arrest him. Sextus felt a surge of hope, as the story came back. Rachel might easily have chosen this as her hiding place.

'There, master; that is where the woman was.' The boy stopped and pointed to a little hut which probably belonged to the gar- dener. 'Keep your promise and free me, master.'

'You will be free when I know you have told the truth.' Even as he spoke, Sextus let go of the cord and moved forward alone. Beyond the hut was a spur of rock, and on it a man was standing, staring out over the valley, as if the whole world belonged to him. A man whom Sextus would never forget.

'So, I have found you at last, Maker of Tents,' he said, as the still figure turned and the moon lit up his face. A small man who appeared tall; a young man who looked old; a face with thin, bitter lines, but the eyes above them were kind.

Also, a man who would not be alone. On every side, his followers would be preparing to show themselves, but there was still time for revenge. One quick stab through the heart, and then the sword would go down on the rock to receive his own body.

'We have a debt to pay, Saul, or Paul, or whatever you call yourself.' The cross on his palm burned again and Sextus walked towards the man who had put it there.

'No, Sextus.' Rachel rushed out of the hut and clutched his arm. 'Put down your sword, for I belong to him now.'

'You belong to him – to the man who branded and shamed me for life.' He threw her aside and the sword edge lay steady under Paul's beard. One sudden movement, one hint of an attack from behind and this throat would be sliced open.

'You misunderstand the woman, Sextus Ennius. She does not mean that she belongs to me personally, but to the one I follow: to God.' The little man's eyes mocked the death beneath them.

'And it seems you will give me an easy end. That is merciful. I thought your revenge would be much harder to bear.

'No, do not touch him, Rachel.' Paul raised his voice as she scrambled to her feet. 'Sextus Ennius fears that we have arranged a second ambush and I have no wish to die from a trembling of his hand.'

'Turn and walk to the hut, both of you.' Out of the corner of his eye Sextus saw the boy making his escape up the hillside. To the right, every olive tree looked as if it were hiding an attacker, and he swung round and lowered the sword against Paul's shoulders.

'Walk very slowly, and at the first sign of a trap you will be dead.'

'Does that satisfy you?' The hut was quite empty and Paul turned and smiled at him. It was a miserable cramped place housing the gardener's tools and lit by a rush lamp and a few dying embers in the grate.

'Yes, my lord, there are only the three of us here, and you may enjoy your revenge slowly, if you wish. After all, you have a heavy debt to settle.'

'That at least is true.' Sextus put his back against the wall. If anybody approached the doorway he could run Paul through at his leisure.

'Now why? What devil's work are you up to now? You tortured me; you put your mark on me; you must know that I have sworn to kill you. So, why did you send a messenger and meet me here alone?'

'That is an easy question, my friend.' The Jew was still grinning at the sword. 'I need your help; it is as simple as that.

'Oh, yes, it was I who branded you, and you have every right to hate me. You bear the most honourable mark in the world, but I put it there for the foulest reason.' There was a slight impediment in his speech which reminded Sextus of Eros Dion.

'I was brought up very strictly in our religion, and I was blind, you see. I and my fellows thought the Master was an apostate sent by Satan. I swore to destroy his followers, and you yourself know how I went about it: arrests by false evidence, torture, murder; and what happened to you was my last blow against him.' He reached out and his fingers brushed the scar for an instant. They were cold and hard and Sextus felt his skin tingle at the touch.

'I am a Roman too, my lord Ennius, and I wanted my fellow citizens to work with me against the Church. Your hand was the tool I used and it succeeded, didn't it? The attack on you made the Governor give us all the powers we needed and the High Priest sent me to Damascus.

'I was so pleased with myself then; so proud and happy. At last the cult of the Apostate would be destroyed and his people return humbled to the faith of their fathers. I can remember every mile of that journey. The long straight road across the desert, the heights of Anti-Lebanon rising like the pillars of smoke which guided Moses, and a dust cloud snaking across the horizon. Then suddenly, behind the cloud, I saw . . . I saw a great . . .' His words broke off and Paul stared silently at the floor with tears streaming down his cheeks.

'And you, Rachel?' Sextus turned to her. 'What are you doing with him, and why did you send for me?'

'Because I have found peace, my love, and I want you to share it. I hid in the city when you released me, and there I met Paul. He listened to my story and absolved me. Whatever my father may have done, it is not ordained that I suffer for another's sin, and he has accepted me into the faith.'

'Faith in a dream, Rachel.' Her face was very appealing in the lamplight and Sextus forced himself to look away from her. There was a debt to be paid and nothing must weaken him.

'Well, tent-maker,' he said. 'What help do you want from me? What possible service would I perform for my worst enemy?'

'A very simple one, Sextus.' The man smiled again and there was no trace of a stammer in his voice now.

'The organization you serve has finally decided to take open action against us, and I want to know what their plan is.'

'You told him, Rachel.' The confirmation of her betrayal was like a physical blow, but Paul shook his head.

'She told us nothing she had promised to keep secret, Sextus. Being a woman, tainted with the curse of Eve, Rachel's carnal loyalty to the man she loves is almost as great as her love of God. She merely arranged for you to come here and give me the information yourself.'

'You imagine I would!' Sextus fought back the urge to kill him then and there. 'What do you think I am, fellow? A slave hoping for idleness in another life? A Jewish blasphemer? A traitor to my country?'

'I think you are a fool, my friend. A child who kicks against a wall, thinking he can bring down the building. A proud, ignorant man who imagines his Empire is all important when its whole existence has been shorter than a single blink of God's eyelid.

'And your superior, Eros Dion, was a fool too, though a cunning one. He thought that he could pry into the hidden life of our master and find something to discredit him. But he found nothing, because he was not intended to. Those years are closed to mankind and will never be opened.'

'No, one day we will know the truth.' Somehow the sword seemed to be growing heavier and Sextus rested the point on the floor. 'The man must have been somewhere and we are bound to discover it.'

'Will you?' Paul stared out through the doorway, at the clear sky with the lamps of the planets and stars shining down on the earth.

'The concentric spheres of Aristotle, Sextus Ennius, which enclose each other like the skins of an onion. We stand on the roof of Hell in the second lowest of them. But beyond us stretch the layers of the moon, and the sun, and the planets and fixed stars till one finally comes to the sphere of the Prime Mover himself.

'Can your organization search those spheres, my lord? Have you the power to penetrate the Heavens? No, for two brief periods God was revealed to us, and that is all we will ever know.'

'You lie, fellow.' Sextus shouted the denial. 'Your master was not a god, but only a man. An impostor who hid himself somewhere on this earth till he felt ready to come out and proclaim his evil gospel.'

'That's right. Cry it aloud, Sextus. Shout to calm your fears. Search till the end of your life, and every day of it will make you more frightened as you realize failure.

'Drive yourself insane, as I did, but all you will find is that which has already been revealed. The Good Shepherd who laid down his life for the sheep; the Man of Sorrow who suffered for his people. And at last, the Risen God who shows that Death may be conquered.

'Oh, I know what the priests will have told you. That the method of crucifixion differed from the usual practice and the officer in charge was bribed. Does that matter in the slightest? The point is that the Master did die on the cross and three days later he returned to his disciples and revealed himself by the breaking of bread.

'Must you still deny him, Sextus? You and Dion have searched so long and failed so often. The power of the whole Empire has been at your disposal, but it didn't help you in the slightest. Will you go on shaming yourself by fighting the new creation? The son who suffered death and the father who harrowed Hell to bring hope to his children. The God of the Morning who can never be resisted.'

'The Nazarene was a human being. An ordinary man like you and I and his teaching has possessed you.' Sextus' words came gasping out and the sword point trembled as he raised it from the floor.

'Then prove it, Sextus.' Paul's eyes looked bright and metallic; steel needles boring into his brain. 'Serve his enemy and kill me now. Follow the tempter who struggles against him but is always defeated. Serve the one who rules an even lower sphere than our own. Show that Jesus of Nazareth is powerless to protect me and push your weapon into my body.'

'I will prove it.' Sextus could hear another voice giving the same order. It came from somewhere inside his skull and it was a whining voice with a plea and a threat and a sneer in it, which reminded him of tiny feet pattering over dusty floors, and sharp teeth gnawing through timber. The orders it gave were clear enough, though, and he knew they had to be obeyed. Standing in front of him was the leader of the movement, the man who had offered the gospel to the Gentiles, and if that man died his followers might become a leaderless rabble.

That was how it had to be. The sword came swaying up against Paul's tunic. Personal revenge was unimportant, the scar on his flesh didn't matter. The Empire alone mattered, and behind that smiling face was a brain which could destroy it.

'Just a single firm thrust, Sextus, and the battle will be won.' The little voice grew louder and he struggled to obey it. 'Kill him and there will be nothing to fear any more. Nothing in life except honour for you, Sextus, and the enjoyment of Pilate's fortune. Kill him, I tell you, and don't worry about the girl. Take her as a slave, and soon she will learn to love you.' He had to do what the voice told him, but why was the sword so heavy? If only his muscles would obey him, if only his hand could hold the hilt more firmly, if only his palm would stop burning, if only . . .

'Come on, my son. I am waiting, so prove the power of the enemy.' The sword fell clattering on to the floor and Paul's hands reached out and held Sextus upright as he started to topple forward.

'All right, it is finished, and there is nothing to fear any more.' He helped him on to a bench at his side. 'Give him some Posca, Rachel. I am afraid that is all we have to offer.

'It is no good, Sextus. You are no stronger than I was and you cannot fight the power of God. Drink this and you will feel better.'

'Thank you.' Sextus had to use both hands to lift the flask to his mouth. Posca was the vinegary wine only drunk by peasants and common soldiers, and its taste mocked his rank, as did the sword at his feet. 'You bewitched me?'

'Not I, Sextus.' Paul shook his head. 'I am just a mortal man, though faith has given me power to serve.' His body seemed to grow bigger as he spoke.

'My master is the shepherd and I am his dog; the fangs of the flock. I have fought with beasts at Ephesus for him, and I will fight them in Rome itself, if it be his will. I am also a wind sent to fan the flame of his gospel till it burns all evil from the world.

'Now, listen to me, my son.' He gripped Sextus' arm and the lines of his face showed like deep scars in the lamplight.

'Eros Dion has prepared a plan to use against the Church; that much we do know.

'He will fail of course, because men and women with faith can withstand any amount of physical persecution. They can stand ridicule as well, Sextus.' Paul's fingers felt as cold and hard as ice.

'But before Dion fails, he may cause great suffering, and I want to prevent that. That is why I risked being killed by the Zealots and returned to Jerusalem, and why Rachel sent for you. You must tell me exactly what those plans are. It is an order, Sextus Ennius, and you cannot fight fate any longer.'

'An order.' The possessed eyes held him as a serpent's hold a sparrow, and then they suddenly turned towards the door and Sextus was free.

'No,' he said. The sour wine was clearing his brain, and the generations spoke through him. A thousand years of authority and trust and devotion to the ideal of government asserting themselves.

'No, Little Maker of Tents, you may be a citizen, but I am a native-born Roman, once the officer of a legion, and my loyalty cannot be bought. Even if your master is a god who can punish with eternal pain, or reward with everlasting joy, I will not sacrifice honour to him. You will never hear our plans from me.'

But Paul was hardly listening. He was staring out of the door and Sextus saw why. The village below was not empty any more and lights were coming towards them: torches moving up the slope with the rattle of armour and the whimper of dogs following a scent.

'So, the revolt has finally begun.' Sextus stood up and looked at the approaching lights. There was no chance of making an escape, because another line was coming down from the hill above to cut them off. His prisoner had obviously met a party of rebels and told them he was there.

'Now, you can listen to me for a change, Paul.' Though the man's death would benefit Rome, Sextus knew that he had to help him. Also, there was Rachel, always Rachel. He took her hand, as the lower lights started to move faster and the noise of the dogs increased.

'These people are only interested in me, and there is a good chance that you can save yourselves. I shall pretend to hide in the hut and you must run down and tell them I am here. They may not recognize you, and accept that you are fellow insurrectionists. Go now while there is time.'

'And how much shall I ask them to pay me, Sextus? Thirty pieces of silver?' Rachel's lips brushed his cheek. 'Before Eros Dion showed me the monster he made, I thought I might love you, and now I know that I do. We have never slept together, my dearest, but death is a kind of sleep, so let us accept that.'

'She talks like a besotted woman, Sextus, but her conclusions are right enough.' Paul walked out of the hut and stared across the valley with that strange air of ownership. 'There is no chance of escape. Almost every Zealot knows me, and I am not running. This is the very spot where the master was arrested, and it will be my honour to follow his example.' They both saw the blaze of pride on his face, as he turned and looked back at them.

'And now, I will promise you something. You both refused me the information I wanted, but you are forgiven, because I know it is ordained that you serve Jesus. There is no death, even though the body rots, and I tell you now that before your hearts stop beating, be that in a few minutes, or many years, or when you are very old people, you will see God.' Paul moved away on to the spur of rock and bowed his head in prayer.

The torches were almost up to the wall at last, and Sextus laid his right arm on Rachel's shoulder. There was a dagger in his right hand, because the sergeant's warning had been quite superfluous and he knew how the Sicarii treated prisoners. Once Rachel had saved his life, and all he could give her in return was an easy death. He held her tightly to him, as the sound of dogs increased to pan-

demonium, and heavy footsteps clattered through the wicket gate.
As soon as the first man reached the clearing, he would stab her
through the heart.

Here he was now. The dogs had been halted, and one man was
coming on alone. A huge figure in armour, striding through the
olives like Mars himself. It would be pleasant to have such a man as
his companion on the long journey, Sextus thought. The best way
to die would be to pick up his sword and face him, but he couldn't
risk that. He raised the dagger, ready to kill the woman he loved,
and then the man stepped out into the clearing and he saw who it
was.

'You! It was you all the time.' Sextus grinned with relief and the
knife dropped from his hand. 'I thought you . . .'

'You thought we were Zealots come to take you, my lord?' Beric
smiled back and motioned his followers to come forward; cavalry
troopers and a slave holding three hounds on a leash.

'That was what I thought, and can you blame me?' Sextus
stepped out of the hut. 'Why are you here though? With the revolt
due to start at any moment, Marcus Cato said he would send out
no more patrols.'

'Oh, I wouldn't call it a patrol, my lord. A detail might be a
better term, and the revolt is not going to start after all.' Beric suddenly noticed Paul and crooked his finger.

'I suppose this is the gardener who has sheltered your woman.
We had better take him back with us and hear everything she told
him.'

'One moment, Beric.' The cavalry officer was young and nervous,
but obviously of good family. 'My orders from the Colonel were
quite definite. No Jewish civilians are to be molested in any way.'

'So you have told me, but in this case . . .' Beric was about to
protest, and then shrugged his shoulders as the young man laid his
hand on his sword and the troopers followed suit.

'Very well. You may go, fellow.' He pushed Paul aside and then
grinned at Sextus again.

'Yes, my lord,' he said. 'I am happy to tell you that the revolt is
already a thing of the past.' The torches glinted on his breastplate
which was beautiful and erotic, with carved Maenads and Satyrs
disporting themselves on the polished brass.

'Two galleys put into Caesarea early today, at almost the same time. But one of them had made a much faster passage than the other and they both brought letters from Rome. The first letter gave orders that Caesar's statue was to be removed from Jerusalem forthwith. Does that please you, my lord?'

'Naturally it pleases me. The people will be content now.' Sextus looked towards the city. In the moonlight he could just see that the gates were open and the smoke of cooking-fires was rising above the walls.

'Very content indeed. It is looked upon as an act of Jehovah and the next three days have been proclaimed a public holiday.

'You are admiring my armour, Sextus Ennius.' Beric's fingers ran across a goat-footed figure with enormous genitals preparing to mount a nymph. 'Do you think it becomes me, my lord?'

'It suits you remarkably well, Beric.' Sextus frowned at the tiny twinkling eyes in the rock-like face. 'But what news did the other ship bring?'

'Greetings, my lord. Greetings from an old friend and I hope they also will please you.' Though Beric bowed, he was still half a head taller than Sextus.

'Eros Dion is our master again. He has regained Caesar's favour as Thassi said he would, and been given both the Vigiles and the Praetorian Guard.' There was no mistaking the triumph in the Briton's voice. 'It was Eros Dion who sent me this breastplate as a gift and with it our new orders. Yes, my lord. Thassi and I jointly command the Department in this country.'

'And now you have come to keep your promise, Beric.' Sextus glanced at the dagger at his feet. Beric's sword was sheathed, and he might just manage to deliver one blow.

'You disappoint me, though. You have come armed when you said you would kill me with your bare hands.'

'So I would like to do, my lord. That would give me more pleasure than anything I can imagine.' Obviously reading Sextus' thoughts he kicked the dagger to one side.

'Unfortunately, another fate is in store for you, Sextus Ennius. It appears that Caesar has heard of your treachery and intends to deal with you personally.

'Doesn't that please you, lord? The Emperor is a great artist and a most amusing man. You should be flattered by his interest; you too, my lady.' Beric laughed at Rachel and his armour rattled.

'A very great honour, isn't it? Merely because you let one Jewish slut go free, Caligula himself will decide on your punishment.' Still laughing, he waved the troopers forward.

'I think the details of your deaths may be rather interesting.'

# Six

As it had been for Eros, the voyage home was long and hard, with rough seas and a contrary wind, but unlike Eros, Sextus saw very little of it.

They kept him chained in a compartment at the bows of the galley, between the starboard timbers and the ram, and most of the time he was alone in darkness with no knowledge of anything except the movement of the deck, the crash of the sea against the bows, and the thresh of the oars.

Once a day, Beric brought him food; figs and dried fish and a little sour wine. Either he did not wish him to have contact with the crew, or enjoyed watching his misery.

'Well, lord,' he would say, crouching low beneath the timbers and holding a lantern at his face. 'I hope you find the accommodation worthy of your rank and station.' He smiled at the foul matting which served Sextus as a couch.

'You do not smell as sweetly as a nobleman should, but we will remedy that when you reach Rome.

'But I have told you so many times.' Beric shook his head at the constantly repeated question. 'Your woman is aboard this vessel, and being well treated. My orders were to deliver both of you in good health and I will obey them.

'How you remind me of my first master, Sextus Ennius. Like you he was young and handsome, but he suffered badly from cramp in the back till he found a way of treating it. He dismissed his trainer at the gladiatorial school, and took on the job himself. I have often heard him say that a brisk half hour at the whipping post was the best cure for his complaint.' Beric was naked to the waist, and turned the lantern to show the marks on his body. 'This he did with a splintered cane, this with a steel-tipped lash, and these came from the teeth of a dog he was fond of.'

'It is strange how closely your face resembles his, my lord.'

'Beric, I have never tortured anybody in my life, and please listen to me.' Sextus had forced his voice to sound pleasant and friendly.

'The Department pays you well, but you are not a rich man. I am though; all Pilate's fortune came to me, and I will give you half, in return for one service.

'Let the girl go free, Beric. Put her ashore before we reach Ostia, and say that you misunderstood your orders.'

'You think I am a traitor like yourself, my lord? You think that you can buy me?' Beric had craned forward and spat in his face. 'Let me tell you something, then. Where the Department is concerned, I am incorruptible, and soon you will not have one brass piece to call your own, because the property of a traitor is forfeit to the state.

'But I wish I could keep my promise, Sextus Ennius! How I long to kill you with these.' He had clenched his fists and then drawn back, probably fearing that he might be unable to restrain himself.

So, time passed. There was a tiny chink in the deck-head which allowed Sextus to distinguish night from day, but the only other physical sensations were movements of the ship and the sea. Plenty of sensations ran through his head, however; memories of his slow acceptance of failure, the fear that they were fighting something too big to be defeated, which had grown into certainty when the sword dropped from his hand and Paul helped him up.

What was it that the man had said at the end? 'There is no death, even though the body rots.' That was a lie of course, the great illusion which gave the cult its strength. Jesus of Nazareth might be a deity, but there was no escape from Caesar, and as the poet had said, 'The Wrath of the Prince is Death.' All the same, the words gave him a crumb of comfort as the ship struggled on against the wind.

Then, at last, they were there. The beat of the oars was replaced by a scream of ropes and pulleys, and the deck became still as the big galley was tied up against a jetty. Beric and two soldiers led him up into sunlight which blinded him; but he didn't see the sun for long. The last stage of the journey was made in a closed litter, and though noises and smells told him he had reached the city, he didn't know in which district they finally halted.

After that, there was a room below ground; small and cramped, but not actually a cell, because it had a chair and a table, as well as a straw pallet, and a barred window high above through which he could see shadows moving across an opposite building. There was a privy in the wall, and a hatch through which food was lowered, so that he spoke to nobody. He tried to record time by scratching on the bricks with his nails, but they were very hard and he soon gave that up, and relied on memories to keep his sanity, and told stories to a mouse which sometimes appeared to share his food.

He had almost given up hope of seeing a human face again, when the door suddenly opened and two jailers appeared. They were rough but kindly men, and they helped him along a passage which ended in a bathroom. There were slaves, not guards there, and a barber to shave him. The water and oils were very hot, and, as the filth of weeks or months left his body, Sextus almost felt young again, though he knew that this was the preparation for the end. The stink of the dungeon would offend Caesar, and he was to be like the Fatted Calf of the Jews; clean and groomed for the sacrifice.

They dressed him in a toga of green silk, and green leather sandals were tied to his feet, and they gave him a draught of some very strong wine to restore his strength. Then he was led up stairs and along more corridors till he reached a marble hall full of scribes and secretaries and messengers. At the end of the hall was a dark, musty room where a little wizened man sat writing at a table.

'Leave us alone and shut the door.' The man went busily on with his work, as the guards left them. He looked stunted, rather than merely small, his hair was a patchy white and grey, and his left hand trembled convulsively as he turned the pages. Sextus recognized his voice, but he had never imagined anybody could alter so much.

'Well, my friend, what am I to do with you?' The man looked up with a smile, and Sextus struggled to conceal his astonishment. The eyes were the same as he remembered them, the smile was still bitter and cynical, but the whole face had a lop-sided appearance, and the mouth was twisted. It resembled a sculpted image that had fallen from its stand before the clay was set.

'It is I, Sextus.' Eros Dion motioned him to a chair. 'I hope my appearance does not shock you, but I have been unwell. A condition which Doctor Cinna describes as a "sickness of the soul". It appears that my mind not only wishes to control the movements of the body, but intends to alter its shape too. I have learned to put up with it, however, and Cinna assures me that I will not die before my work is finished.' There was a glass phial on the table, and Eros removed the stopper, and sniffed at it.

'What am I to do with you, Sextus? You disobeyed my orders by releasing Rachel, and I was very angry with you for a time.' His left hand drummed on the table top as he talked. Not as a man's might do while he concentrates, but almost as if the fingers had separate wills of their own.

'Though I am still angry with you, my friend, it does seem that you may have been punished enough. From our latest news from Palestine, and also from what Rachel herself told me, I am inclined to believe that she kept her promise to you and reported nothing about our dummy Nazarene.'

'You tortured Rachel, of course.' Sextus saw a paper knife on the table and judged the distance. Weak as he was from captivity, Eros looked even weaker, and he might be able to revenge her before the guards rushed in.

'Rachel has not suffered at all. I have never believed in torture except as a punishment for the guilty, and a reward for the obedient who inflict and witness it.' The twisted smile widened like a wound spreading open across his face. 'In a moment, you will have her own assurance that she was well treated.

'All the same, Rachel has told us what we wanted to know. Cinna is not only a brilliant doctor, but he has travelled widely as well. Somewhere in a valley of the High Atlas, a plant called Radix Sicancae is cultivated. When ground very fine and mixed with certain herbs, it produces a strange sleep in which the sleeper will answer any questions which are put to him or her. The interesting thing is that the answers are always true. That is what we used with Rachel, and I am almost certain she told nobody of our intentions.' Eros clapped his hands and a slave appeared in the doorway.

'Bring the woman to me, boy, and see that she is dressed in the manner I ordered.

'Yes, Sextus. In a moment you will see for yourself that Rachel has not been harmed at all, but first I want you to listen to me very carefully.' He took another sniff at the phial and leaned back in the chair.

'Are you still on our side, my friend? Do you still agree that this cult of the Nazarene, this gospel of human equality, is a poisonous thing which must be destroyed at all costs?'

'What does it matter what I think, Eros?' Sextus couldn't take his eyes from the Greek's face, and again he had the odd feeling that a complete stranger was sitting before him.

Was the Nazarene's movement a poisonous thing, he wondered, or was the real poison here in the room with him? Somehow that unnatural sleep brought on by drugs appeared even worse than torture. The destruction of human dignity, privacy wiped out by one mouthful of a powdered root.

'Why should my opinion interest you, Eros?' he said. 'Beric made it clear that the Emperor himself had decided on my death.'

'That was before we knew that Rachel had kept silent. Now, I would like to avoid . . .' Eros broke off in a sudden, coughing stammer.

'You see, even after what you did, I have a fondness for you, Sextus. No, not love, not affection, those feelings have never touched me, but I like having you near me. Perhaps it is because we have known each other for a long time, and faced many dangers together. Perhaps it is because I was once a slave, and you are the first well-born person to call me "friend". Whatever the reason, I want to help you.'

'But what does it matter?' Sextus felt horribly embarrassed, and tried to look away, but Eros' eyes held his like lodestones. 'Caligula has decided I shall die, and he is all powerful.'

'No, no, you can still escape him.' Eros got up and gripped his arm. His fingers were as hard and cold as Paul's had been.

'Caesar is a wild animal, but for the time being, I think I am his master. Give me a promise, Sextus, and I will help you. Swear on the names of your parents and your family gods that where this business of the Nazarene is concerned, you will always obey me.'

'I swear it.' Sextus forced out the words and Eros beamed with relief.

'Good! We are friends again. Your woman has also made the same promise, and she will tell you so herself.' He clapped Sextus on the shoulder as the door opened.

Rachel really did look as if she had been well treated. Her face was a little pale, her eyes were tired, but she was smiling, and her hair streamed over her green dress like flames. She paused for a moment, not realizing who Sextus was in the dim light, and then rushed forward into his arms, kissing him on the lips, crooning endearments, and holding his body tight against her own. And, as she did so, Eros Dion watched with the same cynical smile on his lop-sided face.

'Very well, children,' he said at last. 'You have said that you love each other, so let us now see if it is possible to save your lives. Please sit down and listen to what I have to say.

'Rachel knows what she has to do, Sextus, and you must follow her example. Like her, you wear the Emperor's favourite colour, and you must learn the words to please him. This is what I have prepared . . .'

Eros talked for almost an hour, and as he did, the day died. The sun sank behind the hills of the city, mist drifted in from the Pontine marshes, and the lamps had been lit in the street before he finally finished.

'That is how you must behave before Caesar,' he said, and his breath was as dank and cloying as the mist outside. 'Your fate is in your own hands, so act as if you really believe your lines.

'Tomorrow afternoon, in the arena, I strike my first blow against the Nazarene, and now I will introduce you to his successors: the shadow you have already met, and the wild beast which only I can control.'

The hall was green; it was green all over. The floor and walls were green marble, the furniture was upholstered in green silk, and the slaves wore green tunics. The only contrasting colours were the scarlet and black uniforms of the German guards, but the torches some of them held gave out green coppery flames.

'Wait here and remember to do exactly what I have told you.' Eros left them in the centre of the hall and walked towards the dais and the swollen figure who lolled on a canopied throne. Two creatures who might have belonged to either sex crouched at the Emperor's feet, and a scribe stood beside him holding a roll of parchment. He took great care never to raise his head above his master's. Little Boots was very proud of his physical appearance, but he was losing his hair. A single curious glance at the balding scalp could mean death.

'Ah, Eros, come here. I want to show you something.' Caligula held out his hand to be kissed. 'I am afraid I have decided to go against your advice and restore Marcus Pertinax's fortune to him, after all.' His face was compressed, as if concealing mirth and, in the strange, olive light it resembled an over-ripe cheese.

'I am sorry to hear that, Caesar.' Eros bowed deeply. 'Pertinax was extremely insolent to the Lady Julia before witnesses, and deserved to be punished. Also he is a very rich man, and your generosity at the last Games has left the coffers dangerously low.

'But who am I to tell my master what to do?' He bowed again and spread out his hands in a gesture of abject humility. 'Who am I to question the mercy of Caesar?'

'Naturally you would not question my actions, Eros, and there is no need to concern yourself about the Lady Julia. My sister is a filthy whore, and unless she learns to control her lust, I shall find some physical drudgery to quench it. Pertinax only spoke the truth, and though you are a good, faithful servant, Eros, you must try to follow my example. Learn the quality of mercy, my friend. Soften your heart and show kindness and love to all men.' Caligula's face trembled and he covered his mouth with his hand for a moment.

'Now, I would like you to look at this document. It contains instructions to the Treasury telling them to hand back the fortune, and is an exact copy of one which has just been sent to Pertinax. Please tell me if it is in order.'

'Of course, Caesar.' Eros took the scroll from the scribe. It was heavily sealed and bore instructions that it must only be opened in the presence of a senior Treasury official.

'Yes, an exact copy, Eros. Remember that.' Caligula leaned forward expectantly, as Eros cut the seals and started to unwind the roll and then broke into a whoop of laughter. The parchment suddenly cracked into a hundred separate fragments and fell to the floor.

'We baked them, Eros. After they were rolled we put both letters in an oven and baked them till they were as brittle as glass.'

Tears of mirth trickled down his cheeks. 'Julia is a slut, but any insult to my family is an insult to myself. Try and imagine Pertinax's face when he opens his copy in the Treasury.'

'Sextus, listen to me.' Rachel leaned towards him, as another gust of laughter rang across the hall. 'Do you realize why we are here, my dearest? Can you understand that we are instruments of God and he has brought us here for a purpose?'

'All I know is that we must follow Eros' instructions, if we hope to live.' Sextus stared up at the throne. When he last saw him, Caligula had been a handsome boy, but now he was prematurely aged by disease and debauchery. The insane root in his family had flowered with a vengeance, and Eros was right in describing him as a beast who could be controlled by cunning.

'Does life matter so much to you, Sextus? Remember Paul's promise to us at Gethsemane; there is no death if we serve the master.' She reached inside her dress and then gripped his hand, and he felt something hard and sharp pressed into his palm: a thin surgical knife which she must have stolen from Cinna.

'Take it, my love, and when the time comes, use it well. Remember that we are the instruments of Fate, and there is no other choice left for us.'

'Stop it, woman. Whatever you say, however strongly the Nazarene has possessed you, we cannot do this. Life is valuable and I have given my promise to Eros.' She withdrew her hand and Sextus hid the scalpel in a fold of his toga. If Caligula caught one glimpse of it, their deaths would be instantaneous.

'Do what Eros told us to, and we will come out of this alive.' He understood now why Rachel had looked so happy when he first saw her. Cinna's drugs had rotted her mind, and she expected him to be her accomplice in some pathetic attempt at assassination.

'Very amusing, Caesar.' Eros had stopped laughing and wiped his eyes. 'A joke worthy of the Gods, but there is a more serious matter to consider.' He whispered in his ear, and Caligula motioned the scribe and the nearest guards to withdraw to the end of the room. Only the two painted creatures remained where they were; crouched at his feet like dogs.

'So that is the woman.' He crooked a finger for Rachel to approach. 'Yes, you were right, Eros. She really is a beautiful

animal.' His hands shot out and he tore open her dress, grinning as
he saw the curves of her body.

'The face of an innocent child perched on the fullness of Venus.
But what a pity, Eros! Such an end I had planned for her. A death
which would make her memory immortal till the end of time.'

'A death planned by a God, Great One, though I am still in ignorance of its details.' The Greek put a hand on Rachel's shoulders,
as she tried to draw back from the exploring fingers.

'But does God destroy his disciples, Caesar? There are plenty of
women just as handsome to take her place in the arena, and this
girl has faith. I have talked for hours to her and Sextus Ennius, and
I am convinced they have told me the truth.'

'Master, forgive me.' Rachel suddenly threw herself down
before Caligula, and her hair flamed against the green marble. 'I
did not know. I could not understand the mystery of who you
were, and how you could appear to mankind in many different
forms. Give me any death you please, lord, and it will be nothing
compared to my lack of faith.'

'Look at me, girl.' Lust had vanished and Caligula's face
was full of patient suffering. 'Do you understand now? Do you
really recognize me for what I am? The god of a thousand forms
and names? Jove, Mithras, Osiris, and even the Messiah of the
Jews?'

'I recognize you, lord, but do not ask me to look at you.' He
had grasped her hair forcing her face up to his own and she struggled against him. 'I am only a mortal and the sight of you blinds
me.'

'That sounds like the truth and I forgive you, because God is all
love.' Caligula released her and lay back on his throne. Sweat and
tears of self-pity were pouring down his face.

'Yes, all love, girl, and how do they repay me? With jeers and
taunts, and finally the cruel death of a slave.

'And now, they lie and defile me, don't they? They say that I
returned to Palestine like a beggar, and then vanished into the
heavens.' His voice which had been almost inaudible rose to a
scream. 'They refuse to admit that I am here, sitting on my throne
and judging the world.'

'But tomorrow they will be destroyed, Caesar. Before the sun

sets over the arena, we will have started to discredit them utterly.'
Eros motioned Sextus forward.

'This is Ennius, the man who was with me in Palestine. Like
myself, he wished to shame and hurt you, but now he has found
faith. He and the girl will see that our plan succeeds. She will recognize our mock Nazarene, and he will lead our agents against the
sect. Sextus has a motive for revenge too, Great One. Show him,
my friend.'

'If Caesar wishes it.' Sextus held out his scarred hand. The
effects of the wine had worn off long ago, and he felt weak and ill
and on the verge of collapse. The smoke of the torches against the
green stone, the insane face studying his palm, Rachel beside him,
and Eros' lop-sided grin could have been images from a nightmare,
but something much stranger was going on in his head. A distant
voice trying to give him an order he couldn't understand, and he
seemed to see Paul's bearded lips moving in front of him while the
steel scalpel grew heavier and heavier in his robe. He had to force
himself to keep his hand steady till Caligula leaned back satisfied.

'Yes, that is a worthy motive of revenge, Ennius.' The Emperor
held out his own hand to be kissed.

'Like myself they tortured you, but that is finished now. You
are my first disciples, the first loyal followers who will share my
kingdom. Just three at present, but after tomorrow . . .' He turned
to Eros. 'Tell me again about tomorrow, my friend.'

'I will do better than that, Caesar. I will show you.' Eros waved
over a major-domo and gave him an order.

'At the Games tomorrow, you have given free seats to the rabble
and ordered that all domestic slaves must be allowed to attend.
The early entertainments will be as good as anything the city has
seen. A pitched battle between five hundred German prisoners,
your best gladiator, Aesis, fighting three Gauls at once, a chariot
race, and the deaths you prepared for Sextus and Rachel given to
substitutes.

'It is the last act that matters, however. A spectacle which will
be repeated in every city where the cult of the Nazarene is known
to flourish.

'I have an orator well versed to tell the story simply. An
account of the most monstrous fraud that has ever been foisted on

mankind. The tale of a man who was taken alive from his cross, and paraded as God by your enemies, people who have only one aim and ambition, the destruction of the Empire.' Eros' face was flushed with hatred.

'They wish to destroy everything, Caesar. All that Rome and Greece have built up over the centuries; law and order and civilization. They would take all that from us, and raise the meanest slave as an equal to yourself.

'But we shall stop them. We shall show this risen god to the rabble and they will laugh till they roll in their seats.

'Look at him, Caesar. Look at the thing which threatens you.' The major-domo had returned and two men were approaching. Doctor Cinna, pompous and strutting, and the tall, limping figure he had made. There was a russet robe over its thin shoulders and thorns were plaited around the forehead like a crown.

'Though this is a deception, the stories must be the same. They took him down alive to defraud humanity.'

'Bring the fellow here, Cinna.' The Emperor's mania obviously changed its form from one instant to the next, and he appeared bored with Eros' tirade.

'Good; very good indeed. Nobody would suspect that those wounds were fresh.' He gently prodded one of the crouching eunuchs at his feet, and leered at Rachel.

'You are a clever fellow, Doctor, and I wonder if you could perform a service for me. A simple operation turned Olenus and Medon here into very lovely girls. Would it be possible to make a boy out of this beautiful creature?'

'I am afraid that is beyond my small skill, Caesar.' Cinna shook his head. 'It is easy enough to remove a part of the body, but I have never heard of an addition being made successfully.'

'What a pity.' Little Boots fondled Rachel's throat. 'All the same I think you will attempt such an operation, Cinna. I am in love with strange things, and would like my first priestess to be the strangest one of all.

'And now, let us see if our actor knows his lines.' He smiled up at the tall figure before him. 'How are you called, fellow? Where do you come from?'

'My name is Jesus . . . Jesus . . . Jesus of Nazareth . . .' Again and

again the automatic answers came gasping out, and the lips moved
as if a dead man was speaking.

So it was, of course. Sextus had thought that he was about to
faint when Caligula revealed his plan for Rachel, but all at once, he
became strong again and his mind was clear.

The thing which spoke was no longer human – it wasn't even an
animal. The limbs moved, the lungs breathed, and the lips could
repeat a formula, but it had no will of its own.

Its masters were just as impotent too. A maniac who had gained
his throne by murder and his father's popularity: a doctor who had
broken his vows, a freed slave who imagined that he and his kind
could govern the world. They were all powerless and doomed to
failure, because the being they struggled against was too strong to
be resisted.

Sextus had no feeling of sudden conversion, but memory told
him what he had to do. Stories of someone who had tempted the
Nazarene and always failed, and the knowledge of his own destiny.
His ancestors, who had conquered every nation that faced them,
spoke to him; Greek and Gaul and Carthaginian; Lake Regulus,
Cabira, Syracuse. Battles might be lost, but they had never lost a
war, and he had to be on the winning side.

'Eros,' he said. 'From this moment, I take back my promise and
have become your enemy.' He heard Caligula scream as the scalpel came out, saw the Greek reach for his own dagger, but Rachel
grasped Eros' arm and there was plenty of time. Cinna cowered
away before him, while his creature still repeated the only words
it knew. 'Jesus of Nazareth . . . King of the Jews . . .' The German
guards were bounding across the hall, but there was no need to
hurry.

'Yes, Eros, we are enemies because I cannot live with failure any
longer. Once I have removed your single weapon, you and your
masters are powerless.' He tore open the russet coloured robe
while the mindless repetitions ran on and on.

'. . . of Nazareth . . . The King of the Jews . . .' The thin blade
entered the heart and twisted before they finally stopped.

Apart from a loin-cloth the man was naked. A short, coppery-
coloured man, no longer young and with a body that did not look

especially powerful. Only those spectators seated above the gate through which he entered the arena saw the muscles of his arms and shoulders and were mildly impressed.

'Yes, this might be amusing.' Caligula grinned down from his balcony and acknowledged the man's salute. His sister, Drusilla, sat between him and Eros, and at his other side was Cassius Chaerea, the Tribune of the Praetorian cohorts. 'And you say he is a volunteer? I imagine that he must also be insane.'

'Perhaps merely poor, Caesar.' Eros felt drained of strength, as if recovering from a serious illness or a long debauch. At the very moment that Sextus had killed the mock Nazarene, some strange force had left his body like wine pouring out of a torn skin. The nervous tic had vanished, the stammer had gone, but he knew that he was as naked and unarmed as that small brown figure striding slowly across the sand.

'He is an Arabian merchant who lost all his money in a dice game. He offered to fight if they paid him one gold piece for each kill.'

'Then let us hope that he is killed himself after showing us a little sport.' The Emperor was feeling pleased because it had been an enjoyable day so far. His faction, the Leek Greens, had won the chariot race, a satisfactory number of German prisoners had dispatched each other, and the wild beast show had been most stimulating: wolves maddened by hunger set against a gigantic white bear from the end of the earth which had killed all its attackers before being shot full of arrows.

'But, be of good cheer, Eros. The man Ennius and his girl were clearly possessed and this is not a battle lost, but only a skirmish. We shall produce another Nazarene and that one will be well-protected. Forget your fears and let us enjoy ourselves.' He smiled at the sun already starting to go down over the hills and then at a huge circle of wooden hoardings at the far side of the arena.

'You have a silly notion that these people will face death with nobility, but I assure you that they won't. The end that awaits them behind those boards is very special, and you will hear them scream and curse this Messiah when they realize he has deserted them.

'Isn't that so, Hermann?' Caligula turned to the captain of his bodyguard. 'Your people roast their prisoners slowly in wicker cages, I believe. Have you ever known one of them die in silence?'

'Never, Caesar.' The German's lips curved through his blond beard. 'All of them cursed their gods before they died.'

'Of course they did, so be patient, Eros. My machine is far more subtle than anything a barbarian could devise and in less than an hour you will hear them cursing their false deity to the heavens.'

'As you say, lord.' Eros looked at Beric standing at the end of the balcony like a statue. At least he had been rewarded for his loyalty. His former master, the young nobleman who resembled Sextus, had been arrested on a trumped-up charge of embezzlement, and soon the years of pain and humiliation would be paid for by his death. Below the balcony, the man was still walking on across the blood-stained sand, and once again Eros felt a sense of kinship. Like him, that Arabian was naked and alone and probably soon to die. Already Little Boots was beginning to lose interest in his divine claims. When he found another interest to replace them, the disciple's head would be the first to fall.

That would be the end of resistance. He was the only one who really understood the dangers involved, and after he had gone, the words from the Galilean hillside would spread unchecked. In his mind's eye, Eros looked into the future. Anarchy taking the place of law and authority, and finally the barbarian hordes pouring in through the unguarded frontiers. Civilization wiped out by dreams of slaves with their fishes and love feasts and crosses.

'Now, let's see what this fellow can do.' Caligula leaned forward expectantly. The crowd were silent now, all watching the small, lonely figure and wondering what an unarmed man was expected to fight. He halted in the centre of the arena and the far gates opened. Out of them came three attendants leading dogs; huge, ravenous creatures, Nubian fighting dogs which in many cases could better a swordsman. The man's body must have been coated with some substance to excite them, and they bayed and tugged at their leashes as they caught the scent.

'You say he volunteered?' The Lady Drusilla yawned ostentatiously. 'The death of one maniac is boring sport, brother.'

'Shut your mouth, woman. If you are bored we shall find some means of keeping you occupied. Yes, healthy employment is what you and Julia need, and I know the very thing. You both pride

yourselves on being strong swimmers, so a year spent diving for
sponges will entertain you.' The Emperor sniggered at the notion
as the first dog was set free and came bounding across the arena
with a deep, slavering roar.

I am like him, Eros thought, watching the small, naked figure
facing death. I also am fighting something too strong and it is
bound to destroy me. He watched fascinated as the man remained
motionless, apparently indifferent to the brindled body hurtling
towards him. The dog came in a straight line, and at three paces
leapt for his throat. Only then did the man move. He ducked under
the open muzzle, grasped the forepaws, and his arms swung back
in line with the shoulders. It was too quick for anybody to see
exactly what happened, but the crowd rose cheering to their feet
for the animal's body had split into two pieces and fell quivering on
either side of him.

'Good! Yes, our Arabian really is clever and deserves his gold
piece.' Caligula nodded approvingly. 'I wonder if he can do it
again.'

The second dog had been released, and as he watched, Eros
started to feel hope again. Was this a sign, he wondered? He had
felt as defenceless as the man looked, but the man had a great
power at his disposal. Once more his hands shot out, caught the
legs and his arms swung back like doors to tear the beast apart,
while the crowd roared out its appreciation.

He would go on fighting. Sextus was possessed, but the demon
might still be driven out. 'Love thy neighbour as thyself,' Jesus had
taught. Well, Sextus would realize how much that meant when
he saw the death which had been prepared for him. Soon they
would hear him scream for mercy and curse the dream which had
brought him to it, and plead that another victim might be found
to replace him.

And once he had heard that, he would know what they had
to do. There would be no more waiting for evidence against the
man himself, no more attempts at ridicule. His orders would go
out, and every dungeon, every arena and torture chamber of the
Empire would be packed with the Nazarene's followers.

The last dog was free now and bounding across the sand. It was
even larger than the others, and it didn't approach in a straight line,

but circled the Arabian as though its companions' fate had taught it wisdom.

'Let him win. Please let him win again.' Eros muttered aloud as he watched the crafty approach. 'All I need are two signs: that man's life and to hear Sextus plead for his.' He saw the heavy body leap into the air and closed his eyes knowing that this time the hands would miss and the jaws meet in his throat. The noise of the crowd was deafening, and for a moment he didn't know if it meant defeat or victory. Then he felt Caligula rise to his feet and forced himself to look at what had happened. As his eyes opened, a fanfare of trumpets joined the roar of applause and he knew that the first sign had been given him.

Six pieces of carrion lay smoking on the sand and the man had turned and was trotting towards the royal balcony: a short, slightly built figure from the chest down, but the arms and shoulders could have belonged to Hercules. He bowed deeply before the Emperor and then suddenly spread out his arms in the same motion which had torn the dogs apart. His face was smiling, but horribly mutilated, with the right eye socket puckered and empty.

The left eye was there though, bright and twinkling in the coppery flesh, and as he looked down at him, Eros distinctly saw it wink.

The prison was lit by torches and the stench of burning pitch mingled with the smell of men and animals and blood. Stronger than all these was the smell of fear. Fear of pain and death and, above all, fear of the shouts and cheers and laughter ringing down from the packed benches which formed the roof. Whenever the crowd was silent another sound replaced theirs; the whimper of the wounded from an adjoining dungeon. Most of them had been dispatched to provide fresh meat for the animals, but a few would be sewn up and live to fight again.

At least they were together. Eros had allowed them that single mercy and Sextus gripped Rachel's hand. The wall behind them was glass-smooth, polished by the skin of other victims who had wept and sweated and trembled, and clutched each other for comfort, as they were doing.

'Once I shouted like that.' Sextus looked up as another burst of

applause rang down from the ceiling. 'Once I loved it all, Rachel. I
remember seeing a Dacian net and trident man fight a Gaul years
ago. The Gaul looked slow and clumsy, and cowardly too, and the
Dacian obviously thought he had nothing to fear from him. He
played with the fellow and taunted him before preparing for the
kill. Then the Gaul suddenly appeared to stumble, fell down on his
knees, and before anybody knew what was happening, the sword
came up into the Dacian's groin. All the crowd laughed at the look
of surprise on the man's face, and so did I, may the gods forgive
me.'

'God will forgive, my dearest. Everything will be forgiven.'
There was just enough slack on her chain for Rachel to kiss him.

'My adopted father had a maid called Sarah. She was a very
good old woman; kind to children and animals, and she would
share her last crust with a beggar. But Sarah proved to me that
pleasure at another's suffering was a common human vice.'

'She never missed a crucifixion, and said that the sight of a dying
criminal was a compensation for the hardship of her life.'

'She sounds a wise woman, girl.' Beric stepped out from behind
a pillar. There were two men with him; the Master of the Games,
and a short dandified person with an air of great self-importance.

'Demonstrations of pain have two purposes, as I am sure Eros
Dion must have told you. To awe potential malefactors and to
reward the obedient. Do you begrudge the rabble their pleasures,
my lord?' He grinned as feet pounded on the benches and more
cheers rolled above them.

'But you were wrong about it being a Gaul who killed the net
and trident man, Ennius. He was a Briton and his name was Beric.'
He put his foot on Rachel's chain and dragged her to the ground.

'Why did you do it, you fool? Why did you betray us again? Has
this woman bewitched you, or do you honestly believe that the
dead Nazarene can save you?'

'He may do, Beric. When I destroyed that dummy Cinna made,
I felt I was obeying an order, but all I know for sure is the certainty
of your defeat.' One end of the cell was covered by a sackcloth
curtain and a few beams of sunlight mottled Sextus' face.

'Men like you and Eros, the sons of slaves and freedmen, think
you can rule the Empire. You helped the Caesars to break the

power of the nobility and the senate which made Rome great. Now you imagine you can control the Emperors themselves. You are wrong, Beric, and Eros is as blind as the god whose name he bears. Very soon Caligula will look for another favourite, another pander to his insanity, and then you will die, barbarian.'

'Not as horribly as you will die, my lord.' The big man's fist crashed into his chest. 'Oh, you can talk bravely now, but very soon it will be different. In under an hour you will scream and curse this woman who brought you here.'

'What if he does, Beric?' Rachel twisted her face up to his. 'What will the screams of a man under torture tell you? That your Empire will last for ever? That Caesar is a god ordained to rule the world? That you can keep humanity in chains till the end of time?' She laughed as he kicked her.

'Yes, we will scream, and we will probably curse too, but it will signify nothing.'

'Stop it, fellow.' The short man stepped forward. His voice was high-pitched and as self-important as his expression. 'The Emperor will be very annoyed if either of them are damaged before their appearance.

'There is no need to lose our tempers. What does it matter what these people say to you, or what absurd religious beliefs they hold? To me they are merely subjects for philosophic demonstration and I hoped you would feel the same way.'

'A demonstration which I do not like, Mercurius.' The Master of the Games was old and bald with a long grey beard that waved like a banner as he shook his head. 'It is not only dangerous, but reeks of blasphemy as well.

'The people will not like it either. It is less than a hundred years since our worst enemy was finally destroyed and we Romans have long memories. I think there may be a riot when they see this engine of yours.'

'The people! Who cares what the people like or dislike.' Mercurius raised a scented handkerchief against the prison smells.

'I am not responsible for that engine, as you call it. That was the Emperor's idea and all I provided is the stuff it contains. A substance which may well be part of life itself. My father was killed searching for the secret, and it has been left to me to discover perfection and demonstrate a great power to the world. Is it my fault if Caesar wishes to house it in a foolish toy?' He grinned at Sextus and Rachel.

'And you, my friends, are to be part of the demonstration. Oh, you will scream all right, as Beric has said. You will curse this Hebrew god of yours who sounds a very poor fellow indeed. If he could not prevent himself from being nailed to a cross, how can he possibly save you?' Mercurius' blue eyes twinkled in the thin light.

'All the same I can give you a crumb of comfort. You are not going to die in vain, but for the service of philosophy, because you will demonstrate a marvellous thing. The very fire of Jove which I, Mercurius Caepo, have given to mankind.' He made a little smiling bow and glanced at an hour-glass by one of the torches.

'We still have a short time, my lords, so would you like to come and inspect the contrivance?' He walked forward towards the curtain.

'I would like that very much, Caepo.' Beric started to follow him and then turned back and put his face close to that of Sextus.

'Do one last kindness for me, Ennius,' he said. 'Scream well. Scream so that I can hear you above the noise of the crowd, man with a face like my first master's.' He moved away and helped Mercurius to draw back the curtain.

So, that was it! That was the way they were going to die. The sudden sunlight dazzled him for a moment, and then Sextus gasped in horror as his eyes cleared and he saw what the curtain had hidden. Beyond the gate of the dungeon, screened from the crowd by tall wooden hoardings, was a monstrosity. Its features were turned away from him, but the brass horns rising out from the human skull told him what he had to face.

'You cannot do this to me,' he shouted, struggling against the chain, and staring at the thing whose legend had terrified him as a child.

'Fellow citizens, do not shame me. I am a Roman too, and my ancestor, the Consul Metellius, died on one of those at Syracuse.' Sextus had expected a hideous death; a fire, a cross or an animal, but this was a mockery too, an obscene jest at Rome's dead which only a maniac would dare to show in the city.

'Don't touch me, woman.' He pulled his hand away from

Rachel and he knew that Beric had spoken the truth and she had
bewitched him. Yes, Rachel alone had brought him to this. It was
her will that made him stab the creature in the palace, and the
power of the Nazarene was just an illusion. Even the lowest of
the gods would not allow his servant to die like that. He rubbed
his palm against the wall, trying to erase the scar that lay in it, the
mark of a slave and a criminal, the sign of the great deception.

'You do not care for the manner of your death.' Eros came
smiling through the gloom of the prison. 'That is your heel of
Achilles then, Sextus. To all men there is one thing which is intolerable, a fear that cannot be faced, and it appears that Caesar has
stumbled on yours.'

'Please, please, Eros.' Sextus' eyes kept flicking between the
Greek and the huge horned skull glinting in the sunlight.

'I have wronged you, Eros, and you have a reason for revenge,
but please spare me that. Burn me at a stake, let me fight with
animals, but do not give me that death.' He remembered how the
young Zealot had cringed when Thassi had stated how he was to
die, and he also remembered his own childhood. An old wrinkled
nurse who sat in the shadows of the bedchamber telling stories.
She had a great fund of them and they all concerned the same
thing; the man-beast from across the sea, the devourer of children,
the brazen god who had ravaged Italy for nine years. On and on
her toothless mouth had mumbled the horrible legends, while the
rush lamp sank lower and the shadows became faces that glowered
and leered at him.

'He really frightens you, then.' Eros nodded. 'Your new master
is no defence against the god of the old enemy.

'And what will you do to escape him, my friend? Just how far
will you go? Will you curse the Nazarene in your heart, perhaps?
Will you laugh if the woman dies without you? Will you accept life
from me, Sextus?'

'Life!' The word had no meaning to him, and only the manner
of death was important, but Sextus pushed Rachel aside as she
tried to grasp his hand again and he grovelled before Eros. 'You
will help me? Even after what I did, you would still help me?'

'I will save you, Sextus, but not from any affection this time. You
see I need you, my friend. I want to have you with me again. I want

to look at you every day as a reminder that the Nazarene can be defeated. You will be the proof, Sextus. All the proof I need.' Eros came closer and grasped his wrist with fingers which were colder than the wall behind him.

'Listen to me, Sextus. Listen to me very carefully. The only thing you must do is obey me. Denounce this Jesus now. Tell me that it was the girl who possessed you. That is all you have to do and someone else will take your place in the arena.' He turned and clapped his hands and two slaves appeared dragging a chained figure between them. They halted by one of the torches and Sextus cried out as he saw his own face looking at him.

'Yes, another deception, my friend. That is Beric's former owner who resembles you closely. He will take your place with the Hebrew sorceress and Caesar will never know of the exchange.

'Well, do you agree, Sextus? Will you accept my offer? All I want is to hear you curse the Nazarene now, and laugh with me while we watch the girl wither. Answer quickly because we have little time.' He pointed to the open curtains. Workmen had filed in through a gap in the palings and Mercurius was giving them his instructions.

'It is as simple as that?' Sextus glanced at the man in front of him. A face like his own which was also weak and cowering and terrified as he saw the fate prepared for him. A man who would die with Rachel so that he might live.

'That is all I have to do, Eros?' He turned towards the monstrous engine outside. The thing which had obsessed him since he was a child. The worst death a Roman could die.

But the sunlight must be affecting his eyes, because it appeared to be shrinking. He rubbed them with his free hand, but the process continued. The thing really was shrinking, and all at once it didn't seem nearly so frightening. Smaller and smaller it became, as did the human figures around its base, till they looked like ants beside a toy.

'Just two favours, Eros, and you will save me.' Fear and the blows he had received from Caligula's guards must have driven him insane, because he suddenly felt that another person was speaking through him, and his heart beats sounded as loud as drums.

And something strange was happening in the dungeon itself.

Though the far wall was in shadow, a beam of sunlight was start-ing to spread along it.

'Your price is too heavy, Eros,' he said, and though he didn't know why, he was laughing. 'I must watch the woman I love die by torture and send another human being to a death I cannot face.' Details of the Nazarene's ministry flicked through his mind. The struggles of the tempter against a being who was beyond temptation.

'You want a living corpse to reassure you, Eros. A thing with no soul and nothing in its mind except shame and despair.' The Greek's reply was drowned by his laughter and he saw him stagger back as though he had been struck.

'You can offer me nothing, Eros, nothing at all.' The sound of his heart was far louder than the noise of the crowd and the light on the wall was not caused by the sun. It was white-hot metal, slicing open the brickwork, and something was coming out from behind. He laughed again as he watched, because he knew what it was; the power which could not be resisted; a great, shining pyramid of flame and colour spiralling up to the roof and cutting through it with a noise like tearing parchment multiplied a million times; a thing so vast that he could only think of it as the spirit of hugeness itself. A colossus to which Rome, the Empire, the whole world and the heavens themselves were less than a few grains of blood-stained sand on the floor of the arena. There were bricks and stones and timbers in its arms now, the rubble of palaces and temples and prisons swirling away into nothing, and below them trees reared up through the marble pavements and grass grew on the ruins which were left.

'Alpha,' he said, knowing that he was looking into the future and the past and all time rolled into one. 'You are Alpha and Omega; the beginning and the end.' The chain dropped from his hand, he heard Rachel laugh beside him, and then everything tilted into oblivion.

For perhaps a count of ten Sextus lay back against the wall and, when he opened his eyes, the world had returned to normal. Eros and his companions were moving away, the chain was in place, and the engine outside was as monstrous as ever. Slaves were approaching to take them to it.

Only two things were different. Sextus and Rachel were without fear and both of them realized the reason for their failure. They had been looking for the story of a single man, but Jesus-bar-Joseph had been God-made-Man. Not a man, or the man, but Mankind itself. During his life he must have been countless person-alities which existed in countless situations, sharing the hopes and fears of all humanity till the time came for him to reveal himself as a being who was beyond temptation. It would have been easier for Eros to have reached the farthest star than to have pierced the mantle of those hidden years.

They gripped each other's hands and stared at the tiny beam of sunlight still flickering on the wall. It faded to a speck and van-ished. But just before it vanished they saw that it had the shape of a crowned head.

'Very soon we shall witness a miracle.' The gladiator, Aesis, had dispatched the three Gauls with ease and Caligula was feeling even more pleased with himself.

'My fellow, Mercurius Caepo, is a wonder worker, and for months he and his assistants have been building an engine to dem-onstrate the strange power he has developed. I hope we will find the spectacle impressive.'

'I hope the people will, Caesar.' The Tribune, Cassius Chaerea, glanced at the crowd, who were all staring at the circle of hoard-ings, impatient to know what they concealed. It was some time since the last event and many of them were becoming restive, but Caligula had insisted that the final spectacle must take place during sunset. Chaerea could see discontent in some faces too. The Gauls had been poor, untrained swordsmen, unworthy to be shown in the city, and there had been a few boos and jeers when Aesis was presented with his staff of liberty.

'The People, Cassius! The Rabble! What do they matter?' The Emperor took another cup of wine from his slave. He had been drinking all day and his pale face was laced with little red lines.

'Remember what Eros Dion here said. "Let them hate me, as long as they fear me." Isn't that so, Eros?'

'It is true, my lord.' Eros sat hunched forward on his bench and he felt bitterly cold, though the day was still warm. That last defiant refusal of Sextus had shocked him even more than the killing of the mock Nazarene, and it had taken all his strength to return to the balcony.

'Of course it is true, and the people will be amused by the spectacle, though they will not comprehend what they see.' Caligula scowled impatiently at the sun which was sinking very slowly behind the city.

'Mercurius is a great man. The philosophers stated that no substance can burn without air and he has proved them liars. The stuff he discovered is based on the ingredients of Greek Fire, nitre and powdered charcoal, but he has added another preparation to these, which allows them to combust in an enclosed space. You will see a mass of metal become red hot for no apparent reason, Cassius. And you, Eros, will watch your friends roast without fire.'

'Not my friends, Caesar. Sextus Ennius and his woman are the enemies of the whole world.' Eros turned away from the grinning face and stared across the arena. The hoardings were mounted on wheels and slaves were positioned at cross-bars to drag them away as the sun set.

Had Sextus ever felt for him as a friend, he wondered? Had he ever really liked him at all? Though he himself was incapable of deep affection, it would be pleasant to know that one human being had been fond of him. The bowl of the arena faded for a moment and he was a child again; frightened and quite alone, on a straw pallet in the brothel listening to the grunting, animal noises behind the curtain.

But, though Sextus had refused his offer, he and Rachel would break very soon. Eros' natural resilience came to his aid as he looked at that circle of timber and considered what was behind it. Sextus was possessed, but no human being could suffer such agony in silence. They would both scream and curse before they died, and he would know that the power of Jesus-bar-Joseph was a delusion.

And why had he even considered the possibility of defeat? Long shadows were creeping across the sand below him, and with every hand's breadth they travelled, his confidence returned. He had been foolish once. He had imagined that a faith could give men the power to withstand any persecution, but in a few minutes he would know that it was a lie. Soon he would hear Sextus curse the false god which had betrayed him and the way would be clear. His orders would rush across the Empire and the Christians would be hunted down like rats in a field of stubble.

At last the sun was below the rim of the amphitheatre and Caligula raised his hand. Trumpets blared out, the slaves bent on the cross-bars, and the hoardings were drawn aside. Behind them something glittered in the fading light and started to move forward. When the fanfare stopped, the crowd was strangely silent, the people craning out over the benches as if unable to believe their eyes. To his left, Eros heard Cassius Chaerea give a single bitter curse.

The thing was an enormous, metal statue seated upon a wheeled throne. Its body and face were human, but the teeth were the fangs of a dog, and bull's horns sprouted from the skull. Sextus and Rachel were chained naked between its chest and long, brass-clawed fingers.

'My lord, it is Moloch and you shame us all.' The Tribune was on his feet, flushed with loathing and horror as the monstrous thing groaned on towards the centre of the arena. 'It is less than two hundred years since Carthage was finally defeated.'

'Moloch – Moloch the burner of children – the great beast who ate our prisoners after Cannae.' Every member of the audience was standing up, for there was not one amongst them who did not know the story. 'It is an insult to the dead to bring him here.'

'You fool, Gaius.' Drusilla screamed at her brother. 'You mad, blasphemous fool. The god of the enemy! Moloch who ravaged Italy for nine years and made us hate his people so bitterly that we destroyed their city and sowed its fields with salt. They burned the wounded in Moloch's arms and now you exhibit him in Rome itself. Have you no respect for your own ancestors?' Her voice was drowned by the roar of the crowd, and it was obvious that a full scale riot was about to start. Men, women and children were shaking their fists at the royal balcony and some had torn up benches as weapons. The roars of 'Moloch' were like waves pounding a rocky coast.

'Stop them. Why don't your men take action, Cassius?' Caligula's face trembled in terror and he clutched the Tribune's arm. 'Make them do something, man.

'Ah, at last. At last the cowards have remembered their duty.'
Two lines of archers trotted out of a gate and formed a circle
facing the crowd with their bows drawn. Slowly the noise subsided
and there was complete silence, except for the sobbing of children
and the rumble of the gigantic wheels moving across the sand.

'That is much better.' Little Boots scowled over the balustrade.
His teeth were oddly canine, like the grinning thing below him.

'You would dare to abuse your Emperor, would you? You would
shake your fists and curse me?' He capered up and down in his
fury.

'Oh, I wish, how I wish that the Roman People had only one
neck and I could cut it.' He was answered by a sullen murmur of
disbelief from the crowd. So, this was the son of Germanicus: this
was the boy they had called their star and their nursling when he
was carried into the City. This was the one who had delivered them
from Tiberius. King Log was dead, and King Stork had revealed
himself with a vengeance.

'Silence, dogs.' Caligula turned to the commander of the
bowmen. 'You will kill the first man, woman or child who so much
as whispers. Starting now.' He pointed to a baby which was still
sobbing, and an arrow pierced its heart before the mother could
silence it.

'Good. See that your archer gets this.' He threw a gold piece
down. The brass image had halted at last, and the slaves were hurrying away.

'Now, listen to me, all of you. Moloch is here, because his is
the worst death there is, and those creatures in his arms insulted
Caesar.' He pointed to Sextus and Rachel. 'They are going to die in
shame and agony, and you will watch their death silently, as I wish
to hear their last words.' He sat down again and looked at Eros.

'It will not be long now, my friend. Soon you will hear them
curse their false prophet, and know that his sect can be broken.'
Caligula appeared to have regained his good humour as quickly as
he had lost it.

'I pray that you are right, Caesar.' The man, Mercurius, was
walking towards the statue with a burning torch in his hand,
but Eros hardly noticed him. He stared at the naked figures held
between the brass hands and the chest. Their faces were com-

pletely without expression, and they might have been spectators bored with the whole proceedings.

'You don't need to hope, Eros. Just trust me.' The Emperor laughed as Mercurius lit a wick at the side of the statue and moved away, bowing.

'In a short time that thing will start to get hot and you will hear them.

'Yes, it is beginning already.' He pointed at the metal head. A little smoke was rising between its horns, and a soft hissing sound rose over the silent arena.

'Very soon now, Eros. The stuff is contained in leather coils; fuses, Mercurius calls them, and it burns fast. Try and imagine what is happening inside. Fire without air; heat spiralling up, cracking the leather coils till it reaches the outer casing. They will only feel a pleasant warmth at first, but soon, so very soon . . .' Little Boots sucked his lower lip as he watched.

The smoke kept drifting out from the horned skull, the sun sank lower over the city, but there was no sound except the hiss of escaping gas.

'Surely it must be working by now? Surely the heat will have reached the surface?' The Emperor frowned. 'If Mercurius has deceived me, his own death will be even more horrible.

'Ah, look closely, Eros. Look at Moloch's mouth.' The grinning teeth were becoming dull, the brass ceasing to shine in what little sunlight there was left, and a breeze sprang up, bringing the smell of hot metal.

At that moment, Eros Dion realized utter defeat. Rachel and Sextus had been looking at each other, but they suddenly turned their faces towards him, and he knew that he had lost. The brass casing was glowing with its own light now, turning to a deep cherry red, but it might have been he himself who was burning on it.

'Mercurius didn't let me down.' The stench of burning flesh joined that of the metal, and the maniac at his side cackled with glee. 'Their bodies have started to shrivel, and it is finished.'

'Finished! Look at their faces.' Eros screamed with the terrible rage of despair, and his arm swung out like a flail, crashing into the Emperor's throat and knocking him from the bench.

'Their faces. They are . . .' Something struck him in the back, something came out through the centre of his chest, but he hardly noticed. Another spear from the German guards ran him through, and another. They were not important. The only important things were those two faces which smiled up at him as their bodies withered.

'No,' he said, pitching forward beside Caligula. Blood was pouring from his mouth, choking him, but he had to make his last statement clear.

'Can't you understand, you poor, crazy fool? It is not finished. It has only just begun.'

## ALSO AVAILABLE FROM VALANCOURT BOOKS